No ROAD MAP

To Marie,

Happy Reading

Marie

087 2402391

NO ROAD MAP

Marie Mellett

authorHOUSE®

AuthorHouse™ UK Ltd.
1663 Liberty Drive
Bloomington, IN 47403 USA
www.authorhouse.co.uk
Phone: 0800.197.4150

Published by AuthorHouse   05/13/2014

ISBN: 978-1-4918-9247-3 (sc)
ISBN: 978-1-4918-9248-0 (e)

Acknowledgements

I would like to thank all my wonderful family, my friends and neighbours for their help, support and comfort during a difficult time after the death of my dearly beloved.

My life has changed drastically and without their support I could not have coped.

I have two wonderful sons who, despite having their own lives and their own families, are always in contact and always worrying about me.

Thank you all
Marie Mellett

Chapter 1

As I GLANCE around my bedroom, my eyes rest on my mam's photo, and next to it a photo of Dave and me taken on our twenty-fifth wedding anniversary. Of course there are also various photos of our dear children, now grown up.

My mother died of breast cancer shortly after I was born; my dearly beloved Dave died of cancer also just two years ago. I would like to live for a few more years, perhaps to see my grandchildren grow and to spoil them just a little like all grannies do. Am I asking too much? Obviously, yes. Well, as things stand at the minute, I am ready to say goodbye.

I have always been fond of photography. I have lots of framed photos all over our home. I used to stop and look at a photo in the hallway and say to myself, *I remember that day. It was good*, or something to that effect. I'd always smile to myself about good memories. Every place we went, and for every event in our lives, I always had my camera with me. Dave used to always say, 'Here comes David Bailey!' He was a famous photographer, and a very good one. I always admired his work.

My childhood home was void of photographs. Dad had one old black-and-white photo of he and Mam when they got married; a neighbour took it with his old Brownie.

Considering how old that photo was, it wasn't in too bad a state . . . only faded a little with smoke and age. It's amazing how old photographs can be given a new lease of life by modern technology. I have always treasured that photograph. I took it to a photographic shop and asked the young man there if he could do something with it—enhance it a little. He said, 'Sure. No problem. Leave it with me for a few days.' I went back a few days later, and I was amazed at what he had done. He had enlarged it and enhanced the colour, and even put a lovely authentic frame on it. I could have hugged him, he did such a fabulous job. I told him so. He told me he could see how much it meant to me, so he gave it special care and attention. I was impressed and very grateful. I proudly took that photograph home that day and gave it pride of place with all my other family photographs on my bedroom wall.

When I stood back and admired it, I saw my mother in a different light. I would have given anything to have known her. Dad always told me I was like her in many ways. He used to sit me on his knee when I was little and tell me stories about Mom. From a very early age I knew my Dad had loved Mam very much. He married her when she turned sixteen. He used to tell me he missed her so much that he had an ache in his heart. I did not understand what he meant until I fell in love myself; then I really knew what he'd meant all those years ago. Even though I never met her, I always felt I knew her intimately. Dad used to describe her in detail—her manner, what made her happy, and what made her sad. He used to say she was always singing while she worked. I think I inherited that from her. I have always love music and singing.

When I was in national school, I begged my dad to let me learn how to play the piano. He said he couldn't afford it, but the following year he did manage to scrape the money together. I loved him to bits, and I felt proud to be his daughter. He was never afraid to show his affection towards me. He was a small farmer living in a rural village in the west of Ireland. He was a shy, modest man. His dad had died of pneumonia when he was only fifteen, and a few short years later his younger brother drowned trying to save a newborn calf.

My dad and his mother ran the farm together for a number of years. They relied on each other completely, and there was never a cross word between them. They were doing well on the farm with everything ticking over nicely. Prices were good, and the weather was favourable. All the work got done according to plan, but life always has something unexpected around the corner. One day as he was coming home for his dinner, singing away to himself with his faithful dog, Bruno, by his side, he stopped in his tracks when he got to the top of the hill behind the house. There was no sign of life—no smoke from the chimney, and the hens were still locked in. *Something indeed is wrong*, he said to himself. He started running and calling his mam's name. He didn't know what to expect. When he reached the door, he saw her lying on the floor. She was unresponsive, so he tried the kiss of life. He knew in his heart it was too late. She was already dead, poor Mam.

She had been his friend as well as his mam, bless her. And she had been the best in the world. He got out the bike quickly and headed for the doctor's. He was lucky the doc was at home. With the doctor's help, he put the bike in the boot of the doctor's car, and they headed back to the house. The doctor, who was an old family friend, explained on the way that his mam had had a heart condition for a number of years. My dad was surprised she hadn't mentioned it to him. She had never been one to complain or seek pity. She just got on with life. The doctor examined her and said, 'She's been dead for a few hours.' My dad was upset that she had died alone; he felt he should have been with her.

The doctor helped my dad get his mother onto the bed and prepare her for the priest, who had arrived shortly after them. The doctor had called the priest before they left the town, but he had completely forgotten him. The doctor said, 'She had a massive heart attack. She didn't suffer.' At least that was some comfort to my dad.

For the next couple of days all but the essential work was put on hold while my grandmother was waked and buried. When everything was over and things started getting back to normal, my father realized his situation. He needed a companion. He wanted to share his life with someone who could love him and take care of him; perhaps they could take care of each other. My dad used to go to the pub at weekends for a couple of pints. He'd have a chat with his neighbours and catch up on the local gossip. Sometimes there was nothing of interest going on.

My dad lived in a tight community where sometimes people knew what a person was going to do before the person actually did it! So he sort of kept himself to himself. Now he needed to change all that. He did not want to end up an old bachelor; he wanted to get married and have a family before it got too late. He was in his middle thirties then, and time goes by so quickly. Soon he was surprised that, in one week, it would be a year since his mam had passed. He found that hard to believe.

My father told me the story of his life with my mother many times. Here, in his words, is how I remember his tale:

> As the saying goes, time waits for no man, and that's for sure. *I am lonely*, I thought. *My dog is my companion. How sad is that?* I had never been serious about any girl when I was younger. I used to go to the local dances, but somehow I'd never become serious about anyone. Looking back, it all seems so long ago to me. I thought I had left it too late. I didn't think I could really start dancing again. The word would soon get out that I was looking for a wife. I needed to make some discreet inquiries before it was time to go public. The problem was, where was I to begin?
>
> Truth be known, I had never wanted to upset my mam or her routine. And our situation suited me too. I suppose I was like a lot of men thinking, *There's plenty of time.* In the back of my mind, though, I always knew I wanted to marry someday. Well now was the time, and I was scared! *How stupid*, I thought. I needed someone to help with the housework and the day-to-day running of the house. I needed to put on my thinking cap, and pretty soon. The house was in a mess; I had just been doing general tidying up—no dusting or anything like that. And I hadn't had a proper dinner since Mam passed. I must have burned half a dozen pans. To me, the handiest cooking was to just put something in the pan. But then I'd walk away and end up burning it. Sometimes I got so

frustrated. Sure, I had no one to blame but myself. Putting down a fire was a chore I didn't like either.

The only thing on my mind at the moment was how I was going to get a wife; it was beginning to become an obsession. One night, as I was preparing supper, it came to me in a flash. I knew this very tall guy called SeanFáda, who lived across the field as the crow flies. I knew that Sean had a daughter, but she might be too young. I would discuss it with Sean. The man might be agreeable. One never knows; it was worth a try. The only problem was that I hadn't seen Sean in ages. How was I going to get around that? I always went to the fairs, and there was a fair in two weeks' time. *Brilliant*, I thought, *that's my chance!* I would take the calves to the fair, and I would surely meet Sean there.

The weeks seemed to drag on. At last it was Friday, the fair day. It was a big social date on the calendar. Everyone loved the fairs; there was something there for everyone. There were street traders selling all sort of wares in their stalls—clothing, shoes, material, curtains, wool, delftware (all sorts of pottery dishes), ornaments, baking ware— anything. You name it, and you could get it at the fair.

I got up at five o'clock and did the milking and the other jobs around the house. The night before I had put the calves in the garden beside the house so they would be handy in the morning. I set off on foot with my dog for the fair. The dog would keep the calves from straying or taking a wrong turn.

When I arrived, I found a handy spot to pen in the calves. I was dying for a mug of hot tea. Just as I was approaching the tea wagon, whom should I spot but Sean. Fada I couldn't believe my luck! I said, 'Good morning, Sean. Are you selling or buying?'

'Buying,' answered Sean. 'I'm looking to buy a cow. One of mine went down on me after having a calf. I'm hoping to come across one today.'

I asked, 'Would you care to have a mug of tea with me, and a sandwich?'

'Why not?' said Sean. 'While it's quiet.'

We sat down on a bench together and concentrating on our tea and sandwiches. I was anxious to steer the conversation towards my problem. I didn't know how I was going to do that. Finally I asked, 'How are all the family?'

'Fine,' was Sean's reply.

Not much help there, thought I. Then Sean opened up and told me that his son was getting married soon. He was in a bit of a dilemma as to what to do with his daughter, Nora. He was thinking of making a match for her, but she wasn't too agreeable. Maybe I could just give her a nudge in the right direction.

I couldn't believe what I was hearing, it was music to my ears. This was the chance I had been waiting for. I explained to Sean that I was on the lookout for someone to do the housework and laundry, and maybe if things worked out between us, I might be agreeable to marry her. Sean was delighted. He said it was the answer to our prayers! We shook hands on it and went about our business. I got a good price for my calves and went home on cloud nine, thinking of Nora and what she would be like. I went to bed dreaming of her even though I hadn't even met her yet.

Two days later I hadn't been too long up when the dog started barking. There was a knock at the door. I thought to myself, *What the hell?* I opened the door and stopped in my tracks at the sight of this beautiful creature standing there. She said, 'I'm Nora. I think you are expecting me.' I was gobsmacked—and speechless—for a few minutes. Then I started to splutter. I was overcome by her beauty.

When I finally stopped staring at her I said, 'Please come in.' In my mind I was saying, *And never leave.* I said, 'Nora, sit down. I have only just made a pot of tea. Would you like some?'

She said, 'Yes, John, I would, thanks.'

I thought to myself, *Have I a clean cup to give her tea in?* I did find the last clean one, and poured her a cup. We both sat there sipping tea and not saying a word. We were just eying up each other. I was trying to think of something to say. At last I said, 'Nora, I will tell you what I need doing—general housework and laundry.

She seemed very agreeable. She said, 'I can cook and bake.'

'That's all I need to hear,' I said.

Then she said, 'I will have your dinner ready at midday.'

I said that would be fine. I looked around and realized I had let things slip since my mam had passed. 'I have work to do,' I said. I bid her goodbye, saying, 'I will see you at midday.' I left with a spring in my step and a song in my heart (as the saying going). My chores that day were daging the sheep (that's clipping the dirty wool from around their bums) and dosing them and checking their feet. I had noticed that a few were lame. Sheep can be prone to sore feet; one has to keep an eye on them and make sure they are healthy, which is why they needed to be dosed also.

I might get through them before dinner, I said to myself, *if I get a move on*. I didn't get through all the sheep, though, because I was distracted. I was dying to get back to the house to see Nora again. It was lovely to come over the hill and see life in the house once more. It had been looking sad for too long. *Let's hope Nora will breathe life back into the house—and myself too.* As I came near the house, I noticed the net curtains on the line. I could smell freshly baked bread, but that was nothing to the aroma that was wafting out the kitchen door. I said to myself, *That girl is for keeps.*

Nora had helped herself to vegetables from the vegetable patch, and had cooked stew for dinner. It smelled delicious. 'How you doing, Nora?' I asked, as I pulled out a chair from the table. I could not wait to try the stew.

'I'm good, John,' she replied. 'You must be hungry!' We ate dinner together like old friends; she was easy to talk to. We had a cup of tea after dinner with homemade apple pie—my favourite. I could have kissed her. We chatted for a little while after dinner.

I didn't want to leave, but I had to get back to the sheep. I explained to her that I was letting out the ram next week. I started chatting about the sheep. I told her I'd heard about a new breed of sheep around these parts called Texel. I had invested in a Texel ram, and I was hoping to have a fine flock of sheep if the ram proved his worth. I explained to her that the Texel ram had been more expensive than the Border Lester, which I'd always used, and my father before him, but now I felt it was time for a change. 'Texels have hardier lambs,' I explained, 'and they are good mothers. Plus they have a tighter fleece, so they are a cleaner sheep and require less work.'

Nora seemed very interested. *All I needed*, I thought, is someone to listen, and I can speak for hours about my flock of sheep. They are my pride and joy. 'I hope I am not boring you, Nora.'

'No,' she said, 'not at all.'

I said that I had to go back to work and that I would see her when I had finished. It was later than I intended when I got back home, and Nora had left. I was very disappointed, but that was the arrangement. It wouldn't be proper for a young lady to stay in a house with a bachelor. She had been at the house for only one day, and I could already see the difference she had made.

Nora arrived bright and early the next morning to get my breakfast and set about working straight away. I got out of her way as soon as I had eaten. The house had taken on a new lease on life. Nora washed, cooked, and cleaned—and sang while she worked! She always seemed happy. On Friday, she gave me a list of what she needed for the following week. She baked beautiful homemade soda bread and scones. They were better than my mam's, and that was saying something! She was a very pretty girl, with lovely, long, blonde hair, which she wore tied back. She had lovely green eyes. She was very skinny, but she was young, and I thought she would probably fill out with age. I couldn't find fault with anything she did.

'Nora, there is an old Singer sewing machine in Mam's bedroom,' I told her one day. 'You are welcome to use it if you wish.'

She said, 'Thanks, John. That is wonderful news! I will put it to good use.'

The next time I went shopping, I decided to buy material for her to make a new dress for herself. I wanted to show her that she was special—not just someone who did my housework and my laundry. I got nice material, hoping it was something she would like. I gave her the parcel when he got home. 'Nora,' I said, 'I got you something.'

She was surprised. 'Is this for me?' she said as she opened the parcel carefully, carefully folding the brown paper away and not tearing it. When she saw the material, she cried out with delight, saying, 'John, it's lovely! Just what I like!' She threw her arms around my neck just like a child and hugged me.

I said, 'Nora, now you can try out the old Singer and make the dress here.'

She said, 'That would be great.'

I took a deep breath and said, 'Nora, there is a dance in the parish hall at the end of the month. Would you care to come with me?'

She said, 'I have never been to a dance. I would love to go!'

I couldn't remember when I'd last been to a dance. It had been such a long time ago. I thought I'd best check on my old suit to make sure the moths had not eaten it. And perhaps I should hang it on the clothesline to let the air go through it and freshen it up. I was excited about the dance. The old suit looked fine, and I ironed my best shirt and polished my shoes so well I could see my face in them.

We arranged to meet at the dance; she wanted it that way. Our first dance was a great success. We both had a smashing time, and I was even teaching her to waltz. After that, we went dancing on a regular basis, and we both looked forward to it.

I met Sean in town some months later. 'Hallo, Sean,' I said. 'How is life treating you?'

'Grand now,' he said. 'How is my Nora doing?'

'Great,' said I. 'No complaints. We're getting on like a house on fire. I think I'm in love with her. I was thinking of proposing, if that is agreeable to you.'

'Leave me out of it,' said Sean. 'If Nora is happy, I am too. We will sort out something about a dowry.'

'Never mind a dowry,' I said. 'I'd be proud to have her as my wife.' Sean said, 'I will see her right—not to worry.' We shook hands and parted.

On my way home, I thought to myself, *I can't wait any longer. I'm going to ask her tomorrow.* After breakfast the next morning I left the house in a hurry. I didn't know which was the best way to propose. I thought about it all morning; I could hardly concentrate on my work. In fact, I was so deep in thought, I almost chopped off my finger! On my way back for dinner I noticed lovely wildflowers growing in abundance in the garden near the house. I decided I would pick a bunch for Nora. Women liked that sort of thing. I was excited at the thought of getting married. *But what if she says no? Better not dwell on that. Think positive*, I thought.

When I reached the house, she was singing at the top of her voice. I stopped outside to listen. *She has the voice of an angel*, I said to myself. When she had finished, I stepped inside the back door and applauded. She blushed and said, 'Were you listening?'

'Yah,' I said. 'You have a beautiful voice.' I kept the flowers behind my back and said, 'Nora, would you mind sitting down for a minute? I need to ask you something important.' She did as I asked without question, though she looked puzzled. I went down on one knee. 'Nora, will you marry me?' Then I gave her the flowers.

She said, 'Yes, John. I would be honoured.'

I picked her up and kissed her and danced around the kitchen. 'Nora,' I said, 'you have made me the happiest man on the planet!' And she started laughing. I put her down and gave her a passionate kiss and almost got carried away. I just managed to stop myself in time, as she was a very desirable woman. I thought to myself, *I have a lifetime to make love to this divine creature, why rush things? I have taken the first step, and all has gone well so far. Things can only get better.*

If my mam could only see me now, she would be so happy for me. I asked Nora when she would like to get married, and she said late September. 'I love the autumn colours,' she told me.

I said that would be fine. Then I told her that we would need to see the priest. 'But,' I told her, 'the first person we needed to tell is your dad.' I knew we would have to tell him out of courtesy before we told any of the neighbours.

She agreed with me and said, 'John, will you come to visit my home on Friday night? You could have your supper with my family, and we could have a family get together.

'That would be great,' I said. 'I will look forward to it.'

When I got to Nora's home, everyone was ever so nice, and they all wished us well. Nora's father was very accommodating. He was nobody's fool. He was honest and sincere, and a straight talking guy. He seemed very happy that Nora had met someone of her own choice . . . someone she liked and fancied and wanted to marry. I was introduced to the family members—the son and his wife and some aunts and uncles.

After supper, Sean got out 'the old mountain dew' and started passing tumblers of the stuff around. I was not a drinker as such. I would have the odd pint, but never touched spirits, but now was not the time or the place to refuse a drink. I just hoped I could stick the pace. I took his first sip and thought, *This stuff is horrible, best keep drinking*. The neighbours started gathering, and the drink kept flowing. I was not feeling too good; I thought I might go outside for some air. Nora went with me. I said, 'Nora, I feel sick.' And right then I *was* sick! Suddenly I felt better and started drinking again. Everyone was congratulating us. The music began, and the singing commenced. A good night was had by all. Finally, sometime early in the morning, I said my goodbyes and kissed Nora goodnight. I took a few tumbles before I reached home. All I wanted to do was fall into bed and sleep for a week.

Nora was at the house the next morning bright as a button, and my head was spinning. She was bursting with excitement. She made me a strong cup of tea, and I sat and tried to listen to her plans. She explained that her dad had given her some money for her dowry which was an old tradition (daughters were often giving dowrys when they wed if the family could afford one). I told her that her dad had given her that money for herself, and that she was to do with it what she wished. I said, 'Nora, take the day off and go to town and treat yourself. See you on Monday. Now go and enjoy yourself.' Actually, all I wanted to do was go back to bed! She said okay. She would buy material and make a coat dress for her wedding. It would be warm against the cool autumn days. I was impressed with her and kissed her. She went on her merry way planning in her mind about buying all those little extras that girls like to buy when they get married. I got to go back to bed and slept off my hangover.

Nora bought material to make new curtains and cushions for the kitchen. She wanted to put her own stamp on our home. She did the same with the bedroom. We purchased a new double bed on her orders, and she made the bed covers and everything matching. It was a credit to her—she worked flat out, sewing late every evening. I used to walk her home when she was finished.

On Nov 1st 1960 our wedding day finally arrived, it was a beautiful sunny day with a slight chill in the air, which is to be expected for November. I could not wait to marry the light of my life. I was up early to get all my jobs done. The ceremony was at eleven o'clock, and I had asked a cousin of mine to be my best man. We were at the church with lots of time to spare. I was so nervous. I don't know why. I am usually quietly confident, and I knew Nora loved me, so what did I have to be nervous about?

Nora arrived on time, looking an absolute picture in her blue coat dress and a little hat sitting at an angle on her head. With a veil covering her face, she looked absolutely beautiful. Her sister-in-law was her maid of honour. Nora gave me a big smile when she joined me at the altar, and she squeezed my hand for assurance. I knew then we were made for each other. We had asked only the neighbours and close friends back to the house after the church. You should have seen the spread Nora had prepared the night before—all covered up to keep it fresh. The house looked wonderful. We had moved the table to one side so that we could take to the floor and dance the night away. We had a fantastic time. Nora was a radiant and beautiful bride. The neighbours provided the music—great music—and craic (fun!). Everyone had a good time. It went on till the early hours, and by then we were feeling tired. Everyone eventually started going home. 'Thank God,' I said under my breath.

Nora went to bed, and I locked up after the last one had gone home. The light was off in the bedroom, but that didn't really matter as it was almost light anyway. I called out, 'Nora, are you asleep?'

'No,' was the answer. 'I'm tired of waiting for you.'

That's a good sign, I thought to myself. I hopped into bed beside her; she was warm and cosy and very inviting. I knew this was her first time, so I would have to be gentle with her. I kissed and cuddled her and caressed her lovely body. She felt so good. Soon we were making love, and it felt so good, I could have cried.

Later, while we cuddled, I asked her if she had enjoyed it and if it had been okay for her. She said, 'John, it was good, and I did enjoy it.' I told her it would get better as we learned to satisfy each other and got to know each other better. 'Okay,' she said. 'Stop worrying. We have a lifetime to perfect our lovemaking.'

I kissed her, saying, 'That is for sure.'

She said, 'John, right now I need sleep. I am shattered.'

'Me too,' I told her. We woke up much later wrapped around each other. We made love again, and this time it was special. It was slow, sensual, and passionate. We explored each other's bodies with a longing to die for. She may have been a novice, but boy she was a quick learner! I knew we would be happy, and that married life would be one hell of an adventure. I was looking forward to it.

We got up late the next morning. Sure, who cares? It was the first day of our lives together, and we were going to savour it. We got up together every morning and started each morning with a kiss and a cuddle. Who could want for anything more?

Nora was a wonderful wife and partner. She helped out with everything. Nothing was too much for her. One morning when we had been married for about six months, she got very sick after breakfast. She kept apologizing, saying it must be something she'd eaten. I told her to go back to bed and rest for a while; she would feel better by dinnertime. Off she went, and I attended to my chores. I let out the hens and ducks and fed the calves. I went herding the rest of my stock and checked how the ram was performing, and changed the raddle on him (that's a device that holds a colour marking device on a ram. It's used rather than raddling their breast wool with colour). I came back early to check on Nora; I was worried about her.

When I reached the top of the hill, I saw smoke coming from the chimney. *Good*, I said to myself. *She must be feeling better.* She was sitting by the fire when I entered the kitchen. I enquired, 'How are you feeling, Nora?'

'Great,' she replied. 'I'm feeling very hungry. I could eat a horse.'

I said, 'Why not eat the stew, and we can have a go at the horse later for supper?' She nearly fell of the chair laughing. I noticed she didn't eat much even though she'd said she was hungry. I didn't pass any comment. I kissed her and told her to take it easy. I decided to head for the bog and make a start at cutting peat for the fire. It was a lovely afternoon.

When I got there, I discovered almost all my neighbours had had the same idea. I spotted Sean. *I'd better have a word*, I thought, *before I begin*. I said, 'Hello, Sean. God Bless the work. How are things?'

'Good,' he said. 'And how are things with you? How is my little girl?'

'Great,' I said. 'She is a gem. Can't complain, but she has been sick every morning for the last couple of weeks.'

He started laughing. 'John,' he said, 'you are going to be a daddy! Good luck to both of ye!' Then he said, 'God, you didn't waste any time! As it's her first, make sure she goes to the doctor for a check-up.'

'That's a good idea,' I said. We parted company, and I started working. I couldn't be happier at the thought of having a baby. I was running through my work. It wasn't until I stopped and looked about that I realized that I was the only one left; they had all gone home! I was amazed at how much I had done.

On the way home I was grinning to myself saying, *I'm going to be a dad!* I felt like shouting it out loud. I could hardly wait to tell Nora the news. When I got home I asked, 'How are you feeling Nora?' I planted a kiss on her lips.

She said, 'Fine . . . a little tired.'

I said, 'I was speaking to your father, and I mentioned you were unwell in the mornings. He said you could be pregnant; that's why you are being sick. Isn't that wonderful news?'

'It is,' she said, 'but I am a bit scared as well. I don't know what to expect.'

I took her in my arms and kissed her. I said, 'Nora, I love you. We are in this together. I will help out as much as I can to make life easier for you. Stay sitting. I will get the tea. Where is that horse we were saving for supper?' She started laughing; so did I. I also told her she would need to have a check-up just to be on the safe side. She asked if I would go with her, and I said of course.

After tea we listened to the radio for a little while. I was falling asleep. I must have overdone it in the bog. We decided to have an early night. We had a kiss and a cuddle and fell asleep. I was fast asleep some time later when I was awakened by Nora screaming. I sat up startled. I wasn't sure what was going on. Nora was very distressed. She said, 'The bed is covered in blood!'

Oh my God, I thought. *Poor Nora is losing our baby.* She was crying and very upset. I covered her up saying I was going to fetch the doctor without any delay.

As I was cycling down the road at a mile a minute, I said to myself, *It's at times like this that I wish I had a car. That is something I have to give some thought to, as I am now a married man with responsibilities.* When I reached the doctor's house, I was out of breath. I started banging on the front door urgently and calling out to him. All of a sudden he put his head out the top window inquiring as to what all the racket was about. I explained about Nora. He said he would be down directly, and he surely was.

Once again, he helped me put the bike in the boot, and he took off like a jet engine. We reached the house in a matter of minutes. Nora was very ashen faced and quite weak. He examined her and said she had lost a considerable amount of blood. We would need to elevate the foot of the bed to stem the bleeding, which we duly did. He said her pulse was very week. 'You need to change the bed linen,' he said, 'and make her comfortable and warm her up.' He gave her an injection and put up a drip so that she would not go into shock. He explained the baby was outside the womb. It was an ectopic pregnancy—Nature's way of correcting things. The doctor said she needed to go to hospital in the morning for a blood transfusion and an internal examination to make sure everything was okay. He said he would make all the arrangements. He would return again early in the morning to check on her before she went to hospital. I made him a hot cup of tea and gave him a slice of Nora's soda bread. We filled a hot-water bottle and put it in bed with Nora, as she was very cold. The doctor had his tea and left, and I went to bed. Nora was fast asleep; it must have been the injection the doctor gave her.

It felt as if I had been in bed for only five minutes when the doctor was at the door again. He came in and examined her. Her blood pressure was stable, he said, and the ambulance would be there within the hour. Would I prepare a bag for her. He put on the kettle, and I went to sort out the bag. We just were having the tea when the ambulance arrived. The doctor had a word with the nurse, and they were on the road within a very short time. I went with them in the ambulance; I would get the bus home later. Nora slept most of the way. She was very pale and tired. I sat next to her holding her hand. I wished I could kiss her better. I felt so helpless at the moment. I had my mind made up that I was going to stay close by her side.

When we reached the hospital, the staff were expecting us. Nora was rushed in and checked over and then prepped for theatre. The nurse told me it would take some time before she would be back, and when she did she would be very drowsy, so I could come back later. I said I was staying. I decided to go to the canteen and have some breakfast and pass some time while I was waiting. I had no intention of going home until I had spoken to her and seen for myself that she was okay. I realized I was hungry, so I went in search of the canteen. According to the directions on the plaque on the wall, it was on the second floor. I decided to take the stairs; I was not in a hurry. As I was walking along the corridor, I noticed a little church. I stopped and went in to say a prayer and light a candle for Nora that all would be well for her. I stayed there in silent prayer for some time, forgetting about my hunger. My tummy started rumbling reminding me it was way past time for refuelling. I left the church and followed my nose along the corridor; I could clearly smell food. I was absolutely starving.

The canteen was pretty quiet except for a few student nurses and one or two doctors; I figured it probably got very busy for lunchtime. I decided to go the whole hog and have a fry with all the trimmings, a pot of tea, and a couple of slices of brown bread. That should keep me going until I had dinner later when I get home. I took my tray to a nearby table; I could not wait to get stuck in. It smelled delicious. I poured myself a mug of tea and started on the bacon and then the sausage; it did taste good.

As I was eating, my mind flashed to Nora. I was wondering how things were going for her. The only good thing for her was the fact that she would be sleeping through the whole procedure. I was wondering if she would be long in theatre. I took my time over breakfast; I had no place to be. I just took my time and savoured the food. I wished Nora were sitting opposite me, chatting away. I had become so used to having her by my side, it seemed strange to be eating without her. I did find it hard to finish what was on my plate, as my mind kept going back to dear Nora. I persevered and finally I did finish it. I got a fresh pot of tea and just lingered there a little longer. The clock on the wall seemed to be on a go slow.

I had satisfied my hunger. I now had nothing else on my agenda except Nora. I decided to make my way back to reception and find out if Nora was back from theatre, and if so, which ward she was on. I was told that she was on her way back and that she would be going to the gynaecology ward; I would be able to see her soon. I reached the ward with some reservation, worrying about Nora. Would she be able to have another baby? Would she be okay? Often women suffered depression in such circumstances. If that happened, what was I to do? There I was thinking the worst, hoping for the best.

I was eventually called into the ward when they had her settled. She was having a blood transfusion. She had not woken up properly, and she still looked very drowsy. I sat in the chair beside the bed and waited until she woke up. I was inclined to dose in the chair; it was very warm in there. I had just dosed off when she called my name. I jumped up, startled and not realizing where I was. My heart went out to dear Nora. She looked like a ghost she was so pale. She looked completely washed out. I moved closer to place a kiss on her lips. She smiled at me and started crying.

She was terribly upset and said it was her fault she had lost the baby. I tried to explain to her that she'd had an ectopic pregnancy, which meant that the baby was outside the womb and could not possibly have survived. The doctor came to chat to both of us and explain what he had done. He said there was no medical reason why she could not have a healthy baby some time down the road. He said her body needed time to recover and that it was very important she did not get pregnant for a least a year. She had lost a considerable amount of blood. She needed a lot of rest, to put on weight, be in general good health when she got pregnant in order to deliver a healthy baby. He told us not to rush things. I assured the doctor that I would take good care of her and make sure she had a good rest. He said she could go home in a couple of days after she was rested.

When the doctor had left, I said to Nora, 'I have to go, love. You understand. 'I have to check on things at home.' She told me to go on, that she was okay and just needed a good sleep. I told her, 'I will pop in this evening just to see how you are doing.'

She said, 'No need, John. I'll be fine after a good sleep.' I kissed her and left for home. I was rushing to catch the bus.

It was almost dinnertime when I reached home. The hens, ducks, and chicks were making a racket to get out; they were glad to see daylight. I set off to check on the rest of the stock. I couldn't believe my eyes when I saw my first Texel lamb. *God*, I said to myself, *You look bonny!* Suddenly emotion took over, and I started crying. I cried for the loss of our baby and for poor Nora. The sight of the first lamb was a bit too much. I could not control my emotions. I composed myself after a few minutes. I would need to start checking the sheep morning and night now that they had started lambing. *I could do with the lambing starting a couple of weeks later*, I thought to myself. I was feeling tired; I hadn't got much sleep the night before. I decided to go into town around seven to see Nora, then come back home to check the sheep and have an early night. I got all my jobs done in plenty of time; I even had time to put on dinner. I was feeling tired after dinner. So as not to fall asleep, I put the hens and ducks in for the night. That was a struggle, as they were protesting. I knew they'd had a short day and hoped their day would be longer the next day.

When I arrived at the hospital, I found Nora in good form, considering what she had been through. I wondered if she was putting on a front for me. She was a little tearful as we were chatting. I was unintentionally enthusiastic as I described the first prized Texel lamb, completely forgetting about Nora's loss. (I could have kicked myself.) She fully understood how I felt. When I explained that I had momentarily forgotten how she was feeling, she said she knew I was not deliberately been insensitive. I kissed her and told her how much I loved her. I knew she was struggling to stay awake, so I decided to leave.

After getting off the bus, just as I was heading home, I noticed that the local garage was still open. I thought to myself, *I wonder if is Mike about. Only one way to find out!* I knew he occasionally had the odd car for sale. As I approached the premises, I noticed Mike inside. 'I'm in luck,' I said under my breath. I approached him, and we talked about the weather and other small chit chat. Then I asked him to be on the lookout for a small car for me and my Nora. I said, 'Mike, we have lost a baby. Nora is in hospital. A car would be a lovely surprise for her.

'John,' he said, 'I am so sorry. Ye are young. There will be more babies. Not to worry.' Then he said, 'You know, John, you are in luck! The parish priest bought a new car just a week ago and left the old one to me to sell. You know it yourself. It's a Volkswagen, only three years old, and a good runner. It doesn't have high mileage. It would suit you just grand, and it will last you for years.' We haggled a bit about the price, and in the end came to an agreement and shook hands on the deal. I was really pleased with the purchase. *Nora will be surprised*, I thought. *It's just the thing to take her mind off things. Let's hope it works.*

I asked Mike to give me a quick lesson, as I was unable to drive. He showed me how to start her up, change the gears, and move off. 'Nothing to it,' Mike said. 'You'll get the hang of it in no time.' I thanked him, saying I would be in the next day to settle up. 'No problem,' said Mike. I told him I hoped I could stay between the ditches on my way home! Again Mike laughed, saying, 'I'll give you a tow if you decide to kiss the walls on the way home.' We both laughed. I started her up, and with a crunching of gears moved off. I drove home very carefully. I got out and said to myself, *That was not too difficult.* But then the car started rolling away and I had to run after it. I'd forgotten about the hand break! Thank God I was not on a hill, just a slope, or that could have been an expensive mistake. I said to myself, *Ah, I will get the hang of it.*

I had a quick cup of tea. I debated with myself, wondering if I should check on the ewes or go to bed. I was absolutely shattered. The bed won. I set the alarm to get up early to check the sheep in a couple of hours, hoping I'd made the right decision. The alarm woke me at three o'clock. I got up without protest, and off I went, singing to myself. I was so happy that I would have my beloved Nora home in a couple of days. I decided to keep busy so the time would slip by quicker.

That evening, I took Nora's dad into the hospital to visit. I made him promise not to say a word about the car; I wanted it to be a surprise for her. He said he would keep my secret. Nora was pleased to see us both. She looked brighter. I was surprised she had got her colour back, and I was pleased that she seemed to have accepted what had happened and was getting on with it. But maybe it was just an act for both of us. Deep down I was grieving for my firstborn, but I was hiding my feelings. At that moment, all I was concerned with was Nora and how she was coping with her loss.

On the way home Sean said, 'How are you coping John? You suffered a loss also.' I was a bit taken aback that he was concerned.

I said, 'Sean, I feel this terrible loss. I also feel cheated. But I have to be strong for Nora.'

Sean said, 'I understand well, laddie. I have gone through it myself a few times.' Then he said, 'John, you have got to talk about it together when Nora gets home. It is the best way to heal the hurt.' I was touched by my father-in-law's concern. We decided to stop off at the local pub to have a drink. I felt I needed one. We had just two pints of Guinness. It was not so much the drink; it was more the comfort we got from each other. I dropped Sean off and thanked him for his company. We embraced, not uttering a word. All the emotion was in the gesture. I felt more relaxed when I got home. The chat I'd had with Sean had done me a world of good. I had a cup of tea, checked the ewes, and had an early night.

I woke up early and checked the ewes again. They were lambing grand; no problems. *Thank God*, I said to myself. *At least something is going right for me*. I was thinking of Nora and wondering how she would be when she got home. Deep down I was worried about her. I was just hoping it would all work out well. 'Trust in God,' my mam would have said. I had changed the bed linen on the bed and put a hot water bottle in the bed before I set off for the hospital. I just wanted everything to be just right for her. I intended making a fuss of her; I wanted her to know how much I loved her. I felt proud picking her up from hospital in our very own car. What a pity, though, that she was not bringing home a baby. *The next time, please God*, I said to myself. I was struggling at times to keep the tears in check. I decided to be extravagant and buy Nora a bunch of flowers when I picked her up from the hospital.

When I got to the ward, Nora was sitting by her bed dressed and waiting for me with a smile on her face. I greeted her with a smile and a kiss. On impulse I took her in my arms, gave her a loving kiss and a cuddle, and told her how much I had missed her. There were tears in her eyes. She said she'd missed me too, and that she'd missed my cuddles at night. Without me, she said, she'd found it hard to get to sleep. I said right then, 'What are we waiting for? Let's head for home and take care of each other.' I picked up her bag and thanked the nurses for all they had done for Nora.

We left the ward holding hands and chatting away. Nora was anxious to get home. We walked out to the car park together. I walked over to the car and put her bag in the boot. She said, 'John, who did you borrow the car from? There was no need. I would have been fine on the bus.'

I laughed and said, 'This car is not borrowed! It belongs to us!' I opened the door for her, saying, 'Have a seat, Mrs.'

She said, 'John, you are wonderful. What a lovely surprise!' She kissed me and said, 'Thank you. It is a lovely gesture.' I told her she deserved the comfort—we both did—and what's more I got a great bargain. 'I love it!' she said. 'Will you teach me to drive?'

'Hold on,' I said. 'Let me get this thing home without knocking any walls, then I might think of giving you some lessons.'

She laughed and said, 'You are always joking.'

'Not this time, darling,' I replied.

I drove home carefully, trying to impress Nora and prove that I was a good driver. I stayed well away from the walls. There was very little traffic on the road, which was an added bonus. When we got home, I made her a cup of tea. I sat next to her and told her how much I had missed her and how glad I was to have her home. I promised to take great care of her. I kissed her tenderly, and she responded with a loving kiss. She told me she loved me too, and that she had missed me. And she told me that we would always look after each other. I put some more turf on the fire. It was not cold; the fire just made the kitchen more inviting. I told her to take things easy and have a rest. I had jobs to do outside, and I would be back later. I kissed her and left. I was going to take Bruno with me, but believe it or not, he wanted to stay by Nora's side. He had missed her also. I knew how he felt.

I went to check on the ewes, and I had two more couples. They seemed okay. *I am pleased*, I thought to myself. *If they continue dropping like this, I will be through in no time.* I checked on the rest of the stock and checked on the hens and ducks. I gathered the eggs and put in fresh straw for them. I was just mending walls on my way back to the house when I noticed Bruno coming to find me. I thought to myself, *Nora must be having a lie down.* I patted the dog on the head. I knew all was well. The dog was not distressed or anything, just bored. We strolled back home together. I knew in my heart that Nora would be fine after resting and taking life east for a while. I was just happy to have her back.

The kitchen felt cosy when I got back. Nora had put extra turf in the range before she'd gone to bed. I put the radio on while I was getting some tea for myself. I had a boiled egg and brown bread—nothing compared to Nora's.

I had bought it in the shop before I picked her up from the hospital. I had not wanted to delay our trip home with errands. After my small meal, I went up to check on her and see if she needed anything. She woke as I entered the bedroom. I said, 'How are you feeling now? Do you fancy anything to eat or a cup of tea?

'I feel rested,' she said. 'I think I will get up for a little while and have some tea with you.' I told her that Bruno had come to find me after she had gone to bed. 'He is like clever like his master,' she said. I laughed. Nora and I listened to the radio for a little while, and she started dosing. I tapped her on the shoulder and suggested we hit the sack. 'Sure,' she said. 'I am feeling sleepy.

'Me too,' I said. We had a little cuddle and went to sleep.

When I awoke the next morning, I spent a few minutes admiring Nora as she slept. I thought to myself, *What a lucky man I am. I don't know how I would have coped if anything had happened to her. I cannot express how much I love her. I am going to take good care of her and build her up and help her get her strength back.* I got up quietly so as not to wake her up. In the kitchen, I put down the fire. When the kettle was boiled, I brought her a cup of tea and a bowl of porridge. She greeted me with a smile and a kiss. 'I'm hungry,' she said. 'I could get used of this pampering.' And she laughed. I told her to stay in bed till later. 'I might just do that,' she said.

I headed out after I had eaten. About half the sheep flock had now lambed. I needed to separate them. I put the ones that hadn't yet lambed in the garden next to the house. I put the rest into a fresh paddock with lush green grass so that they would have plenty of milk for their lambs. Then I had to check on the rest of the stock. We had three cows that were due to calf, and I had to keep an eye on them also. I was thinking to myself that I would pop back to check on Nora when I had checked on the cows. So far they were okay. There was no sign of any of them being sick.

When I went back to the house around mid morning, I half expected Nora to be still in bed, but she was up by the fire having a cup of tea. I was surprised to see her up. I said, 'Nora, you are supposed to be resting.'

'I am,' she said. I kissed her and sat with her and had a cuppa too. I thought to myself it was lovely to come in and see her sitting there in the kitchen where she belonged.

The next six months were hard going for me. I would get up early and put down the fire, take breakfast up to Nora, and then have my own before I set off outside to do my chores. At times Nora seemed so far away in her thoughts. I would wonder what was on her mind. I often tried to get her to talk, and she eventually did. It turned out that deep down she was blaming herself for the miscarriage, and she was worried she may not carry another baby to full term. I explained it could not have been helped. I reminded her that the doctor had told us there was no reason that she could not have a healthy baby—lots of them, in fact—and that seemed to cheer her up.

Nora started going out for short walks if the weather was favourable, and she often picked up the eggs. She was slowly getting back to the Nora I loved dearly. I would take her out for a spin in the car and give her a driving lesson, just to cheer her up, and it seemed to work. In no time at all she could drive better than I! I was delighted. She seemed to be improving. I was longing to see that spark back in her eyes again.

One day, out of the blue when I came back at dinnertime expecting to get something ready myself, I was greeted with an aroma of dinner wafting out the back door and inviting me in. I was over the moon. I rushed in and scooped her up in my arms and danced around the kitchen with her and kissed her. 'Welcome back!' I sang.

She laughed. 'You daft thing! Put me down!' We were so happy together. I was delighted to see her on the mend. Every day I could see an improvement in her. She started going for longer walks, and Bruno would go with her as if he was taking care of her. She seemed to suddenly get her strength back. She even put on a little weight, which suited her. We started going dancing again—every other week to start off with. We enjoyed it; it was something to look forward to now that she was feeling much better. She did love dancing, and she had become very good at it. One would have to admire her when she danced the waltz. She was graceful and elegant and, of course, beautiful.

She used to make the most beautiful dresses for herself. She was gifted with the sewing machine. Everyone used to admire her clothes; she was the best-dressed woman in the church on Sunday, and the best looking. She made dresses for the neighbours for special occasions like weddings and such. She made Communion and Confirmation dresses also.

One night when we were in bed, she said, 'John, let's have a go at making a baby. I am ready.' I was a bit apprehensive, but I went along with her wishes anyway. She didn't get pregnant for at least six months, but, oh boy, we had some fun trying. She was an absolute gift, always happy and singing away no matter what she was doing. She always made me feel special. She always listened to what I had to say. She never dismissed me. If she did not agree with something or other, she steered me towards a different way of thinking or suggested a different means of doing something, never making little of me. She loved me to bits, and me her; we were in complete harmony. When she did fall pregnant, we were both over the moon. This time she felt different. She said she could not explain it, but everything seemed different. She did not get morning sickness. She was full of energy, and we had sex in every position possible. We were having the time of our lives. She was radiant, oozing sex appeal, and she looked absolutely stunning. The extra weight she had put on had done her justice. I was so proud to be her husband.

Nora sailed through her pregnancy without a bother. One night we were both feeling tired and had an early night. Sometime during the night I heard Nora getting up. *She's going to the toilet*, I thought to myself, and just rolled over. She had been up and down a couple of times during the night. I just turned over and went to sleep. Sometime later, Nora tapped me gently on the shoulder. 'John,' she said, 'I think it has started.'

'Oh my God!' I said. 'What shall I do?'

'Get up and get dressed!' she said. 'That would be a start. No need to rush. We have hours yet.' I decided to have a quick look around outside to make sure the stock were all fine. It would probably be some time before I would be back from the hospital.

When I got back inside, Nora was sitting down, looking very ashen faced. I said, 'Would you like to head off to be on the safe side? We can leave now. You look very uncomfortable.'

She said, 'I think that would be a very good idea. I'll get my coat.' I fetched her bag and put it in the car, then I called out, 'Are you ready, Nora?' I was getting nervous. She said the contractions were every fifteen minutes and very severe. I assisted her to the car and made her comfortable, and we set of for the hospital.

Every so often she would wince. I knew it was best to get a move on. We would be there in ten minutes. I was driving a lot faster than I normally did; I wanted to get there before the baby came. Thank God we did. The staff were very efficient. They took her directly to the labour ward. They wanted me to come back later, but I said I would rather stay. Nora was in labour for hours, and she was exhausted. I stayed by her side. I refused to leave. The staff did try to get me to go, but I wouldn't leave her. She gave birth to a beautiful baby boy. He was small even though he was full term. He was put into an incubator—as a precaution, they said. They told us there was no need to worry; he would be there for just for a few days. I waited until Nora was settled back in bed before I left for home. I kissed her and said my goodbyes. I went back to the baby unit to check on our baby before I headed for home.

I was so glad to have my own transport instead of having to wait for a bus. When I got home, I checked that all was well before falling into bed sometime in the early hours. I awoke to loud knocking on the door. I could not comprehend what on earth was going on. It was the local guard. Our baby had taken a bad turn. He was really sick with a raging temperature. I was shocked. Everything had seemed fine when I left. The guard said he would take me, as he could travel with the siren on and get there quicker. I was in no position to argue. I dressed quickly, and off we went. We rushed to the hospital. Poor Nora was in a state. We both headed to the baby care unit together. On the way we passed the church in the corridor. We went to pray for our baby to survive. There was a priest inside praying.

We explained the situation to him, and he said he would baptize the child for us. We were very pleased. We called him Daniel. Don't ask me where the name came from. It just came into Nora's mind. We had not decided on a name yet. He had viral pneumonia, the poor little mite, and was finally responding to treatment. It was a long night, but he was finally out of danger. We were elated, but exhausted.

I went home to get some sleep, and Nora had some rest also. But sleep would not come to me. I had gone through such an emotional time in the last couple of hours. I had been praying that we would not lose our baby—or Daniel as he was now named. Later, I tended to my chores. I had neglected my duties for the last couple of days; it's hard to keep focused in times of crisis.

Mother and baby were ready to come home at the weekend. I was up early on Saturday morning. I tidied up and put down a fire. I was beginning to allow myself to feel happy about the birth of my baby son. Before this I had been scared to feel anything, but now I knew my wife and son were going to be coming home in a couple of hours. I felt I could afford to be happy. *I am a proud father going to the hospital to pick up my wife and child*, I thought. It had a nice ring to it. I couldn't explain how proud I felt at that moment.

Nora was ready to go when I got to the ward. To me she looked absolutely adorable. On impulse, I took her in my arms and kissed her passionately. I told her I loved her dearly. All the patients and visitors clapped, and we both laughed. We were both very happy going home together. Daniel was fast asleep in his mother's arms.

When we got home, Nora put him in his crib by the fire. Her father had lovingly made the crib for us. It was on a stand, so we could gently rock the baby to sleep. We had a

Moses basket for the bedroom, which was more convenient. Nora was a wonderful homemaker, wife, and mother. She used to sit at the old sewing machine and turn out the most beautiful things for the home. She made curtains for all the windows and matching cushions, and patchwork quilts for the beds, which were cosy and warm. She also made lovely baby blankets for Daniel.

He was a very quiet child. He seemed to cry only when he was hungry, and of course Nora was always singing to him. He seemed to enjoy it. She was completely besotted with him, and why not?

The first year seemed to pass in the blink of an eye. We were blissfully happy. I gave up going to the pub altogether after Daniel was born. I had everything I needed at home. I couldn't bear to be parted from them. I used to sail through my work. I cannot describe how happy we were. Nora fell pregnant when Daniel was just gone the year. She was very sick for the first three months, but after that it became easier for her. Also she used to get very tired. The doctor advised her to lie down for a nap after dinner. Her blood pressure was elevated, and her ankles were swollen. I had to take care of Daniel so she could have her rest. Sometimes Sean would oblige and give a hand. He was a devoted granddad. Nora and I both felt the pressure; we were both exhausted. She gained a lot of weight. The doctor said it was fluid. She found it very uncomfortable. Towards the end of her pregnancy her blood pressure shot up so high the doctor was concerned for her. She had to stay in hospital until the baby was born. She did not like that at all. I used to take Daniel to the hospital every day to stay with his mother. That gave me a chance to get my chores done. Daniel was starting to walk, and he was into everything. He used to crawl through the fence to play with the lambs and chase the hens and ducks. He was a right busy body. There was a playroom in the maternity ward, so toddlers could spend time with their mothers. That was an excellent idea. It relaxed the mums as they didn't have to fret about the toddlers. I would pick up Daniel after visiting Nora and then head for home. After his bottle, Daniel was ready for bed and so was I. I would get my dinner at the hospital canteen to save time. I often fell asleep reading Daniel a story, and I'd wake up frozen with the cold, missing Nora.

She went into labour in the early hours, a day before her due date. The hospital rang me to let me know she had started. I got Daniel dressed and dropped him off at Sean's house and went straight to the hospital. Nora was not as long in labour as the last time. She gave birth to a lovely baby girl. She said, 'John, you can name this colleen whatever you like.' I said, 'What about the name Angela?'

She said, 'That is a lovely name. Angela it is then.'

Nora was in good form after the birth blood pressure had settled. Everything was just grand. She was allowed home after three days, and she was delighted. She could not wait to get home. The day after Angela was born, I took in Daniel to see his new sister. He wanted to play with her straight away. Once again we were on our way home with a new baby. Daniel was so excited, and so was I. We were both glad to have Nora back home again.

Angela was not a bit like her brother; she made her presence felt. She seemed to demand everything, always crying. One could easily wear out a pair of shoes trying to get her to go to sleep at night. We used to take turns pacing the floor. I used to say, 'We are in this together.' I sure did my share of the work. Boy, it was exhausting, but worth it. After a couple of months, our daughter seemed to settle down, and we got our lives back again.

When the children got a little bigger, Nora used to give me a hand with the chores—flocking the sheep and dosing them. It was great to have the company. She often brought tea and sandwiches so we could have a picnic in the hayfield or the bog. The kids loved that. She was great with the newborn lambs as well; she brought many a one back from the brink.

Nora had two miscarriages before she had another baby. Our second daughter was tiny, and I mean tiny— just five pounds. We called her Emily. She had to spend almost two months in an incubator at the hospital. She got stronger, and was finally able to breathe on her own when she reached her target weight. We were eventually able to take her home. It was difficult for Nora when she had to come home and leave the baby behind. She had to go to the hospital every day to express milk to feed Emily. We had to take the other two children with us as well. It was not easy. We got through it together though.

Emily was a delightful child, easy to please. We had to keep checking her to see if she was okay. The two little ones were fascinated with the new baby. I suppose it was because she was so small. Mind you, she was growing by the day, a real bonny baby. She was a delightful child, always smiling.

Poor Nora was not having a good time. She suffered two more miscarriages before she had another baby. She was advised by the doctor to take a break from having babies, but like all women, she did not take his advice, claiming she was fine. She was back to where she had started years earlier weight wise. She was very slim; not an ounce of flesh on her. I was really worried about her and constantly tried to encourage her to eat more. She did take my advice and began to look healthier. And she fell pregnant soon again.

The next one was a boy. We called him Timmy. He was a very contrary child, always crying. Nothing would satisfy him. Again we had to take turns trying to get him to sleep. I decided one night to give Nora a break because she looked exhausted. I took Timmy for a spin in the car and it did the trick. After that, if he would not sleep, he got a spin in the car.

Nora had another girl a year later. We named her Ann Marie. She was as good as gold and cried only when she need something. Nora was looking wrecked. I told her she needed a break from babies, and to my surprise she did agree with me. I looked after the children as much as my work would allow, so that Nora could have a break and a rest. She seemed to thrive for a while, even putting on that elusive weight. We were happy and never spoke a cross word. Daniel used to love to come out and help me round up the sheep or let the hens and ducks out; he had stopped chasing them.

We did not have any more children for four years, and then in the late 1980's Rose Mary was born, Rosie for short. We had a very happy life together, but also a sad one. Nora lost six babies and had six that survived. She suffered mentally as well as physically.

This is the end of my father's story.

I—Rose Mary, Rosie for short—was the last baby born. I was loved and adored by my father. My mother never recovered after giving birth to me. She was very tired and not able to cope. She could not even hold me. She was in pain all over, just deteriorating before everyone's eyes. Tests done at the hospital confirmed that she was in advanced stages of breast cancer. It had gone to her glands. She was so ill, she never left hospital after my birth. She did not show any interest in me, the new baby. It was so unlike her, Dad was really worried about her. All the nurses and doctors could do was make her comfortable. All the family were devastated, and Dad was inconsolable.

All of the children rallied around to help Dad. They helped each other get ready for school. Daniel was a great help to Dad, who seemed to go around in a trance, not able to take it all in. He felt they should be happy after having a new baby; instead they were preparing for the death of the love of his life. It was so difficult to understand it all.

My mother passed away in a matter of weeks. The neighbours were absolutely brilliant. They helped Dad have a wake in the house. All rallied around with food and whatever our family needed. Everything was attended to, even the digging of the grave.

Poor Dad, he could not believe just twenty odd years ago they had celebrated their marriage. Where had the years gone? And more to the point, why had his dear Nora been taken from him? How was he going to get through life without her? Daniel was now eighteen and worked alongside his dad on the farm. Angie was a year younger, and Emily was fourteen. They were as thick as thieves, those two. They did everything together. Timmy was ten. He had been very attached to his mother, and he was the one who would struggle most at her death. Ann Marie was nine and very close to Timmy.

My father had a sister in America. She had no family. When she heard of his plight, she thought she would step in without any bother and take a few of the kids. Dad soon put her straight: he would take care of his family. He did not know yet how he would manage, but he knew he would. His sister was none too pleased. John asked her, 'Where were you all those years? And more to the point, you never even came to our wedding. You never knew my Nora. So why would you want any of our children? How come you did not put in an appearance before now?' Vehemently he told her, 'I love my family. I will take good care of each one of them. I do not know how yet, but I am pretty sure that we can manage.'

Things were different now without our mam. The children really didn't know how to express their grief. They just went through the motions of everyday life. Mam had been a wonderful mammy; we all missed her dearly, especially Dad. Granddad Sean passed away not much later. He was a good age, in his eighties. He had been dearly loved by the children, and indeed by my mother and father. He seemed to be always there if ever they needed advice, but he never interfered. He was a dear friend to my father as well as his father-in-law.

Chapter 2

Dad did not know what he was going to do with a newborn baby. He didn't want to hold back my two older sisters. He wanted them to have an education. That's what he and Nora had discussed. Perhaps he would keep the two lads on the land and try to increase his acreage. With more land, he could specialize in sheep or cattle. With his sons working by his side, they could decide what they wanted to do together.

A young couple, Kate and Mike, had built a house not far down the road from our house. Dad did not know them very well. He knew she had been pregnant around the same time as Nora, but he did not know any details of the birth. He had been too consumed with his own grief to get involved with anyone else. At mass one Sunday he learned that they had lost their baby. He went over to the house to sympathize; it seemed the right thing to do at the time. The woman, who was called Kate, was inconsolable. It was her first child, and he had been born with a heart defect.Kate invited him into the house and Dad explained his situation. She thought for a little while. She said, 'John, maybe we could help each other out. Let's talk over a cup of tea.'

'How?' he asked. She explained her idea: 'I could care for Rosie during the day. Looking after her would help me get over my own loss.'

John thought for a moment. 'That would be brilliant,' he said, 'and my older girls could get on with their plans.' They chatted for some time, and he told her of the wonderful life he'd had with Nora. 'She was a wife in a million,' he said with a tear in his eye. 'I felt privileged to have been her husband. I could not have felt more loved if I tried, and she was wonderful with the children. She cocooned us in a bubble of love. She never argued and always found solutions to problems She was always willing to help. She was a brilliant cook; she could turn her hand to anything.' Kate listened sympathetically. 'Sorry to go on,' he said, 'but she really did have all those wonderful qualities.' He shook her hand and thanked her for listening and for the tea.

Kate took me under her wing. She loved me and took good care of me. She fell pregnant very quickly after the loss of her own child, and she had a lovely little girl. They called Bridget. We were reared together; we were just like sisters. We played together and did everything together. We stayed in each other's houses; we were never apart as we grew up. For me, it was like having two dads and sharing a mam.

Kate was brilliant. She took me shopping with her when she was shopping for herself; she never left me out. I loved her like a mam. She had a baby boy when Bridget and I were three. She did not need to worry about us girls; we held hands every place we went. We often kept an eye on the baby for her when she was busy. He was a lovely baby. We used to help her when she was giving him a bath; we got everything ready for her—towels and other things she needed. We started school on the same day. Kate took both of us together, and we were so excited. I was almost a year older than Bridget, but it didn't matter. She was taller than I and looked older. My dad used to say I was petite like mam. At playtime we would play together; all we needed was our own company. We had similar likes and dislikes. I loved singing and dancing. We did Irish dancing together, and we loved it. We were very good at it too. We used to practice in the backyard. Our school used to have a concert at Christmas to make money for the school funds. Both of us would dance, and I would sing Christmas carols. Dad was very proud of me. He would say, 'If your mam could see you now . . .' That used to make me feel sad, but I didn't let Dad see. Bridget and I always did our homework together, and we did our reading with Dad; he loved that.

Dad was special—very caring and always reminding me about my mother. He would talk about her and how she used to sing her songs. I think he wanted to keep her memory alive as much for himself as for me. We used to sing '(How Much Is) That Doggie in the Window?' together. It was her favourite, and mine too as a child. Bridget and I got into mischief and all sorts of things together. As we got older we could not bear to be apart. We used to sleep in each other's houses. Nowadays it's called a sleep over.

We spent all our time laughing and giggling and singing. We were the happiest little girls in Ireland. In the summer holidays, we amused ourselves in our own way. We built a bus with scrap from our backyard. We used old chairs for seating, sheet iron and wood for the side panels, and branches and old sheets for the roof. We travelled all over the world on that bus without ever leaving the backyard. We used cardboard boxes for our cases and buttons for money. We had a shop at the end of the garden where we did our pretend shopping. We saved all the empty cartons from tea, sugar, biscuits, and anything else we found around the house that we could 'sell' in the shop. We used to dress up in old clothes and pretend we were old ladies. We had a lot of fun. We would look at an atlas and pick out a different location every day for our trip on the bus. We were learning about other countries without it been a task, and we still had fun. Our summer holidays were such adventures! We had more fun than people who get to go away for holidays nowadays.

The years were rolling by, and my siblings and I were growing up fast. Angela had done very well in her leaving certificate and went to England to study nursing. She really liked her work. She came back twice to see us, and when she qualified, she decided to stay in England. She was happy there. Emily had made up her mind to join her sister. She left in the spring. Timmy and Anne Marie were very close. He had one more year to do at school, then he wanted to help on the farm. Anne Marie did not like school. She just wanted to work in a shop. I did not really get on with her. I was the baby, and she did not want to know me. If it hadn't been for Bridget, I would not have had anyone to pal around with.

Dad used to take me to the graveyard to pray for mam. We would clean the weeds on her grave and plant fresh flowers for her. During the summer months, we went on a regular basis and changed the flowers every other week. Bridget used to always come with us. We would help him with the planting. When we were finished we would say a prayer for her. Even though Kate was brilliant to me throughout my life, I still felt cheated without my mother. I never told anyone that; I didn't want to hurt anyone's feelings.

My older brothers, Daniel and Timmy, eventually took over the day-to-day running of the farm. Dad seemed to be losing interest, or he just was not up to it anymore. He had acquired another twenty acres from the land commission, which he was very pleased about. Daniel had increased the sheep flock to almost double the amount Dad used to have. He kept only Texel sheep, and he supplied all his neighbours with rams. He made a nice little earner from that side of the farming.

Timmy's passion was training collie dogs. He had a flair for it, as he had a way with dogs. He could train them to do almost anything. He used to take part in dog trials at the local agricultural shows. If he didn't win, he surely placed. He used to travel all over to the trials, even to England and Wales. His room was full of trophies and cups. Daniel used to take his best ewes to the shows as well, and was always winning prizes. He was always in the top three; that meant he could command top prices for his stock.

Daniel was going out with a lovely girl from Ballinrobe in Mayo. Her dad was into sheep in a big way. She used to go to the shows with him; he didn't have a son. She was very interested in sheep, and not afraid to get her hands dirty. Daniel was crazy about her. She was real pretty, but she wasn't just a pretty face. They used to meet up at the shows and spend some time together before they started going out together. She was real nice to Bridget and me.

Dad used to do all the housework as we were growing up. After a while, I started helping out; he didn't seem to be too interested anymore. I started cooking the dinner, and suddenly all the jobs around the house were left for me to do. Dad started getting slower in his walk. He didn't go out as much he used to. He would sit by the fire and snooze. On sunny days he would ramble out and collect the eggs, but that only happened on the odd occasion.

Ann Marie got a job in the local hairdressers. She discovered she had a flair for it, so when the summer holidays were over she persuaded Dad to let her stay on and do her training. She seemed happy, so Dad said yes. She was delighted. She finished her training in a couple of years and got a job in Dublin. She could not wait to get away from home. We heard from her only occasionally after she left.

Bridget and I were still the best of friends. As teenagers, we thought we knew everything. We were beginning to take notice of boys. Bridget was tall for her age, with a crowning head of dark, curly hair. She was very pretty, and she knew it. She had a lovely figure with curves in all the right places. I, on the other hand, was skinny. I had no womanly shape whatsoever. I could pass for a boy. Dad used to say I would fill out as I got older, and I couldn't wait. I had long, blonde hair and green eyes. I needed to grow a bit more. I knew I would never be tall, but I would have liked to be a bit taller.

We used to go to the pictures on a Friday night. We were only thirteen and fourteen, so Daniel or Kate's husband, Mike, always picked us up. That wasn't 'cool', but it was the only way we were allowed go. Kate was very good at dressmaking, so she showed us how to cut out the makings of a dress from a pattern. We both loved sewing; it was our new passion. We could make a dress for a fraction of the price of one in the shops. We used to go to town on the bus during the school holidays and window shop, taking note of styles for the season. We would bring pens and notepads with us and roughly sketch out the styles we fancied; we thought we were very clever. We would buy remnants of material or the end of a roll. We always got a bargain, and we couldn't wait to get home to make up our new dresses. We were really into fashion. We would spend ages deciding on what style or pattern we would use. We could even make up our own patterns from old newspapers. We would lay the material on the floor in one of our bedrooms before we decided on a particular style. We would chat for hours as to what we were going to do; we never fell out or disagreed. It used to take an age to decide on a particular style—such big decisions at the time. Once we decided on the particular style of the dress, it didn't take us long to make it up once we had it cut out. Putting in the zip could be tricky depending on the material, but we always got it right in the end. Then we had to model the dress and see if it was okay. Would we make headbands in the same material or just leave our hair as it was? All of this used to take hours, and sometimes days, but we were always happy and never bored.

One day when I came home from school, Dad was sitting in his usual chair by the fire. I spoke to him when I came in, but he didn't answer. I thought he must be asleep. I went around to face his chair and immediately knew he was dead. I dropped to my knees beside him and started crying. My loving dad had died alone. He had been dead for some time, I could tell. I went outside to see if I could see any of my brothers. I saw Daniel coming up the lane to the house. I said, 'Daniel, Dad has passed away. I found him when I got back from school.'

He said, 'Rosie, I am so sorry that it was you who found him.' He put his arms around me and gave me a hug. We went into the kitchen together and comforted each other. He had been such a good dad; we would miss him. Timmy came in, and he too was upset when we told him. Daniel said he would go to fetch the priest and the doctor, but first they would put him on the bed. Timmy went to fetch Kate.

She would know what to do. Bridget came with her mother, so we went to my room. I was feeling very sad. I would really miss him. Bridget was sad also; she was very fond of him too. We cried together.

The doctor came and pronounced him dead, and the priest came also. I had never seen a dead person before. I was just sad that the first one I saw had to be my dad. Kate had changed his clothes and shaved him and laid him out on the bed. He looked so peaceful. He had always been there for me. What was I going to do without him? I loved him dearly. Pity I never got a chance to say goodbye.

The priest said the rosary when the doctor had left. By now a lot of the neighbours had heard the news, and they had come to the house to sympathize with us. Everyone had nothing but praise for Dad. They told us how he had been completely besotted with our mother and would do anything for her, and she had been the same. Dad never got over Mam's death. Life without her was a chore for him. After her death, all that kept him going was seeing me grow up. I was fifteen, so he must have felt it was time to leave and join Nora, the love of his life. He died of a heart attack, but what was so sad was that he died alone. I was not so sure how I was going to cope without Dad. I was fifteen— not old enough yet to stand on my own.

Dad was waked in the house, and we were amazed at all the people who came to sympathize with us. I had never cried so much; I felt so alone without him. The next day he was buried alongside his beloved Nora, my mam. All the neighbours were brilliant. They brought sandwiches and lots of food. They couldn't do enough for us, and of course Kate was on hand to help in any way.

When all was over and we were back at the house, I finally realized how much I was going to miss my dad. My brothers had never been that close to me. I never went to them with a problem. I would go to Kate; I felt I could tell her anything. Daniel spent a lot of time with his girlfriend, Deirdre; he stayed over with her almost every weekend. Timmy didn't have a girlfriend; as far as I knew, he had never been serious about anyone. I usually stayed with Bridget, so Timmy was on his own. He started drinking and leaving the house in a mess, expecting me to clean up after him. With Dad gone, there was no connection. We appeared to be pulling in opposite directions. No one had time to sit and chat or say how we felt.

The first summer without Dad was dreadful. When there was lots of work to do on the farm, I would cook for all the workers, and Bridget would help out. We used to eye up the guys on the tractor and have crack with them. Daniel didn't seem to be bothered about the banter, but Timmy used to be furious, giving out to us for hours. Daniel would tell him to lay off, and it would all end in an argument. I used to think it was all my fault. It got to the point that, when Timmy came in, I usually left. I couldn't bear to be in the same room with him. Dad had always been such a mild-mannered person. He would never pick an argument; he would always find a solution. But Timmy was the total opposite, always finding fault. He was moody and bad tempered. He probably missed Dad, but never said. He just moped about. He and Daniel seemed to be heading in opposite directions too.

Daniel decided to build a new house on the land. He had discussed it with Dad before he passed, and had applied for planning permission. He was just waiting for approval. We were bored, Bridget and I. We didn't know what to do to pass the time for the summer holidays. Oh, we still did our dressmaking and went to the pictures on Friday nights, but we needed excitement. Bridget suggested we apply for jobs in the local hotel for the summer holidays. We went together, and they were only too glad to give us jobs. The owners, Liam and Nuala, knew our parents and our background, so they knew we were honest and trustworthy. We were employed as chambermaids, and we were over the moon. We couldn't wait to get started. We just worked four hours every morning, but we loved it. We could get our breakfast at the hotel after we had finished our work. I had to prepare dinner for my brothers, which was a bit of a nuisance, as I was always rushing home to get started in the kitchen. Bridget suggested I prepare dinner the night before and leave it on the stove on the slow burner so it would be ready when they wanted it. She thought that would save me rushing home and getting all flustered. I did try that, and it worked out okay. It just meant that I had to get up earlier and prepare the vegetables and leave everything all ready. I used to put on the porridge too, so that they only had to reheat it when they got up. It all worked out fine for all of us. I was keeping out of Timmy's way, which suited us both. I used to stay with Bridget most nights; we always had so much to talk about.

Bridget loved working. She loved having her own pocket money. She kept saying she wasn't going back to school, that she was going to continue working. I was a bit apprehensive about leaving school. Without Dad I didn't have anyone to discuss my future with. My brothers only cared about someone cooking for them; they didn't really care about my well-being. Daniel had received planning permission for his house. He had already started on the foundations, so he was completely involved with the building work. Timmy was still doing his own thing; he was still training the collies and winning prizes with them, and still as miserable as sin.

Bridget was beginning to get bored, and we talked at length as to what we were going to do with our lives. We decided we were not going to go back to school. After all, we were grown up now, or so we thought. I was sixteen gone, and Bridget would be sixteen on her next birthday. We decided go to England after Christmas. Kate had a sister, Mary, who lived in London. Kate told us she would contact her and see if we could stay with her until we got settled. She said she wouldn't have to worry about us if her sister could accommodate us for some time. All we had to do was wait for a reply from her. One evening my brothers were at home, so I explained to them what I was going to do. I told them they wouldn't have to worry about me, because we would be staying with Kate's sister. They were a bit surprised. Daniel said, 'Rose, I am sorry I have not had time for you since Dad died. Is that the reason you're leaving?'

I said, 'No, not at all. Ye had your own lives to live, and I want to do my own thing. Only I do not know what that is exactly.' I knew I just want to get away.

Daniel said, 'I understand where you're coming from.' Then he said, 'Deirdre and I are getting married in the spring. Will ye stay until then? We want both of you at our wedding.' I told him I would discuss it with Bridget, and I thought it would be fine.

Timmy was giving out. He said, 'Ye don't know what ye want to do!' He didn't want me to go.

I said, 'It is not up to you. You are never very nice to me anyway.'

He said, 'I am sorry. Please, Rose, let me make it up to you. I will change.'

But my mind was made up. 'Too little too late,' I told him. 'I am not annoyed with you, Timmy,' I said. 'I just want to see a bit of the world and enjoy it.'

'Fair enough, sis,' he said, and he hugged me.

Bridget came over later; we were doing each other's hair. I told her about Daniel's wedding and how he wanted us both to be there. She thought for a little while and then said, 'We will stay for the wedding, but after that we are off.' Once we had made our minds up that we were leaving, nothing seemed to matter that much. All we wanted was some excitement; we felt we were suffocating at home. We were trying to make some positive decisions concerning our departure. What exactly were we going to do when we got there? Go to college perhaps? Get work somewhere? Doing what? Were we crazy? We had a lot of unanswered questions. We had no plan. It was crazy, but we were both adamant that we were going. For the moment, we were going to make the best of the short time we had left and worry later. Very mature. I said, 'Who cares? We have some money saved, so we're not completely stupid.' We wanted a buzz out of life, and we felt sure we would get that in London.

Chapter 3

BRIDGET AND I were really looking forward to my brother Daniel's wedding to Deirdre; we were going to make it special. Neither of us had ever attended a wedding before, so we decided to go all out to make it a day to remember. We went to Galway for the day to shop for material. This time we could afford the best—not the end of a roll or remnants; nothing but the best. We had a little money put away from our holiday jobs; we thought we were 'rich'. I had designed my outfit for the wedding. I discovered it was easy to make trousers, so I had designed a trouser suit for the big day—slim-fit trousers and a long-line sleeveless jacket, which I'd wear with a matching polo shirt and white accessories. We always did each other's hair, so I intended putting ringlets in mine. Then I would thread a white ribbon through it and wear it partially up. I thought that would look nice. Bridget was tall and elegant, so she went for an empire-line dress in blue with a bolero jacket and red accessories. She planned to wear her hair in much the same style as mine.

We took great care in making those garments. We laid out the material on the floor of my bedroom quite a few times before we cut out the patterns so as not to make a mistake and ruin the material. We were very thrifty; we never wasted anything. I used to make the patterns out of old newspapers, pin the pieces onto the material, and cut round. Then the pieces would ready to stitch. It was very simple really, and we got a lot of pleasure out of making our own clothes. Even if I say so myself, we were pretty good at it. We made mine first. Bridget was a dab hand with the iron. She loved ironing. She pressed my suit when I had it finished, then I slipped it on to see what it looked like. It looked amazing! Just as good as one bought in the shop. I was very pleased with the end result. Then I repeated the same procedure with Bridget's dress. It was royal blue, and she looked adorable in it. I then cut out the jacket and the lining. It took a little longer to make the jacket because it was lined, and if the lining is not right, the jacket will not look right. She pressed it and then tried it on. We had surpassed ourselves! It looked stunning. We were delighted with it.

We could not afford to buy new shoes for our outfits, so I hit on the idea of buying one fancy pair of shoes in the latest fashion, which we could dye whatever colour we needed for wherever outfit we were wearing (pretty clever). We were great with coming up with ideas to save us money.

We were up bright and early the day of the wedding. It was a lovely day . . . a little nippy in the morning. We did each other's hair. I also did Kate's hair. She always wore her hair short, so I had put colour in it a few days before the big day, and it looked well. I had also made a dress for her. It was nothing fancy, but she was well pleased with it, and she bought a hat in town to match the dress. She looked really pretty; she was a very attractive woman.

We had a great time at the reception, it was held in Daniel and Deirdre's new house. They had just moved in a couple of weeks before the wedding. The neighbours provided the music, and we had great crack. We danced all night, and we couldn't have had a better time. Sadly, we were leaving for England in two days' time. Even though we were anxious to leave, we were getting a bit lonely, and we were sad at the thought of leaving Kate. Actually, I was a bit apprehensive about leaving Kate. She had always been there for me. It felt a bit strange, like losing my mother all over again. Funnily enough, Bridget couldn't wait to get away. She had fantastic parents who would not stand in her way.

The day we were leaving, all the neighbours came to call and wish us luck and say goodbye. We were very touched by how many came to bid us farewell. Kate was very upset. She could not bear to wave goodbye; she said her goodbyes indoors. Timmy apologized to me for his behaviour and said he hadn't intended to hurt my feelings. He kissed me and said goodbye. I felt a bit emotional. Daniel took us to the station, and we got the train to Rosslare. We arrived in record time. We boarded the ferry and set about getting our seats and making ourselves comfortable.

We were so excited! We had set out on our adventure, and it was just beginning. We were full of hope that life would be kind to us; we intended to make the most of it. The crowds were gathering fast on the ferry, and all the seats were filling up. All the passengers were sorting out their seats so that they could get a sleep later on. The bar didn't open until we set sail. A lot of the younger people were longing for it to open up. Some of them had consumed enough already; they were probably sad at leaving home. We settled down in our seats.

We were just falling asleep when the bar opened and the crowd started congregating. Suddenly the music started up, and we heard talk about a *hooley* (Irish dance and song and merriment) in the kitchen! It was fantastic. Bridget and I joined in with the singing, and lots of people were dancing in the aisles. The time passed so quickly we could spy land before we realized we had even set sail. Bridget and I went on deck. We were so excited! We had each brought only one case with us so that we wouldn't be struggling with oversized bags. We thought we would look more sophisticated with just one bag that we could handle gracefully.

We got the train from Holyhead to London, and that was fairly packed. We were lucky to find a seat. We were still excited. We could hardly wait until we got to London. All we could see on our journey was people's backyards. We didn't see a lot of the countryside. Nonetheless, that didn't dampen our enthusiasm; we were like two kids in a sweet shop. As we approached St Pancras station, we realized we were almost at the end of our journey. We'd had a cup of tea and a sandwich on the train; it was almost lunchtime so we were getting hungry again.

When we got off at the station, we looked around for Kate's sister, Mary. She had told Kate that she would be holding a card with our names on it; we had no other means of identifying her. We walked up and down eying up the crowd that was there to pick up relatives, but we didn't see her. We were beginning to get anxious. What if she had forgotten us? Maybe she'd been delayed. The possibilities were endless. All we could do was sit and wait. I suggested to Bridget that we get a cup of tea and take it in turns to inspect the crowd that was gathering and disappearing before our eyes. *Soon it will be our turn*, I kept saying to myself. We sat and chatted for a while, then Bridget got up and said she would check the crowd again. By now the bulk of the people had left, and we were getting worried. Bridget came back excited. 'In here!' she cried. We grabbed our bags and ran over to Mary.

She gave both of us a hug and said, 'Welcome to London!' We were so relieved, we hugged and kissed her. She explained there had been an accident on the route they usually took, so they'd had to do a detour, which added to the delay. She apologized for being late.

We both said in unison, 'Not to worry!' It was fine.

We got into the car, and she introduced us to her husband, Harold. We were amazed at all the buildings, the traffic, the red buses, and all the people rushing here and there. So, we hugged each other in the back of the car and said, 'Welcome to London!' And we burst out laughing. We were here at last.

When we got to Mary's house, she took us upstairs to our room. She had put her two children into one room to make room for us. At that point, we were starving, and Mary had a lovely dinner ready for us. We ate every morsel. W all chatted for a little, but we were tired so we went to bed early that night. We couldn't wait until morning to go exploring.

We slept like logs, but we were up early next morning. Mary gave us directions to places we might go, and she also gave us a door key. She worked part time, and knew she may not be around later on. Our own key gave us more freedom. We got ready and set off on our merry way. We were amazed at the hordes of people rushing about. We couldn't figure out where they were all heading or what they were all out and about at the same time for. It was so unlike home. No one spoke to us or even looked in our direction. We couldn't understand why everyone seemed in such a hurry; had they all slept in and were late for work?

We got in with the crowd, and soon we were rushing down the street. We looked at each other and burst out laughing. 'This is infectious!' I said. 'Now *we* are rushing!' Then we understood. No one dilly-dallies. They just go about their business, and they don't care what the neighbours are doing.

Mary had given us the names and addresses of people we might look up. They were mostly ladies who needed help with their kids—taking them to school and picking them up at the end of the day. I went to the home of one of the names on the list and knocked on the door. I was greeted by a very nice lady. I explained who I was. She invited me in and introduced herself. 'I am working from home today,' she said. 'I work in the heart of the city, and I need someone I can trust to take my children to school, do light housework, and collect them up later on from school.' She seemed very nice. 'I know Mary's family,' she told me. 'I feel sure I can trust you.' I also had a glowing reference from the hotel where I had worked for the summer, which impressed her. The money seemed more than generous, so I accepted the job. I could live in if I wished, and I thought, *Why not? I'll give it a go.* I explained to her that I would take the job only temporarily, because I was unsure as to what I really wanted to do. I told her I might go back to college. She was impressed and gave me good advice about local colleges. 'You know,' she said, 'you can do any course on a part-time basis. Your time would tie in with my children's school time. Maybe you might like to check out your options. I can give you phone numbers to help you get started.'

I said, 'Great. Thank you.'

I had arranged to meet Bridget down the road in a café later. She was already there sipping her coffee and looking very sophisticated when I arrived. I got my drink and approached her table. 'May I sit here, madam?' I asked her sombrely.

She burst out laughing. 'Sit down, you idiot,' she replied. We were both laughing. I told her I had got a job, and she said she had too! We discovered hers was on the same road as mine and just a few doors away. We hugged and decided that was brilliant. We were delighted, and our jobs were only a few roads away from Mary's house.

After chatting for a while, we discovered that we both started on the same day, we were both living in, and the kids were going to the same school. It was all too good to be true. We were both going to move into our new lodgings the next day. We were going to have our own rooms! I had a lovely room with television and my own shower; it all looked very fancy. Bridget's room was equally as nice. We would meet up together and do the school run.

We also decided to enrol in college. We had a few weeks yet to decide what subject we wished to study. I said, 'Bridget, let's have a look around and see what this place has to offer us, and maybe pick up some information on classes we can take.'

She said, 'What a brilliant idea!'

'Then we could go for a coffee in the canteen and check out the talent,' I suggested, 'Or we could have a coffee in our own lodgings.'

'Excellent,' she said. We continued chatting and enjoying our coffee as we planned what we were going to do.

We decided to go to the local market on Saturday and see what kind of material was on sale there. We both had the whole day to ourselves on Saturdays; we could whatever we wished. We got up early and headed in the direction of the market. It was amazing. You could buy anything and everything in the market. We bought lovely material and toiletries, perfume, and lots of bits and pieces. The material wasn't expensive either. We went for a coffee and to rest our feet. We had done a lot of walking. We needed a gossip anyway. We treated ourselves to a fresh cream cake.

So far we couldn't complain. In fact, we were on top of the world. We would need to find out if we could acquire a sewing machine, as we hadn't brought many clothes with us. We both decided we would meet in my room later and write to Kate and fill her in on our adventures so far. We were still on a high.

On our way back, we noticed a poster for the cinema, and it looked as if it wasn't too far from the market. We could come out later and watch a film. Everything was so convenient—just a bus ride away. We were so lucky. We both wrote a nice long letter to Kate. I wrote to Daniel and Deirdre also. I thought it better to keep a line of communication open. I told them to tell Timmy I would write to him later in the week, so that he would not feel left out.

Mary had rung Kate, telling her we were fine. We just wanted to fill her in on all the details. After all, we were seeing everything with fresh eyes, and we were excited and amazed with so many things. We went to the Plaza Cinema. Oh my God, you would not believe it. It was fantastic— lovely red velvet curtains around the screen, and velvet seating. The foyer was so tastefully laid out, with red being the main colour. One could buy all types of sweets and crisps, drinks and popcorn. We had never had popcorn before, so we indulged, and it was lovely. We could also buy all types of magazines, or just sit at a table and have a cup of tea or coffee. It was a great night out. We enjoyed the film. It was a comedy, and we laughed till we cried. It was good fun.

The area we were living in was called Greenwich; there was also had a quaint little village of the same name. It is just twenty minutes from central London. There were close links with the Royal family going back to the Middle Ages. The buildings were old and fantastic. The Royal Naval College was a spectacular building. Henry VIII was one of Greenwich's former residents. The view from the top of Greenwich Park is still the most impressive in London. Up the hill was the most famous building of all, the Royal Observatory, a scientific site founded by Charles II in 1675 to improve navigation at sea and determine longitude—one's exact position east and west while at sea or on land, based on the Prime Meridian in Greenwich. Until 1954, Greenwich was the home of Greenwich Mean Time, which was based on celestial observations made at the site. It was the centre for the measuring of world and space time—the starting point for each new day at the stroke of midnight.

There was a fantastic park—really huge—called the Royal Park. It was maintained so well; the trees and shrubs and flowers were out of this world. One could stroll around there for weeks and never get tired of it. Bridget and I loved going there on Sundays. We could sit there on the benches or go for a stroll. It was a beautiful place, known all over the world. We felt very privileged for having visited it. There were fantastic old shops in the village—really old-fashioned ones—and lovely cafés and restaurants and a few bakeries, which offered the most delicious bread. There were craft shops and art galleries with the most wonderful paintings One could spend hours walking around admiring the paintings. When you stand back and take in the beauty of a painting, you may see something you did not notice the first time you stopped to admire it. I could spend all day admiring all the work of the famous artists and local artists as well. Bridget was not that keen on the art galleries, but she knew I liked that sort of thing, so she endured our visits. The streets were covered in cobblestones; they are very quaint . . . different.

One Sunday, we went for a coffee and chatted about all we had seen. There were lots of shops we still needed to see, and there were lots of second-hand shops all over the place. We were amazed. If some of that stuff had been back home, it would be thrown out as rubbish! We took our time and enjoyed our coffee and decided which direction we would go next. We decided we would take a left and check out the shops in that direction. The first shop we looked in had an electric sewing machine. I was so excited when I saw it. I enquired about the price, and it wasn't expensive. Between us we could make up the money, so we bought it. It was pretty light to carry. Now we were in business. We could start making our own clothes again. This was brilliant!

There were still a lot of shops to explore, but we were getting tired, so we decided we didn't have to see it all in one day. We decided to head home. We thought we would pay Mary a visit on the way back. We got some fancy cakes in one of the bakeries so that we could have a little treat with a cup of tea. As we walked home to Mary's, we chatted about the great day we'd had and the luck we'd had in finding a sewing machine. We chatted along the way and we were at Mary's gate before we realized. We were really looking forward to a cuppa. Mary said we shouldn't have bothered with the cakes; nonetheless, we enjoyed one each. We chatted for some time. We showed Mary the sewing machine. She couldn't believe we'd got such a bargain. She tried it out with a scrap of material, and it worked perfectly. Boy, were we pleased.

We were each going back to our rooms, and we would meet up later and decide what we would do later on. We usually had our meals with the families we worked for. That was handy. Or if we wished, we could cook our own. We were happy enough living in. We went back to the nearby colleges to sort out the subjects we were going to study. We found we could go to classes two days a week or at night. We decided we would do the two days in the week; we could still pick up the kids from their school. We didn't have to pay for classes, as we weren't eighteen yet. We had chosen the college nearest to us, and we were both going to start classes after the summer holidays. We would study our A levels. We wrote and told Kate, and she wrote back directly. She couldn't believe we were so sensible; she was over the moon.

We made all new clothes for ourselves. We got to know the traders in the stalls at the market, and we always managed to get a bargain. We were chatting to one of the stallholders at the market one day, and she told me she would give us the material for free if we would make some dresses for her for the stall. We decided we would give it a try for a month and see how we got on. It was a roaring success. We were making money, and she was too. We were all happy. But all that would have to change when we went to college in September. We explained that to the stallholder. She was okay about it.

We were thinking we might make the odd garment if we had time and try to build up some stock. We could take a stall in the market and sell for ourselves and cut out the middleman—in this case woman. It was worth a try. We did as we had planned. It took us a couple of months to build up our stock. The only problem was that we didn't have half enough. We were sold out in an hour. Everyone loved our dresses. We were tempted to drop the classes, but we made a pact that we would stick at them until we qualified, and that is just what we did.

We studied hard together for two years and passed our A levels with top marks. It was worth it. Now we could really decide what we wanted to do. First we were going to take a holiday and go home for two weeks and see our families. When we wrote and told Kate our plans she was elated. She said they were going to have a party for us for doing so well with our studies. We felt we had achieved something important even though we were unsure as to what we wanted to do. We were going home in a weeks' time, and we were excited about it.

Chapter 4

KATE WROTE AND told us she and Mike were going to meet us at the station; we thought that was great. Once again we were excited. Just two years ago we had been excited about going to England; now we were going in the opposite direction, and we were over the moon about going home. So far, life had being good to us; we were enjoying every minute of it.

We had bought presents for our families. I got a lovely picture in an art gallery for Daniel and Deirdre for their new house; it would look good in their living room. I bought Timmy a nice shirt. He was not the best for buying his own clothes; in fact, he was usually desperate by the time he got around to buying clothes. I got a long-line cardigan for Kate and a sweater for Mike.

We had a very nice crossing on the way back. It's so different when you know what to expect instead of anticipating what might happen. We felt so confident on that return journey, especially because we had some savings and did not have to worry about money. Oh, we weren't going mad or anything like that. A bit of money just gave us independence and confidence. There is nothing like the feeling of being equal to your fellow man. It is quite possible that we were better off than a lot of them. We relaxed on the boat and acted as if we were seasoned travellers. We got two coffees and sat down and admired the talent or criticized whatever was appropriate at the time. We had a good giggle anyway, and that was all that mattered. We had a snooze during the journey, and we ordered an Irish breakfast in the morning before the restaurant closed for docking. We enjoyed the breakfast; it was filling. We met two nice fellas while we were eating. We told them so many lies we couldn't remember half of them! We had a good laugh when they left. We got the train down to Galway. It wasn't too packed, and we found seats together, which was great.

Kate and Mike were at the station when we pulled in. They hugged us and kissed us. One would think we'd been gone for ten years instead of just two. We were all laughing and crying. We were so happy. We began asking about our friends and neighbours, dying to hear the gossip. When you are at home, nothing seems to happen. But go away, and you miss all the excitement.

We were at the house in no time at all. The weather must have been good over the previous month or so, as we observed that all the silage appeared to have been cut, and a lot of the oats and corn. It's hard to remember about things like that when you don't see the work being done. When we got out of the car and looked around, we looked at each other. 'Home sweet home!' We hugged each other; we were glad to be back.

Kate had a lovely chicken casserole cooked. All she had to do was heat it. We took a short walk outside. It's funny. When you go away you expect things to change, but oddly enough, everything often remains the same. We were just outside when Bridget's kid brother came running up the drive. Oh, how he hugged and kissed us. Brian was fifteen, and boy had he grown! We could not believe it. He had been a lovely child. Bridget and I had both looked after him lots of times, and he had turned into a fine young man. We had dinner with Kate and Mike, which was delicious. We finished off with homemade apple pie and a cup of tea. Mike told us there was a trade dance in town. They were going, and he asked if we would like to go with them. We said yes, of course; we didn't have to think twice. I said, 'I am going to stroll down to see Daniel.'

Bridget said, 'I am coming too,' so we both set off together, chatting away.

We reached the house, and Deirdre answered the door. She said, 'Welcome home, you two. Come on in!' When we went inside she said, 'Would ye like the guided tour?' We both said yes please, so she showed us around the house. It looked lovely; it was all painted and decorated. They had a lovely fitted kitchen with a solid-fuel range for cooking; it was so warm and cosy. They had built-in wardrobes in all the bedrooms, and a lovely bathroom. They didn't have all the rooms furnished yet, but they were getting there. They had a nice-size living room, which was decorated with taste.

I said, 'I got ye a present for the house!' And I handed her the painting.

She looked at it and admired it. I could tell she liked it. She hugged me and said, 'Thanks very much. I know where that is going. In the living room over the fireplace.' I knew she would like it. It was a painting of a young couple walking hand in hand on the beach. It reminded me of them.

She said Daniel should be home soon, and sure he was. He picked me up and danced around the kitchen with me kissing and hugging me, saying he'd missed his baby sister. He kissed and hugged Bridget too, saying she had grown and put on a little weight. He turned to me and said, 'Rose, you must be starving yourself since you left home. You are very skinny, and you don't appear to have grown one inch!'

I said, 'I am doing my best, but nothing is happening.'

'Not to worry,' he said, 'we can't all be giants.' Everyone laughed.

As we drank a coffee in the kitchen, we told them about all the things we had done and seen. We promised that we had a lot more to see. Daniel said, 'I am very impressed with you for going back to school and doing so well.' I believe we deserved great credit. He said, 'Rose, what do you intend to do?'

I said, 'I haven't made up my mind yet. It's difficult to decide what you really want to do. Bridget is thinking of getting a job in one of the banks. I'm half thinking of going back to college. Or maybe I might study to be a nurse. I can't really make up my mind. There's no rush; we have two weeks to think about it, so we will enjoy ourselves for now.' I asked Daniel, 'How is Timmy doing?'

'You will see for yourself,' he said. I wasn't sure if that meant good or bad. We would have to wait and see. Bridget and I decided we would pay him a quick visit before we headed home. We left Daniel's saying we would see them soon.

As we walked down the road toward my old home, I got very emotional. Even Dad's old faithful dog was nowhere to be seen. I sure missed my dad. I kept my feelings to myself so I wouldn't upset other family members. As we came nearer the house, I noticed Timmy coming down the lane. He quickened his step when he saw that he had visitors. As he came nearer, he realized it was us. He stretched out his arms and gave me a big hug when he reached us. With tears in his eyes he said, 'Rose, I really missed you.' I told him I had missed him also. He gave Bridget a hug and a kiss. He asked, 'Are ye back to stay?' We started laughing and told him we were only on vacation, so he started laughing too. 'Come inside,' he said. We followed him.

I started crying when I saw the empty chair by the fire. Tommy hugged me again and said, 'I know how you feel. I feel like that every day. He was a great dad, both a mother and dad to us after Mam passed. He never got over losing her.'

'I know,' I said. 'He used to speak about her all the time when I was little. I hope when I fall in love it will be as special as what they had.'

Timmy said, 'Me too.' I looked about and was surprised how tidy the kitchen looked. I asked Timmy if there was someone special in his life. He smiled and said, 'I have met the woman of my dreams, and I am over the moon.'

I hugged him, saying, 'I am so pleased for you.'

He said, 'I was at a show in Dublin, and this lovely girl called Clare watched me put the dog through her paces. She was fascinated. And I was fascinated with her. I was doing all in my power to impress her. It must have worked. I offered to take her to dinner that evening, and she accepted. We have been together since, and that was six months ago. We are very happy. We enjoy each other's company.' Then he said, 'Will ye have a quick coffee with me?'

I said, 'Yes, sure.' Bridget and I were both amazed at the change in him. He said that Clare stayed over most weekends. She lived and worked in Dublin and came down by train. I said, 'Aren't you lucky?'

'I sure am,' he replied. We said we were going dancing with Kate and Mike later.

He said, 'That's a dinner and dance. Ye best go home and sort out what ye are going to wear.'

When we got home Bridget said to Kate, 'You never told us it was a dinner dance!'

Kate said, 'We wanted to go tonight, not next week!'

We laughed. 'We are not that bad!' I said. Kate told us to sort out something to wear, and offered us a cup of tea or coffee. 'No, thank you,' I said, 'we had one with Timmy.' We went upstairs to rummage through all the boxes that Kate had stored for us. She had washed all the clothes we had left behind and stored them in boxes so we could have them when we returned. She had put our names on the boxes so it was easier to sort out.

We started throwing everything on the bed, looking and rummaging. We needed evening dresses or fancy trouser suits. Among all the chaos I spotted the very dress. It was full length and made in gold material. I had made it a long time ago, but had never had the opportunity to wear it. I had also made a wrap to match the dress. Bridget was still rummaging. At last she said, 'I've found the one!' She picked a lovely red dress. Because of her long legs, she looked absolutely fantastic in it. She was really tall for her age, and she had a figure to die for. On the other hand, I was a year older and looked a lot younger. I was still very skinny with a figure like a young boy. Not a curve in sight. I hated the way I looked. Everyone used to say I was very pretty. I had long, blonde hair, and Bridget had jet black hair. We tried on our dresses and modelled them for each other and agreed that they would do. Then we set about doing each other's hair. I wore mine up at the back and wispy around my face.

I borrowed long earrings from Kate. Bridget gave me her seal of approval. She said, 'You look lovely.' *That will do me*, I thought. I started toying with Bridget's hair to come up with a style to suit her. I piled most of it on top of her head and made ringlets around the back. She liked it. She also borrowed earrings from her mum to complete the picture. I wore black platform shoes and carried a black clutch bag. The inside of my wrap was black, with a black trim around the edge, and I thought the ensemble looked quite fetching. I was ready to go. Bridget wore black accessories as well. Her red dress had a black sash, which made it look even better on her. Kate wore a silver dress that I had made her for her birthday some time ago. I had made a matching tie for Mike with the leftover material, which I had completely forgotten about. It looked great on him. At last we were ready to go.

We got there with plenty of time to spare. There were lots of people gathering and finding their seating. There was a large blackboard in the foyer with lists of the people who were to sit at each of the numbered tables. We found our table number and proceeded to find the table itself in the dining room. There were four other people assigned to our table; we were hoping that they would be nice people and that there might be some young men so that we might have someone to dance with. After a little time, we saw a couple approaching our table. Two young men were strolling behind them. I kicked Bridget under the table. 'Spot the talent,' I said. 'The fellas look great. Very attractive. We may be in luck!' Mike stood up and introduced us, and the other gentleman did the same with his family. They seemed a pleasant family. We started chatting, and the staff started distributing the menus. We made our choice of food, and the others appeared to do the same. Service was very swift. We all had our starters in no time at all. Everyone was chatting and getting to know each other. The main course consisted of beef or salmon with all the trimmings. I had the beef, and it was absolutely delicious—tasty and tender. One can't beat the Irish meat. Some of the others at the table had chosen the salmon, and they gave it the thumbs up, saying it was very tasty. The adults had wine with their dinner while we had water, and the young men had soft drinks. The sweet trolley was unbelievable. I ordered cheesecake, and Bridget had the black forest gateau, and we shared them. I could have eaten every dessert on the trolley and not put on an ounce. Kate did not have anything; everyone at the table had coffee.

The band started to set up their instruments, and finally they began to play. When the tables were cleared, they were moved to the side of the room to give more room for dancing. The band started playing an old-time waltz. Mike got up and asked Kate to dance, and the other couple took to the floor too, as did half the people in the room. We looked at the boys and said, 'Can ye dance?'

'Sure,' said the one called John. He and his brother, Joseph, both stood up, and we were just raring to go. The band were playing the 'Blue Danube' waltz. I loved that one. We took to the floor, and sure enough, the boys could dance. They would match us any day. They twirled us around the floor. John was a really nice guy, very polite. I really liked him. When the dance was over, instead of walking back to our seats, we just swapped partners and started dancing to the music again. It was jiving, and we were up for that. We thought we were experts when it came to jiving. We soon realized we were not alone. They were great dancers also. We had a fantastic night. We just kept swapping partners throughout the night. We had great crack . . . the best of fun. It was the first time we'd been to something like that, and we thoroughly enjoyed ourselves. Mike and Kate and John's parents took a leaf out of our book and swapped partners a few times. Before the night was over, we had both danced with everyone who had sat around the table.

All too soon, the band announced it was the last dance. John got to his feet immediately and asked me to dance. It was a waltz, just what we had started with. I can't explain how I felt. I just wanted him to put his arms around me forever. I felt so safe in his arms. We held each other tight as if we were the only ones on the floor. I couldn't believe the night was over. My heart was pounding. I didn't want the night to end. We came back to the table and sat for a few minutes, then we put on our wraps and said our goodbyes to each of the boys. John gave me a hug and pushed a piece of paper into my hand. 'I need to see you again,' he whispered as we said our final farewells.

Bridget and I were both tired. We announced that we were going to have a lie-in in the morning. We went straight to bed when we got home. There was none of the usual chat. We just wanted to get some sleep. It took me ages to get to sleep. I found I had feelings for John. I had never had a boyfriend; I just didn't understand my feelings. I eventually fell asleep dreaming of him.

I was exhausted in the morning, and didn't get up till late. I had to laugh when I looked around the room. We had clothes thrown all over the place. It looked as if a bomb had hit the place. All the clothes had fallen in an array of colours. We would have to attempt to tidy up before Kate saw the mess; she would think we were used to living in total chaos, which wasn't true. We eventually surfaced and tidied up before getting food. Kate cooked us a big breakfast, which we both enjoyed. We washed up; it was the least we could do.

We decided to go for a walk and try to wake ourselves up a little. We began chatting about the night before—and John and Joseph. I was telling Bridget how I felt about John. She stopped in the middle of the road and said, 'Rose, remember we often spoke about boys and falling in love? We agreed we would have fun for some time before we got serious about anyone.'

I said, 'I understand all that, but you can't just decide to fall in love in two years' time. It doesn't work like that. I know how I feel about him. It might sound stupid, but I can't help how I feel.' We continued walking until we were outside Daniel's house. We knocked on the door, and Deirdre let us in. We told her about the fantastic night we'd had, and I told her about John and how I felt about him. Then I realized I had forgotten about the phone number he'd pushed into my hand as we left. I would need to search for it when we went home.

Deirdre advised me to meet him and see how I felt about him. If our feelings were real, we would find a way to be together. She said, 'Daniel and I will take you two to the pictures if you care to go.' We said that would be lovely. She suggested we might have something to eat before the film started, and we said better again. We went home and lazed around for a while. A few friends called round to see us. We had a chat and some tea. I went to look for that phone number, and sure enough it was in my clutch bag. I was so happy I had found it.

I phoned John that evening and told him we'd had a fantastic night at the dance. He said he had too. They had both enjoyed our company. He said he would like to see me again. I explained that I was going back to London in a little over a week, but he said he still wanted to see me. I said okay, and we agreed to meet on Saturday night.

Bridget and I got ready, dressing casually for the pictures. We had a lovely meal beforehand in a Chinese restaurant. We had a good old chat, then we left and went to the film. We enjoyed that too; it was a comedy. We laughed till we cried; it was great. They dropped us off at Kate's. We had a nightcap with Kate and went to bed.

I told Bridget I had a date with John on Saturday night. I asked her if she minded, and she said no of course not. It was Saturday before we knew it. Time was flying. The phone rang in the morning. It was John. 'I've borrowed my father's car,' he said. 'I'll pick you up at eight if that is agreeable. Do you think Bridget would go out with Joseph?

I said, 'Hang on; I need to ask her.' I did just that, and she said she would go. That was settled. Another night to look forward to.

We had decided we were going to a disco. We each picked out a sexy dress, and we were just going to let our hair down naturally. We were ready some time before they arrived. They were both dressed in T-shirts and jeans. I got into the front seat with John, and Bridget got into the back with Joseph. We both felt nervous. This was our first time being alone with young men; they seemed a little nervous too. We went to the nightclub, and it looked amazing with all the lights. There was quite a crowd there. We got on the floor and danced, then we sat down for a chat and a drink. We danced some more, and before we knew it the night was over. John asked me, 'Rose, do you want to go home straight away or would you like to go for a walk?'

I said, 'Let's go for a walk.' He held my hand, and we strolled down the road till we came to a gateway. He stopped and put his arms around me and kissed me gently on the lips. I liked his lips on mine. We kissed again, and he said we'd best get back. We strolled back again to the car. Joseph and Bridget were waiting for us. We went to MacDonald's on the way home and had some chips. John and Joseph were the perfect gentlemen. They dropped us at the door, kissed us goodbye, and left. I was in dreamland I said to Bridget as we were getting ready for bed, 'It's a pity we are not going to be here for longer.'

She said, 'Don't worry. Things will work out. Love always finds a way.'

We had dinner one night with Timmy and Clare. She was a fantastic cook. We had a good old chat with them, and Timmy dropped us home. We went out together with John and Joseph at the weekend. They took us bowling. Again, we had a good night; we enjoyed ourselves. When we got home, Bridget said, 'I don't want to go out with Joseph again. I don't feel the same about him as he does about me. I don't mind if you go out again with John.'

On my last date with John, he took me out to dinner and presented me with a beautiful bouquet of red roses. I wore a little red dress with black accessories. He said, 'Rose, I can't believe that you made that dress. It's so professionally made.' We had a beautiful meal. At the back of our minds we knew we would not meet for some time, if ever again. We sat in the car for a kiss and a cuddle. We both knew it could have gone further, so we decided to go home. We kissed when we got home, with a longing neither of us was ready to fulfil. If only things had been different. We kissed and said goodbye. Bridget and I were leaving in the morning. John and I promised each other that we would keep in touch . . . ring each other every weekend. We parted with a long, lingering kiss.

Chapter 5

IT TOOK ME ages to get off to sleep after that last date. I kept turning everything over and over in my mind. *I'll be nineteen in a few months' time. Maybe I have fallen in love with John, and he with me. Should we have had sex? God knows we both wanted too.* I had never felt that way about another human being before. I just wanted him so much. I wanted him to be the one to touch me in those oh-so-private places that only someone very special is allowed to touch. I wanted him to be my first love. I eventually fell asleep. I was so tired in the morning. Bridget was as bright as a button. My mind was in turmoil.

After breakfast we popped down the road to say goodbye to Daniel and Deirdre. We had time to have a coffee with them; we didn't need to leave till the afternoon. We left after about half an hour or so and went further down the lane to bid farewell to Timmy. He was very emotional. 'Will you come back for our wedding?' he asked.

I said, 'We both will. Of course. We would be delighted to.' We hugged and said our final farewells.

Back at Bridget's house, we finished packing. We had both brought an extra bag with us; there was no point in leaving our clothes behind. We packed as much as we could. Kate made a light snack for us. Bridget had eaten a hearty breakfast; I had managed only a slice of toast. Kate must have noticed my mood. 'How are you doing, Rose?' she asked.

I said, 'I feel so confused.' I explained how I felt. I told her I had really wanted John last night.

She said, 'Ye were wise not to have gone the whole way. Ye would have regretted later.'

I said, 'No. I'm regretting it now!'

She said, 'You will feel differently in a couple of days. Also, if you miss him too much, you can always come back. There is always a bed for you with us.'

'Thanks, Kate. That is the sweetest thing you could have said to me,' I said. She hugged me, and I began to cry.

Bridget came into the kitchen and joined in the hugging. She said, 'Don't worry, Mam, I will take good care of her. We will take care of each other and heal her heart.' We both started laughing. Mike walked into the kitchen, and he hugged both of us, saying he would miss us. We both thanked them for a fantastic two weeks. We'd had a brilliant time; it just had gone by so quickly. We told them we still hadn't made up our minds yet as to what we were going to do.

We were just about to leave when a car pulled up outside the door. It was John in his dad's car. He said he wanted to have a word. Kate asked him to come inside, and we could talk over a coffee. He explained he was only a first-year engineering student. He had a couple more years before he would be qualified and would be able to take on the responsibility of a family. He asked me to wait for him. He said that we could spend the holidays together and see how things worked out between us. He said, 'I really wanted you last night, but if we had given in, we could have ruined both our futures.' By this time I was in tears. John was so considerate and kind. He kissed me and gave me a big hug. He said, 'Promise me you will write every week. We can take it in turn to phone each other.' He gave me a little box like a ring box. He said, 'Open it.' It was a lovely Claddagh ring. These old-fashioned wedding rings feature a heart held with two hands. You wear the ring with the heart faced in if you have given your heart away, and with the heart facing out if you are available. 'Wear it always,' he said. 'It will remind you of me. One day I hope to give you the real thing.' We kissed for the last time, and he left.

Kate said after he had left, 'He is one special guy. Ye will be happy together one day.'

I said, 'I know we will,' and I started crying.

Kate hugged me again, and said, 'You will be fine.'

Mike and Kate said that they would take us to the station. We were all packed, so we thought it best to leave. We had said all our goodbyes; there was no point in hanging about. Soon we were on the move. My heart was heavy. All I could think of was John. Why did he have to be so sensible? Could he not be reckless? We could take our chance, and to hell with being sensible! We could be lucky and not get pregnant, but then again, knowing my luck, I would get pregnant the very first time. That's when the 'fun' would begin. He would probably blame me and leave me holding the baby. Oh, heck. What the hell? I figured I would probably have to wait until I was an old maid before I had sex, and by then I would have gone off the idea. I came back down to earth with a bang when Bridget said we are at the station. I couldn't believe we were there already. I looked around, and we were surely.

Bridget said, 'No need to ask you what you were thinking; you were in a world of your own. I called you a few times, but you were sitting there with a grin on your face and a faraway look in your eye.'

I laughed and said, 'I only did it in my dream, and it wasn't that wonderful. I don't know what all the fuss is about.' We both started laughing.

She said, 'That's it, girl, keep your chin up!'

I said, 'Sure thing.' We gathered up our bags. We each had two going back with us. We had time to have a last coffee before we left. Inside I felt my heart was broken. I did not know how I was going to cope. I had never felt so empty. I said to myself, *If this is love, why does it hurt so much?* Every guy I saw, I wished it were John. I just could not get him out of my mind. *What will I do?* We had our coffee in silence. We all hated goodbyes, and the time to say them was fast approaching. We both hugged and kissed Bridget's parents, and then we boarded the train. We sat next to the window so we could wave as the train left the station. I glanced at the ring on my finger and secretively said, *Goodbye, my love.* We both waved.

When we had left the station, I burst out crying. Bridget put her arms around me. 'You have it bad, my girl,' she said, but she made me laugh. She said, 'You will laugh about this in a few years and say how silly you were.'

I said, 'I hope you're right.'

We sat in silence for some time, then Bridget spoke. 'What are your plans? Are you going back to college or are you going to look for work?'

I said, 'I am seriously thinking of going back to college, but I haven't made up my mind yet. Have you made up your mind?'

She said, 'I haven't given it serious thought yet. I am planning on applying to the various banks so I can start earning real money.' I told her that wasn't a bad idea.

We had a cup of tea and a sandwich on the train. I hadn't eaten much that morning, and I fancied something. Time seemed to be flying by so quickly. We were boarding the boat in little or no time at all. It looked as if it was going to be well packed, so we thought it best to hurry and secure comfortable seats and get settled so that we could have a little sleep later on. We got our seats on the lower deck. We would be able to sleep, as they were reclining ones, which was great. I felt like sleeping for a couple of years. I wasn't tired; I just wanted to wipe out the next couple of years, and just wake up when John had graduated and we could get on with our lives. Sadly, life is not like that. I did try to sleep. All I could see in my dream was John. I tossed and turned and eventually went to sleep. *Why can't life be simple?* I glanced at Bridget a few times, and she was fast asleep.

We both woke up together, and strangely enough I felt refreshed and hungry. We decided to try to get some breakfast before we landed on dry land. We had a full Irish breakfast—fried bacon, sausage, eggs, tomatoes, potatoes, and bread. It was delicious. 'When in love stuff your face,' I said, and we both laughed. We could see the mainland in the distance. We would be soon coming in to dock. Somehow the time had flown so quickly. It was hard to believe we were almost back in London again.

We were both sitting together looking out to sea. Bridget spoke first. 'Whatever we decide to do we are going to live together.'

I said, 'I totally agree.' I could not possibly have coped on my own. 'That's the first thing we need to do—sort out accommodations,' I said to Bridget. 'Maybe I might apply to the banks like you and get a temporary job until I decide what I really want to do.' Then I had an idea. 'Stuff working for someone else, Bridget. What about working for ourselves?'

She smiled and said, 'Now you're talking, partner.'

I began to get excited. 'We need to think this through properly,' I told her. 'We need to concentrate on the rag trade, make dresses and tops, and sell them ourselves. We'll get a market stall. I think I may go back to college two days a week and do a course in designing. Bridget, we will need to produce a fair amount of stock to get started.'

'No problem,' she said. 'That sounds like a good idea. Maybe we could still do the odd night of babysitting; after all, we have the contacts.'

'Good idea,' I said. We did have some savings, even though we had just come back from a holiday. I said, 'We have to postpone this conversation; we have just landed.'

We gathered up our stuff and proceeded to leave the ferry. We had to wait until all the cars had driven off before it was safe for us foot passengers to disembark. We all left in a very orderly fashion. Bridget turned to me and said, 'Do you think Mary and her hubby will be there to meet us?'

I said, 'I'm sure they'll be at the station in St Pancras waiting for us.'

She smiled. 'I'm sure they will.' The train for London was packed; we could hardly load our bags. There was no way would we be able to get a seat. We were standing just inside the door in the isle, where we were pushed and shoved as passengers got off and got on. This was impossible, but we just had to put up with it; we did not have a choice. I thought we might eventually get a seat, though it seemed highly unlikely. Everyone appeared to be heading to London. Just our luck. We put up with the jostling; after all, we were on a fast train. We would be there in no time, and sure enough, we were. When the train stopped, there was a mad exodus. One would have thought there was a bomb on board. We almost got trampled on—especially me, a midget struggling with two big bags. Eventually we made progress and practically fell out onto the platform.

Now we had to really struggle with our bags to get outside the station. We had escalators to contend with before we would be safely outside, and that was a nightmare. We were now tired; we just wanted to get home. We were hoping Mary and Harold would be waiting for us. We heard someone call our names, and we immediately recognized the voice as Mary's. We turned to each other and said, 'Thank God.' We both hugged; at last we could relax. We were so delighted to see Mary, we almost strangled her with hugs. She was laughing at us. She pointed out where the car was parked. We had to hurry, and that was not easy with two big bags, but we eventually crossed the road. Harold stuffed the bags into the boot, and we collapsed into the backseat, thanking Mary and Harold for picking us up. Bridget said 'We felt we could not have got much farther on our own, we were that exhausted.' I agreed.

Mary said, 'Ye can stay at our house tonight and sort yourselves out in the morning.' We did not argue with that decision; in fact, it was just what we needed to hear. We lay back in the car delighted to be closer to a place of rest and a warm meal, both a necessity at that moment. I opened my eyes with a jolt and told Bridget that I hadn't thought about John since we had left home! She started laughing. 'I thought you were madly in love. And now you have forgotten him. Only joking,' she said. 'Wait until you try to get some sleep tonight. Then you will wish you had forgotten him.'

When we got to Mary's house, she said, 'Go inside. We will bring in the bags.' We were delighted at that suggestion. There was a hot, appetizing meal on the table for us in a matter of minutes; it was just like home away from home, and boy did we appreciate it. We told them all about our holiday—the brilliant time we'd both had—over a cup of tea. I even told them about John. I couldn't believe the things I was saying about him. I hardly knew him! Mary was amazed. Jokingly she said, 'Ye best not go back again for a couple of years.' We all laughed. We had an early night; we were both pretty exhausted. We didn't have our usual chat; we just fell into bed. I think I fell asleep immediately. I don't remember anything until morning. I had a wonderful sleep, and I dreamed of John. It was a wonderful dream; we were both so happy.

When I woke in the morning, I turned around and noticed Bridget was still asleep. 'Hey, sleepyhead,' I said, 'it's time to get up! We have a lot of things to do today.' She woke up, but she wasn't her usual self.

She said, 'I had a terrible night. I had a bad dream, and it unnerved me.' Then she said, 'I don't want to talk about it.' This was very unlike her; she analyzed everything, especially her dreams. We went in search of breakfast. We had a full Irish again, and Mary got top marks. We even had homemade soda bread. It was delicious. After we had eaten our fill, we felt we were ready for anything. We decided first things first: we had to find a flat.

We decided to go out and check the local paper and see what was on offer locally. We bought the paper and checked out all the two-bedroom flats. We wanted to use one room for our dressmaking business and share the other one for the time being. We went for a coffee and scrutinized the local paper and the early edition of the *Evening News*.

Sure enough, we found about five properties that might be of interest to us. We would be able to decide after we had checked them out. We chatted away after we decided which flats we were going to check out. We came up with the idea that we needed to learn how to drive. We would need our own wheels to get our stuff to the markets and for running about. There was only so much you could take on the bus. It was all so exciting! We were going to start our own business, and hopefully acquire own our own set of wheels.

I didn't have a lot of time to think about John. I usually did that when I went to bed. I would be wondering what was he doing at that precise minute. Was he going to bed too? Or was he up studying. We used to take it in turns ringings each other at the weekend and make arrangements for our next chat. We were always there to facilitate each other; so far we hadn't missed a call. We also wrote to each other. The phone calls were often frustrating, each of us trying to say the right thing without upsetting the other. I always ended up crying.

Bridget and I went to look at some the flats that looked interesting. As per usual, some were absolute dumps, but there was one that covered the top of a house. It had a large living room, two large bedrooms, and our own bathroom and kitchen. The bathroom was on the small side, but hey, one can't have everything! We loved it. We had to haggle about the rent. The landlord didn't want to give in to us, but eventually he did. We paid him a month in advance and still had enough money in the kitty to buy material to make more dresses.

We opened a joint bank account and put equal amounts into it. This was our working capital. Whatever we made from sales, we planned to put right back into the account. Our hope was that, after some time, we could allow ourselves a wage. We would just have to see how things were going to work out. We decided to give ourselves three months. We needed to show a profit to be able to buy materials and keep a roof over heads. We agreed we would start work every morning at eight and finish at five, and have an hour for lunch. We worked hard every day. I designed and cut out the patterns, and Bridget ran them up on the machine. At first, we could afford only one sewing machine.

We worked well together and enjoyed every minute of it. I did go to college three days a week as I had planned. I took a design course, which I loved. My classmates were very nice. By the end of only one month Bridget and I felt sure we had enough dresses made to fill a market stall. Time would tell.

We both applied for our provisional licences and started taking driving lessons in the evenings. We were doing fine; we both liked driving. We decided we needed to buy a small vehicle—a minivan perhaps, or a small car. We looked around at local car sales places to check out what sort of money we would have to shell out, and we were surprised to find out that we could get a vehicle that would suit us fine for under one thousand pounds. I was on the bus one evening and spotted a minivan for sale. I took down the phone number and rang it when I got home. We made an appointment to see it next day. We took it for a test drive, were happy with it, and put a deposit on it. The next day we returned with the full amount in cash and drove away our prize. We could not believe our luck; everything was going our way.

Life in London was unbelievable. There was plenty of work, and everything we needed was close by. We accepted cancellation appointments for our driving tests, and we both passed the first time, which was another bonus. We were now mobile and completely independent. How wonderful!

On our first market day, we got up bright and early with an air of excitement as we prepared for the day. We got to Greenwich market full of enthusiasm and excitement. After we set up our stall, we declared that we would make our fortune in the rag trade. We hugged and laughed. A lady came to view our stock. She appeared to be only a year or two older than we were, and seemed very keen. She asked, 'Where did ye get this stock? Did ye buy in bulk, or are they rejects?'

We looked at each other. 'Rejects?' I said. 'You have got to be kidding! We worked hard to get those dresses ready for the market.'

She sounded surprised. She looked at both of us and said, 'This is your work?' We nodded and said yes. 'They are excellent, and the finish is superb,' she said. 'I will buy the entire stock right now.'

We were speechless; this couldn't be happening. I said, 'Okay, are you for real?' We had expected to be there most of the day. She said, 'Will ye pack up everything and put it all in my van? It's parked across the road. I'll go and get it.' As she was leaving she handed me her card. We both looked at it. She was a buyer for a well-known clothes shop. She parked right by our stall and gave us boxes to put the garments in. As we did so, we counted carefully, as we were not too sure how many dresses and tops we had. She helped us to load them into her van. We were still in shock.

There was a coffee shop just down the road from our stall. She asked us if we would join her for a coffee to sort out the details and maybe draw up a contract. We were still in shock. We went and had our coffees and discussed all aspects of our deal. We were so over the moon. She couldn't believe I had designed the dresses and we had made them. She asked us how many we could make in one week. We told her, and she was amazed. She said she would take all our stock. She didn't want us to sell to anyone else. We agreed. She gave us a cheque for the stock we had just loaded into her van. We were more than pleased with the number of zeros on the cheque; we were on to a winner.

We had expected to spend most of the day trying to sell our stock at the market. Instead, we had sold the lot in less than half an hour! We could not believe our luck. The buyer, whose name we'd learned was Caroline, said she needed to draw up a contract. If we were agreeable, we could meet up for dinner, get to know each other, and discuss anything we were not happy with. We said that would be great. She gave us the name of the restaurant. She asked for our address and said a taxi would pick us up at seven thirty, if that was agreeable. We said it was. She said her goodbyes and left. We looked at each other and started laughing. Bridget said, 'Maybe we might make our fortune in the rag trade after all!' We toasted each other with the fresh cup of coffee we had just ordered.

We decided we were going to look like a million dollars for our dinner date. We went to the hairdressers as a real treat; normally we did each other's hair. We were going to push the boat out this time. We had a manicure also for the first time. We couldn't stop giggling. We were afraid it was a dream, and we would wake up and realize how stupid we were being. But, at the time, it was real, and we were having the time of our lives.

When we got back to the flat we had to decide what we were going to wear. I said, 'The sexiest and most stylish dress we can find . . . so start looking!'

Bridget started laughing hysterically. 'Boy,' she said, 'this is like nothing I have ever dreamed of!'

'Me too,' I said. I knew the dress I was going to wear. It was made of white, rather stiff material with a raised pattern. It had a black sash and a little bolero jacket to match. I had put white piping round the edge of the jacket in the dress material. Even though I say so myself, I thought I made a pretty good job of it. One thing I have always prided myself on is attention to detail; I think it's very important. Bridget decided to wear a royal blue dress I had designed for her birthday shortly before we left home. It was a strapless gown. The bodice was covered with sequins in the pattern of a branch. It was very fetching, and she looked divine in it. She wore a black wrap and shoes, and carried clutch bag to match. I also wore black accessories. We had a full mirror on the landing, and we did a lot of twirling, just checking to see if we looked a million dollars. In our book, we sure did.

The taxi arrived on time, and we drove off to the restaurant in a state of euphoria. We felt like Cinderella must have felt! The restaurant was very posh. We gave our names and were escorted to an alcove where Miss Moneybags was waiting for us. She stood up to greet us and told us we looked amazing. That made us feel ten feet tall. We had an amazing dinner and the finest wine—even a glass of champagne to finish up with. We discussed all aspects of our venture. We didn't sign on the dotted line. We were wise enough to say that we needed to check out the contract first. She agreed. We said our goodbyes and left in our taxi.

When we got home we hugged each other. We believed it was a good deal, and we were determined to make it work, and start earning some serious money.

We were not in a hurry getting up the following morning. When we finally did, we chatted about the details of the deal. We needed to discuss all aspects and terms and make sure that we could deliver on time. Also we didn't want to be tied to a contract indefinitely, so we decided we would sign the contract for only one year. We needed to see how things would go; we might want to go our separate ways after a year; one never knows. We agreed on most things, and we made a list. We had arranged to meet Caroline in two days' time at the same restaurant, this time for lunch.

We got to the restaurant in time, but she had arrived before us. She greeted us warmly. She suggested that we have lunch first and discuss the finer details afterwards. We said that was fine. We both enjoyed our lunch. Even though it was a posh eating establishment, we had dressed casually. Again she commented on our dress sense. When we explained we were wearing all our own designs, she was flabbergasted. She wanted to employ me as a designer and Bridget as a seamstress. We told her we needed to discuss that. She went off to make a phone call, and we chatted. Bridget was happy with that arrangement. She said I was the one with the talent and that I should be rewarded for it. Okay, we were both happy.

When Caroline came back, she was delighted that we agreed to her suggestion, but when we told her we would sign a contract for only a year, she wasn't too happy. We compromised on two years, and we were all happy with that. We were amazed at the money she was prepared to pay us, but we were very happy. We had a few more details to sort out, but we had agreed on most things. We would have one more meeting to iron out the final details, and that meeting was arranged for the weekend. We said our goodbyes and left.

We decided to go for a coffee before we went home. When we were settled with our coffees, I said to Bridget, 'Are you happy so far with the details?' She was indeed. She asked if I was happy, and I said, 'Yes, of course.' We finished our coffee and went home. We would need to get started and run up some garments so that we wouldn't be behind schedule by the weekend. We wanted to just make a start. We were expecting a delivery of material the next day. Part of the deal was that Caroline would supply the materials. I was to design outfits, and she would approve them, and we would make whatever amount she required. That was the deal. I had old drawings, which I submitted to her for approval. She was more than satisfied with them, so I went ahead and cut out the patterns. We were on a roll, and we were so happy.

The ring John had given me would often catch the light, and I would just stop and say, 'Oh, John, where are you right now and what are you doing?' I would try to put him out of my mind and not think of him. Sometimes it was easy enough; other times I would get very sentimental and shed a few tears, but usually I got over it. The weekends were the hardest. I used to work right through the weekend just to keep occupied. Bridget had just met a really nice young man called James, and she sometimes went out at the weekends with him. She often felt guilty about leaving me at home, but I didn't mind. I was fine; I would just work. If I wasn't in the middle of designing something, I would make up some garments. Everything was going fine. We were turning out the work, we were getting well paid, and Caroline couldn't get enough of my designs. We were all happy.

Bridget and James were going out to a dance one weekend, so she persuaded me to go out with them. We all left together in a taxi. I had already announced that I wasn't going to stay late. I was planning to get a taxi and come home by myself. I told them I would let them know before I left. The dance was great; I just wasn't in the mood. I needed John there to hold me tight. I wanted to dance in his arms as if we were the only couple in the world. After a while, I went looking for Bridget and James and told them I was going home; I would see them later.

I went outside to hail a taxi. There were a lot of young men outside—some a bit worse for the wear. I had just missed a taxi and would have to hang around until some more came along. I felt a little uncomfortable. Bridget and I were always together; I didn't feel so brave now standing outside on my own. Hopefully I'd get a taxi soon. As usual, about six taxis came all together, so I decided I would go for one of the ones toward the end of the queue. Just as I was about to get in, someone pushed me forcibly from behind, and I found myself on the floor of the taxi. Trying to restore my dignity, I struggled to get up, but my assailant hit me with such force, I must have passed out. I didn't get a look at the gent in question. He must have given an address to the driver, because he continued driving unaware of what was going on in the back of the taxi. The guy jumped out when the taxi stopped at a traffic light. The driver got a bit suspicious and pulled over to check the situation.

He found me unconscious on the floor with my dress torn in shreds I was bleeding heavily from my face. He took me straight to the local hospital. I woke up very sore and unable to speak. I was informed that I had been raped, and my jaw was broken. I was so distressed they had to sedate me. I was interviewed by the police officer who came to see me I was able to write down where Bridget and I lived, and get him to find her and bring her to me. I felt so alone and scared. The doctor came to see me and told me I would have to have my jaw wired and re-set so I would be going to theatre in the morning. He said they had acquired DNA evidence from me, so it was possible they would catch the guy. I would be given something to prevent a pregnancy. That was a relief. I also had to have swabs taken to make sure I hadn't contracted a disease from him. I was sent to a female medical ward for the night.

The more I thought about what had happened to me, the more upset I got. Bridget and James came in to see me. They were appalled when they saw the state of my face. I was black and blue and still covered in dry blood. Apparently I hadn't allowed the nursing staff to clean my face, because it was too sore and tender. Bridget was very upset. I drifted in and out of consciousness. I would wake up in a sweat, see Bridget by my bed, and then fall asleep again

When I woke up in the morning and realized where I was and what had happened to me, I was totally distressed. My emotions were uncontrollable. I couldn't remember a thing. My head was very sore, and my jaw and face was very painful. I had never felt so low in my life. I tried to speak to Bridget, but I was in too much pain. I was very confused; nothing made any sense to me. The nurse came and said I would be going to theatre shortly. She asked Bridget to leave and get some rest; she had stayed by my bed all night. She was exhausted. She didn't want to leave, but the nurse told her to come back in the evening. She promised that I would be feeling better. Bridget kissed me and left.

After she was gone I cried and cried. How could life be so cruel? I had wanted John to be my first love. My life had been ruined by some animal I didn't even know. John would probably not want me anymore. How could this be happening? I looked at my hand and realized my ring was gone. I had lost everything that night. I was so thirsty. I needed a drink of water, but I couldn't have anything. I needed John there. I needed to tell him it wasn't my fault. I needed him just to hold my hand, to say he loved me . . . anything. I just needed him. I needed him there. Oh, God, I needed him.

The porters came to take me down to the theatre, and that was the last thing I remembered before the anaesthesia. In my induced sleep, John and I were happily married and madly in love. We were going to have lots of babies. We would go dancing every weekend, and ask Bridget to babysit for us. Or maybe not. Knowing her, she would want to dance the night away also. I could see all my life flashing in front of my eyes as if I were watching a movie. John was a successful engineer, and I was working from home as a dress designer. We lived in a beautiful Victorian house. We had two boys and two girls, and they are adorable. An au pair stayed with us and took care of the children and did a little light housework. Life was sweet. We had two vacations a year. Life could not have been better.

Chapter 6

As I OPEN my heavy eyelids and look around, I could not comprehend where on earth I was. There were people in other beds next to mine. I was trying to figure out what sort of place I was in. The penny dropped when the door opened and a nurse came in. She checked my vital signs. 'Rose, your blood pressure is a bit on the low side,' she said. 'Is that normal for you? We are concerned about it.'

I said, with great difficulty, 'Yes, that is normal for me. She introduced herself as Sarah. She was to be my nurse for the day. Inooded at her and wished the circumstances were different.' T Cringing in pain I managed to ask what had happened to me?'

She said, 'Rose, I have only just now come on duty. I have not had the nurses' report yet, but I think you were mugged.' She asked me how I was feeling. I was in awful pain and all I could do was move my head slowly, realizing I was on a drip. She said, 'Rose, you are not long back from theatre. Your jaw is broken. It needed to be set with pins to keep it in place until it is healed.'

She told me it could take up six weeks for my jaw to heal.I thought, *Oh my God . . . that long.* She said, 'Rose, you will be able to go home in a few days if there are no complications.' That made me feel a bit better. She went off to get an analgesic to relieve my sore head. I was grateful for that.

I felt so sad, so hurt, and so alone and confused. I could not remember a thing about my assault. I had no idea at all what had happened to me. Nurse Sarah came back directly with the medication. She handed me a glass with a straw so I could take a sip of water with my tablet. I could open my mouth very little, as it was wired in place. I asked, 'How will I eat?'

She explained, 'You will have to be on a pureed diet until your jaw has healed.'

I began to cry. 'How will I cope?' I sobbed.

She tried to reassure me. 'The weeks will go by quickly, and you will learn to cope,' she said. 'You will be amazed how us mere mortals can cope in difficult times.'

I said, 'Okay. I believe you.'

Before she left, Sarah said, 'Rose, there is a detective outside who wishes to speak to you if you are up to it.

I said, 'I'm sure he is a busy man. Tell him it's okay to come in.' I was thinking to myself that he was probably some old grouch, but I was in for a shock. He was drop-dead gorgeous!

He also turned out to be a nice young man. He came and sat by my bed and introduced himself as David. 'My friends call me Dave,' he said. I think he was trying to put me at ease. He asked, 'How are you was feeling?'

I said, 'My head and my jaw hurt real bad.' Then I told him, 'I can't remember a thing.' He said the taxi driver had been a great help. He had been able to give the police a good description, plus the swabs taken from me for DNA testing would be helpful in identifying my attacker. I started to think that could only mean one thing. I said to him, 'Please tell me I wasn't raped.'

He said, 'I'm so sorry. Did you not know?'

'Everything seems so muddled,' I said. He put his hand into his pocket, pulled it out, and handed me my Claddagh ring. The taxi driver had found it in the back of his cab. I started crying big loud sobs as I thought of John. David slipped the ring on my finger. I smiled through my tears. 'I love the guy who gave me this ring,' I said. 'We are waiting until our lives are more settled before we make a commitment to each other. How awful this had to happen to me. What will he think?' I said.

The young officer said, 'It wasn't your fault. We know what happened to you. Your attacker bundled you into a taxi and hit you on the back of the head with a heavy object, which he took with him when he got out of the taxi. He told the driver you were drunk and he was taking care of you. At first, the driver thought that to be true, so he drove on, observing the traffic, unaware what was going on in the back of his taxi. He got suspicious when the guy jumped out at the traffic lights. He glanced in the mirror but couldn't see you. He pulled over at the next available moment, because he felt something was wrong. He saw a vacant space up ahead, got out, and opened the door. You appeared to be unconscious. You were covered in blood, and your clothes were ripped and torn. You looked as if you had been sexually assaulted. Without delay, he went straight to the local hospital with you. He called the police on his way, and we met him when he reached the hospital. We took what was left of your clothes for forensic testing. We may be able to get fibres or something positive to help in the identification.'

Dave was very kind and sympathetic towards me. I liked him. *Maybe he just feels sorry for me*, I thought. When he had gone, I started to go over things in my mind, trying to figure out exactly what had happened. It was no good; I couldn't remember anything. I did remember being inside the venue dancing and then saying goodbye to Bridget and James. After that, my memory was a complete blank. I kept thinking, *How can I tell John what had happened to me? Will he blame me? Will he say I should not have gone outside on my own? That I should have waited with Bridget? Maybe I should have.* I hadn't seen any danger at the time. I clearly thought I was safe getting a taxi and being dropped at my front door. How was I to know there was an animal on the prowl that night? I thought to myself, *When the nurse Sarah comes back, I'm going to ask her if I can have a shower. I might feel more human.* I could still feel the dry blood in my hair. *I know I don't remember, but I still want to wash myself clean.* I hadn't been out of bed yet because my blood pressure was still low, even though that was normal for me. *Perhaps when Bridget comes in she could help me to have a shower*, I thought.

When Sarah came back to check my vital signs, she said there was a slight improvement in my blood pressure, which was good. She gave me some more analgesic—an injection this time. I told her I was very tired and I needed to get some sleep. I said, 'Sarah, when my friend comes in can I have a shower?'

She said, 'It all depends on how you are feeling'

I woke up hours later. I felt quite refreshed until I realized where I was, and the dreadful nightmare came rushing back. I remembered going for the taxi, but nothing else. Thank God I didn't remember! *With any luck*, I thought, *I will never remember. It's just one mega nightmare.* When I looked about, dear Bridget was sitting in the chair by my bed. She got up to kiss me when she realized I was awake. I just burst into tears. 'Please, Bridget, hold me and tell me it's all been a nightmare!'

'I wish I could,' she said. 'I will be here for you every step of the way.'

'I know you will.' I cried and sobbed until I ran out of tears.

Bridget asked me, 'Are you hungry? Have you eaten anything?'

I said, 'I don't feel hungry, but maybe I might have a little soup.' She went to the kitchen and got me a bowl of soup. When she got back I said, without a little sarcasm, 'I will have fun with this.'

'No,' she said, 'I got a beaker for you with a lid. You should be able to drink from that without spilling.'

'Right back to the baby stage,' I said.

'No,' she said. 'It's only temporary. You will be as right as rain in no time at all.'

'If the nurse says it's okay, Bridget, will you help me to have a shower?'

She said, 'Rose, of course.'

I still had a hospital gown on, but I felt that it would be nice to get into my own clothes again. I asked the nurse if it would be okay, and she said, 'Take it easy. If you feel dizzy, get back into bed.' I agreed. I wanted to have a shower at any cost.

Bridget helped me to the bathroom. I got such a shock when I saw my body. It was covered in bruises! My inner thighs were all scratched and bruised. My ribs were also sore and bruised. Suddenly I hadn't the energy to stand up. I think looking at my body made me realize what had happened to me. I told Bridget I would try again to get to the bathroom after a little while. I thought I might sit in the armchair to rest a little. She said, 'Rose, would you like a coffee?'

'Bridget, I would love one.' She had been to the canteen to get one earlier, and she told me that they had nice coffee there. That sounded good to me.

After a bit, I felt someone tapping my hand. I had dropped off to sleep while Bridget was gone fetching the coffee. It was truly a nice coffee. I really enjoyed it. I was the only thing I fancied all day. I eventually got the strength to go to the bathroom, with assistance from Bridget. I had a lovely, warm shower. I had to be very gentle with my head, as it was still very tender. Bridget washed my hair and helped me dry myself. Suddenly I felt exhausted, but a least I felt clean. I hugged Bridget when I got back to the ward and thanked her profusely. She said, 'Don't be daft! Aren't we like sisters? We always will be.'

I started crying again. I still felt so hurt and upset. Bridget helped me into bed. I said, 'I think I need to sleep.'

She said, 'James is coming to pick me up. He will be here any minute.' He came shortly after that. I had started to nod off. I just opened my eyes to see them both walking away out the door. I slept through the night and I woke up early with a thumping headache. But I felt rested.

The nurse in charge came in to take my vital signs. She said her name was Cara; she would be my nurse till the afternoon shift. She was very chatty and seemed in a good mood. I just realized I was feeling a little better in myself. I wasn't just feeling sorry for myself; I was taking notice of what was going on around me. I observed the girl in the bed next to me. She seemed in a lot worse shape than I. She appeared to be in traction, with a bed cradle over her legs. I knew something had happened to her legs; she was unable to get out of bed. She had just woken up and appeared to be in a lot of pain. The nurse left and came back directly to give her an injection. *When she settles down*, I thought to myself, *I will try to talk to her and see if we can strike up a friendship. Maybe we can console each other.*

I managed to get out of bed to go to the bathroom. My ribs were very sore, and I had a lot of bruising in that area. I told the nurse, and she said the doctors would be doing their rounds shortly. I should stay in bed until they came around. I got back to bed. My head still hurt quite a bit, and as for my jaw, it was strange not to be able to do such a simple task as open my mouth. *God*, I thought, *it's amazing how we take everything for granted!* Simple tasks are a marathon if you are unwell. It can be very frustrating. I could manage to drink through a straw; that was no problem. But trying to get some food into my mouth was impossible. I could barely manage a spoonful. I was very slim, and I was worried about losing weight. I could not really afford to lose any, as I would look like a total skeleton.

The doctors came on their rounds, a whole gang of them. (They had no idea of how intimidating that could be!) The consultant spoke. 'How are you feeling, Rose?' I explained how my head hurt and that my ribs hurt also. He said that, to be on the safe side, he would send me for an X-ray. He also explained, 'You will be kept here for a few more days and fed via a drip, as you were a bit underweight to start with.' I was a bit disappointed, but at the same time I didn't feel ready to go home.

The doctors spent longer with the girl next to me. When they had move on to another patient, I introduced myself and asked her how she was feeling. 'I'm Shakera,' she said. 'I'm in a lot of pain, but it's self-inflicted. I tried to commit suicide. It was my second attempt.' I was shocked. I didn't know what to say. I explained to her what had happened to me. She said, 'My family are originally from India. They arranged for me to marry some older guy back home that I have never met. I have a boyfriend here in England; he is a white boy. I am in love with him. We want to marry, but my family would not allow me. My brothers and uncles beat him up a couple of times to stop us from dating, but we still kept seeing each other. In fact, we moved in together and were planning on starting a family.' She stopped for a bit, and then said, 'I can't take it anymore. I intended killing myself. I have broken both my legs and my pelvis. I will be in traction for a number of weeks. It is worth the pain. They leave me alone while I am in hospital.

I said, 'Shakera, I am so sorry.' One never knows how the other half lives. We did indeed strike up a friendship. I told her all about John and how I felt about him. She was intrigued. She couldn't believe how we felt about each other and that we still resisted having sex. She thought it was something to do with religion. I started laughing. 'Hell no,' I said. 'I am not that religious! At least, I wouldn't let it come between me and my fella. For once it was common sense that prevailed.' I told her, 'In this country you can obtain the contraceptive pill only if you are married or have a good medical reason. In Ireland you would have no chance of ever getting it, because it's against the ruling of the church. We decided to wait until John was qualified. Then we could take up where we left off and hopefully have a happy life together.

Then she said something interesting. 'What about life getting in the way?

I said, 'What do you mean?'

She said, 'It's possible you could meet someone else while you are waiting for John to qualify as an engineer.'

I thought for a little while. When I spoke, I explained to her that I had never had a boyfriend; John was the first one. I had such strong feelings for him. I just wanted him to hold me tight and never let me go. I had an uncontrollable urge to have sex with him, to get as close as possible to him and spend the rest of my life wrapped around him. And he felt the same about me. 'He has a lovely, toned body,' I told her. 'I could spend hours just caressing him and he returning the compliment.' I just wanted to go to bed with him. I didn't feel shy or awkward. It just felt so right. I had so been looking forward to that first night with him, and now it had all being ruined. I didn't know how I would react with him. What if I never wanted a man to touch me ever? I begin to cry when I realize how this could affect my outlook on life forever.

Shakera tried to console me. 'Everything is very fresh in your mind right now,' she said. 'Perhaps with time you will feel differently.'

Through my tears I said, 'Maybe you are right. Only time will tell.' I knew one thing. I had begun to realize that I could not tell John. I explained to Shakera that I kept thinking he wouldn't understand. I looked at the ring on my finger and wished things were different. I thought I might tell him later, but at the time I didn't think I could. I said to Shakera, 'I am sorry. I didn't mean to keep talking about myself.'

She said, 'That's okay. You needed to get it off your chest. Things might be a bit clearer in your head now that you have talked about it.'

'Well,' I said, 'my head still hurts and I can't eat or laugh properly. And my ribs hurt. But apart from that I'm fine!'

She said, 'Rose, I will laugh for you, and you can walk for me.'

'Shakera, that's a deal.' I walked over to her bed and we hugged each other as best we could. We promised we would get through this and be better people. We didn't know how things would pan out, but one has to be optimistic in this life.

The nurse came back and did whatever needed to be done. She said I would be going down for an X-ray shortly. She changed my drip and put up a nutritious one. She said, 'You can have an analgesic when you get back for your pain.' The porters came shortly to take me to X-ray. I was back in the ward again within a half hour. Lunch was being served when I got back. I so fancied something, but I knew that was not possible yet. I did manage some soup, which I enjoyed. Shakera was able to sit up and have her lunch, but she said she was in terrible pain. She was waiting for an injection. She said, joking, that her bum was like a pincushion.

It would be visiting time in about an hour, and I was really looking forward to seeing Bridget. She was always the first one in when the doors opened, and I was always so pleased to see her. She hugged me and told me I was looking better. 'How are you feeling?' she asked.

'Still a little sore and uncomfortable, but I am getting there,' I assured her.

She said, 'I am working hard to keep the orders filled. James's sister, Tricia, is helping me out, and we are practically up to date with the orders.'

'That is great!' I said. I hadn't expected her to do all that work.

She said, 'We are well able to cope. We have been getting up early to get as much done as possible. The orders will be completed by tomorrow afternoon. I just have to call

Caroline to have them collected. See?' she said, 'you have nothing to worry about.'

'Bridget, I just had an X-ray. I think I have fractured ribs. The doctor will be coming by shortly to let me know for sure.' I went on to tell her, 'I was having nourishment in my drip. They are worried about me losing too much weight as I am unable to swallow more than a spoonful.'

She said, 'Has your detective, Dave, been in to see you?'

'I haven't seen him today.' Then I told her, 'John will be ringing tomorrow night at eight o'clock. Will you tell him I have the flu and can't speak? Tell him my throat is very sore. I don't think I'm ready to talk to him. I am definitely not ready to discuss what happened. I need to be in a better state of mind.'

'I fully understand, Rose,' she said. 'I have to go now, but I will see you in the evening.'

Shakera's boyfriend, Michael, came to visit her. He seemed a very nice young man. He brought her a big bouquet of flowers. I also had one. Caroline had sent it with a card saying, 'Take it easy. Don't worry about anything.' Gosh, if she had seen me . . . I looked fragile and broken like a china doll.

As the days rolled by, my bruising became more prominent. I looked as if I'd lost by a few rounds in the ring. I ached all over, and I was feeling down in the mouth and right fed up. Nothing seemed to cheer me up. Bridget left me some girly magazines. I just glanced through them. Nothing seemed to catch my eye. I was not interested in reading.

One afternoon, I just decided to close my eyes and try to sleep. I did sleep for a little while, and when I woke up, I was surprised to see Dave sitting by my bed. It was a pleasant surprise; I found myself pleased to see him. He said, 'How are you doing?'

I told him I still hurt and I couldn't eat very much, so I was still on a drip. 'Plus,' I said, 'I'm black and blue all over!'

He said, 'We have arrested the perpetrator of your assault. He's still in custody and will be charged.'

I started to panic. 'I can't identify him!'

Dave must have seen the fear in my eyes. He said, 'Don't worry. The taxi driver has identified him.'

'That is a relief.'

'I didn't mean to upset you. I hope you will I be going home soon.'

'Me too!' I said. He told me goodbye and said he would keep in touch. I lay back against the pillow trying to piece together the events of that fatal night. I still didn't remember anything after I left Bridget and James. Deep down, I hoped I would never remember. I still had another week to wait for results from samples taken to see if I had contacted any disease from him, and that was a worry. I was hoping that, when Shakera's boyfriend left, we could have a chat. I thought it might cheer me up. Or maybe cheer up both of us.

When he had left, she said to me, 'Rose, you have no idea what life is like for a little Indian girl growing up in Southeast London. I was never allowed have English friends at school. I have one brother and sister; I am the eldest child in my family. After school we had to stay in our own garden and not speak with our English next-door neighbour children. We were only allowed to play with cousins during the holidays or sometimes at weekends. I befriended an English girl in secondary school. When my parents found out, I endured a severe beating. Both my parents are very strict. I was constantly being groomed by my mother to get married. I hated it. That was all my mother spoke to me about. I just wanted to live a normal life like the other girls in my class.'

Shakera went on to explain that family honour was very important to her parents, and when she was younger she dared not disobey them. If she did, it was at her peril. As she got older and left school she realized that was not the life for her. She wanted to be like her English friends. She started going against everything her parents believed in, which did not go down well. They tried to take her to India to meet her future husband. She was scared they would not allow her to come back, so she refused to go. She left home and stayed with her English friend at her house. She told her parents that, if she did marry, it would be to someone of her choosing. She wanted to be allowed to fall in love. She refused to marry an old man she had never met. This led to endless conflict with her family. Her brother was continually spying on her, making her life a living hell. Finally she said, 'I fell in love with the brother of my best friend. My family were furious. They ambushed him one night and beat him up so badly he ended up in hospital for weeks. That didn't deter us, though. We continued seeing each other. They continued beating him up I went and pleaded with my parents, but to no avail. I could not see him put in hospital again, so I thought if I attempted suicide, they would leave us alone, but no way. This time I intended to end it for good. I could not take anymore. That is how I've ended up in hospital in the next bed beside you, with terrible injuries.' I was amazed that such cultures still had such weird and outdated customs. How could they be so cruel to their own child? I was stunned. I was getting tired; I dropped off to sleep.

Chapter 7

I HAD A good rest. I woke up refreshed and in a good mood until I realized where I was and why I was there. I felt as if I was doing time for something I had done wrong and had no control over. I had been thinking about my family in the last couple of days. It was amazing but not surprising that I felt more connected to Bridget and her family than I did to my blood relatives. I felt like a misplaced person. I suppose that's to be expected as Kate had practically raised me after dad died. I can understand my brothers not wanting a younger sister hanging around cramping their style, but my sisters . . . that was a different story. Surely, I thought, they must get homesick or think of me sometimes. Or did they just not give a damn. I had three sisters somewhere in America. I had never really known them. Daniel may have been in contact with Angela. One would imagine that one of them could come back home at some stage. Dad had two sisters also in America. None of them had come for Dad's funeral. Maybe they felt bitter that they'd had to go away at such an early stage in their lives. I have often thought about the situation. I think it is sad that they had no wish to come home. Had they become such snobs that they didn't want to know us anymore?

I decided to contact Daniel and Deirdre and explain to them what had happened to me. Maybe I could go home and stay with them for a couple of weeks. I knew I would need to discuss it with Bridget first and see how she felt about my plans. In my mind I didn't feel comfortable telling John what had happened to me. I felt weird about it. At that time, I could not face him and tell him, so I decided to leave it.

Shakera has had a real heart to heart with her boyfriend, and she is in a good mood. They have plans to get married when she leaves hospital, but sadly this will be some time down the road. She will be starting counselling today. The doctors have been worried about her state of mind over the past week or so. Sometimes she was on a high and nothing could touch her or her boyfriend. Then, at other times, she could be like a scared little girl, petrified of what her parents might do to both of them. It made me so sad. She had been born and raised in England, so she should be allowed live her life like an English girl. Why could her family not be happy for her? She had a boyfriend who loved her very much. Why would they want her to marry some old guy she has never met? Her mother must have no compassion. Either that, or she was totally under the control of her husband. One would think she would visit her to see how her daughter was doing and if there was anything she could do for her. Not one member of her family had visited. Not even her younger sister, which I thought was really sad. Shakera didn't appear to have even one of her family members on her side. I could see how hard that must have been.

As I lay back on my pillow thinking of things in general, I spotted my journal. Bridget had brought it to me earlier. I opened it and started drawing. I needed to come up with new designs for the summer season. I started with daywear. I drew lots of different designs—tops and shift dresses—and then I needed to come up with something special for evening wear. I spent a great deal of time drawing and rubbing out until I was satisfied. I hadn't realized I had spent a couple of hours drawing, and I felt rather tired when I had finished. As I looking through the designs, I felt really pleased at what I had done. I hoped Caroline would like them.

As I continued doodling with my pencil, I was just thinking to myself it would be nice if she called to see me, and who should walk in the door but Caroline! I was so delighted to see her, and of course she had a huge bouquet of flowers. She knew I loved flowers. She hugged me and said, 'You look good!'

I thought for a moment, and realized, 'Yes, I do indeed feel better today!' I said, 'Caroline, I managed to do some work.'

She said, 'I am impressed. I didn't want to put you under any pressure.' She said it would be good for me to start taking an interest in things again.

I explained, 'I didn't feel up to it till now.' I told her how I felt—that things were really muddled in my mind . . . that I wasn't sure how I felt about John anymore. 'I think I have feelings for Dave, the detective who is investigating my case,' I said. 'I am a mess!'

She said, 'Rose, you have been through a terrible ordeal. You are doing really well, but maybe you need to speak to a counsellor and explain how you feel.' She picked up my journal and started looking at my drawings. She started to smile. 'Oh, Rose, these are wonderful! They are the best you have done so far!' I was so pleased. I couldn't believe it, and as usual I started to cry. She hugged me. 'Let it out,' she said. 'You're getting there. You're doing so well.'

We chatted for a while. I explained the type of material required for the new designs. She said she would get on it straight away, and it would be delivered to the flat without delay. We chatted for a little longer, and then she left. She had brought me the daily paper. That was something else I had forgotten. I had always like to read the daily paper in the morning with my coffee. This time I actually read the paper; I didn't just glance through it. I was beginning to feel more confident in myself. I was gradually getting through the day without feeling sorry for myself or crying at the drop of a hat. I began to feel a bit tired, so I dropped off to sleep for a little while.

When I woke up, Dave was sitting by my bed. I was a little surprised to see him. He said, 'I'm off duty. I came to see you—not the girl who was attacked, the nice girl down the road. How are you?' He shook my hand formally.

I replied, 'I'm fine, Dave. How are you?' We both started laughing, only I couldn't laugh that well. He handed me a bouquet of yellow roses. I thought they were absolutely gorgeous. He gave me a hug. I clung to him. I don't know if I wanted him to be John or just himself. I think I now realized I desperately wanted someone to love me. I did like the feeling I got when he hugged me. I drank in his odour; it was so manly and comforting. We chatted for quite some time. He told me he had studied hard and got a degree in criminology. Then he'd applied for a job as a detective and got it. He loved his work; there was always something new every day. It wasn't always pleasant, he told me, but then again it was not always unpleasant. It was a job he loved.

I explained to him, 'I still have nightmares about that night, but in reality I don't remember the actual event.'

'Rose, you will eventually be able to live with it, but it will take time. I am here for you if you want to talk any time. I think of you a lot; I can't get you out of my head.'

'At the moment, Dave, I don't know how I feel. I feel very confused. I have been thinking a lot of my family. I feel the need to belong, but to belong to whom I do not know. I need to sort myself out before I can get involved with anyone.'

'I fully understood how you feel.'

'With respect, I don't think you do. I don't really know myself how I feel.'

'Rose, I am not putting any pressure on you. All I'm saying is that I am here for you.'

'I understand,' I said. Then I told him I had an appointment with a counsellor in the morning. 'I am hoping it will help.'

'I hope it will too. Goodbye, Rose.' He gave me a peck on the cheek and left. He also left me his private number. 'If you need anything, ring me,' he said. 'I will keep you informed about any developments in your case.' I shook his hand and he left.

The doctor came by to see me. 'Would you like to go home?'

I thought for a few minutes and said, 'Yes.'

He explained, 'You might be happier in your own environment.'

'I think you may be right.' He told me he would make the necessary arrangements so I could go home the next day.

Bridget came in later, and I told her my good news. She was delighted for me. She said, 'I'll get James to pick you up at lunchtime.'

I told her that would be great. Then I said, 'Dave visited me, and I think he's sweet.'

She started laughing. 'Rose, you *are* feeling better! I need to keep an eye on you.' I also told her Caroline had visited and had liked the new drawings I had done.

She was happy that I had done the drawings and that Caroline had liked them. She said, 'The material has been delivered, and it looks great. I can't wait to start working with it. It will be great to have you to supervise us and be there to help with any problems.'

I couldn't sleep I was so excited about going home. But I was also a little apprehensive. I still couldn't eat very well. I ate loads of yogurt and pureed food, but one can get fed up with that. I eventually fell asleep, but all too soon it was morning. I had to get up and have a shower and try to look alive. Bridget, bless her, came in early with clean clothes and to see if I needed help packing my things. She was willing to help in any way she could. As usual, she was always there for me. James came just before lunchtime, and by then I was delighted to be going home.

It seemed like such a long time since I had been at the flat. Tricia was there making up some of the new collection. I was amazed how far ahead she and Bridget had managed to get. I checked out some of the samples, and they looked great. I was very pleased with them. Bridget said, 'If the circumstances were different, we would be celebrating with dinner and a few glasses of wine, but as it is let's just hope that you are back to yourself in no time at all. We can celebrate when you are better.'

'That's okay. I don't want to celebrate,' I said. I just felt like going to bed. 'I'm going to rest. Give me a shout in an hour.'

She said, 'Okay, no problem.' So off I went. I slept like a baby. Maybe it was because I was back in my own bed, or maybe I was on the mend. I got up and had a little dinner.

Sometime later, there was a knock at the door. Bridget opened it, and who should it be but Dave with another bouquet of flowers. When he saw me he said, 'I wanted to welcome you home.'

I was pleased to see him. We had a coffee together. I hadn't been outside for a couple of weeks, so I fancied a walk. I asked him, 'Would you mind a walk in the park?'

'There is nothing I would like better.' We had a lovely stroll. We sat on a bench and talked for some time. He put his arm around me and cuddled me, which I liked. I had been afraid that I would not like a fella to touch me, but I felt all right about it. The counsellor had told me that, as I had no recollection of the actual event, it wouldn't change the way I felt about men, which was a relief. I asked her why I felt so uncomfortable about telling John, and she said I was blaming myself for what had happened, and I didn't think he would accept that it wasn't my fault, and that would come between us. At the moment, I liked being with Dave. I felt secure and safe and sexy with him. *Let's just see how things work out*, I thought to myself. *Maybe I am just dreaming. He might just feel sorry for me. Who knows?*

Chapter 8

OH, IT WAS good to be home and wake up in my own bed. I was feeling better already. I got up and had a shower. My head was a little tender still, but I felt I was making progress. I had some breakfast. I actually felt ravenous, but I was limited as to what I could eat. A bowl of porridge filled the gap, but I was dreaming of a full Irish breakfast, which was one of the meals I missed the most. I was just longing for one; I could even smell it! I decided to go out for a walk after breakfast, just to the park that was around the corner. It was mid morning. Bridget and Tricia were working hard in the spare room. I popped my head round the door to say, 'I'm going for a walk.'

Bridget said, 'Hang on. I'll come with you.'

'No need. I am fine on my own.'

They looked at each other and said, 'See you later!'

I put on my runners and decided to go for a jog to blow the cobwebs away. I had a lovely, relaxed run. I sat on the bench in the park before I decided to go home. I was trying to trash things out in my head. I made up my mind that I needed to go back home. I wanted to meet up with John and tell him what had happened to me. After that, it would be up to him. He could either accept it or tell me to be on my way. I decided I would tell Bridget of my plans when I got home.

A little old lady came and sat beside. She commented on the beautiful day. 'Even though it's a little chilly,' she said.

'It's only early spring. Isn't it good to be alive?' I said. 'We don't appreciate the good things in life.'

She looked at me in a strange way and said, 'You are a very cynical young lady.'

I smiled at her and said, 'Something happened to me to make me appreciate life more. Don't get me wrong,' I continued, 'I am not a bad person. I've had a lot of sadness in my life, but sometimes I have taken things for granted.'

She looked at me and noticed my jaw. She said, 'I'm a good listener. Do you want to talk about it?'

'No thanks,' I said. I decided to go home.

She shook my hand and wished me luck in my life. She said, 'I will probably see you here again if you are a jogger. Do you usually run here?' I nodded and set of home.

When I got back I felt great. I felt I could tackle any problem. After I had a shower, I made coffee for all of us. I said to Bridget, 'We need to talk, so let's have a coffee break.'

'We could do with a break anyway,' she said. We all sat in the living room and had our coffee.

'Bridget, I have my mind made up. I want to go home to confront John and explain what has happened. I want to see Daniel and Deirdre and spend some time with them. I need to get to know my family. I don't mean to sound ungrateful; after all, your mam reared me and took care of me, but I have a family, and I would like to get as many of them together as possible if I can.' I told her that my jaw should be better in two weeks. That would give me time to write to Daniel and ask him if he could locate the addresses of some of my sisters. Maybe they might come to Ireland for a reunion.

Bridget said, 'I would love to come with you.'

I said, 'Why not?' We had always done things together, why stop now?

She hugged me and said, 'That's great!'

'It will take longer than a few weeks for us to get ready. How about a month? That will give us time to have all Caroline's designs finished before we leave, and it will give Daniel time to contact our sisters and make arrangements with them.' Bridget agreed. I said, 'Let's hope it all works out.'

The girls got back to work, and I decided to write to Daniel. I explained what I was planning and asked him to speak to Timmy and to contact our sisters as soon as possible. I went out and posted the letter and felt good I had made a start to my plan. The doorbell rang a while after I returned. I called out to the girls that I would get it. I opened the door, and who was there standing on the step but Dave. He said, 'Hi! May I come in?' We sat in the living room. He said, 'You're looking much better on the outside. How are you really?' He put his arms around me and gave he a big hug. I needed that. I wasn't sure, however, if the hug was from the right guy, though I didn't say that to him. I told him about my plans. 'I am going back home in a month.'

'That's a good idea,' he said. 'I hope all will work out for you.'

'Yah,' I said, 'I hope it does too.'

'Would you like to go to the pictures with me some night?'

'Why not? We could go as friends. I don't want to complicate things until I seen John and talk things through with him.'

'I understand.'

We sat and chatted for ages. I really enjoy his company. He said, 'I want to take you out for a meal when your jaw has healed.'

I laughed and said, 'Don't push it!'

He squeezed my hand and said, 'Okay.' He left after a couple of hours, but before he left he asked, 'Is it okay to call by again?'

'Sure!' When he had gone, I thought to myself, *Am I playing with fire?* Then I thought, *What the heck. I'm sure John is no angel. God, where did that come from?* I was on a high. I didn't know if it was because I had plans to go home or if it was because of Dave. As one gets older, life gets more complicated. One must be a genius to get it right . . . to read the signals right.

I was up bright and early the next morning. I had a cup of coffee, put on my runners, and went for a run. I felt on top of the world when I got back. Bridget and I had breakfast together. She said, 'You're getting back to your old self again.'

'I can't wait!' I said. I looked at the calendar. I had an appointment with the counsellor in the afternoon. I would go and see Shakera when I was finished with my session. I had a shower and set off for the hospital. The counsellor was very satisfied with my progress. This was my third meeting, and she couldn't believe how positive I was. She said she would like to see me again when I got back. She would leave it to me to make the arrangements. That was fine with me, and I left.

I had a coffee before I went in search of Shakera. When I got to the ward, I noticed her boyfriend outside, and he looked very upset. I spoke to him explaining who I was. I told him I had befriended Shakera while I was in hospital. He looked at me and said, 'Oh yes, I remember. I asked him how she was. 'Not good,' he said. 'Not good at all.' When I asked why, he started crying. 'She has developed a bad infection in one of her legs, and the only solution is to amputate.

'Oh my God,' I said, 'Poor Shakera! How is she taking the news?'

'She is very down. I don't think she can cope. I don't know what to do,' he said.

I was shocked. I didn't know what to say myself. I said, 'Will you come and have a coffee with me and we can talk?'

'I will.'

We went to the canteen and had coffee and chatted for a little while. He was anxious to get back to her. I tried to explain to him that she needed him now more than ever, to reassure her. I advised him to tell her she was the single most important person to him and that he could not live without her. He said, 'I love her. I don't know what more I can do. I feel she has been too extreme . . . that she won't stop until she finishes what she set out to do. I am not strong enough to sit around and watch her do this. I just do not know what to do. I will go back to the ward to say goodbye, and I will come back in the evening.' I told him I would walk back with him. I wanted to spend a little time with her if he thought that would be okay. He said, 'You go in after I have left.'

We walked along the corridor in complete silence. Nothing I could say could possibly change the situation; I felt so helpless. I sat outside while he went in, just going over things in my mind, thinking of the saying, 'there is always someone worse off than you.' How true that is. When he came out, he waved goodbye, and as he left, I went into her room. I had picked up some magazines on the way for her. I gave her a hug asking how she was. I could see she had been crying. I said, 'I know. I had a chat with your Michael outside.'

She burst out crying. 'God is punishing me for what I have done,' she said.

'No, it's just bad luck. You must make the best of things. They can do fantastic things with prosthesis nowadays.' But I got serious with her too. 'This is probably your last chance,' I told her. 'You have been dealt a terrible blow, but you have also found the love of your life. It's up to you to prove to him that you are worthy of his love . . . that you will do all in your power to make him happy. All he wants to hear is that all the suffering has not been all in vain.'

She listened to me and said, 'You're right, Rose. I will do my best.' I told her about my plans, and also about Dave. I told her I liked him, but I didn't know yet if it could be anything serious. I said I would visit again, and I reminded her to give Michael some hope or she would lose him. She said, 'I will.' I hugged her and left.

I got up early every morning and went for a jog in the park before breakfast. I felt good in myself; slowly I was getting my confidence back. All the bruising had faded, and I didn't hurt so much. Sometimes I completely forgot what had happened to me. Sometimes when I saw a guy approaching me in the park, I would say to myself, *I wonder, is it him?* But I had stopped panicking at this point. Occasionally, just for a fleeting moment, I might get a little worried, but it soon would pass, and I would be fine again.

I got a letter from Daniel without much delay. I couldn't wait to open it; I was so excited! I sat down and began reading it quickly. He said Timmy was getting married, and they had already contacted our sisters in America. They were awaiting a reply. He went on to explain that he agreed it was about time we all got together. I hadn't told him about what had happened to me; I felt I needed to explain it in person. He went on to say he would let me know as soon as he had confirmation of our sisters coming. He also said we should be getting Timmy and Clare's wedding invitations any day now. I made a cup of coffee and reread the letter to make sure I had not missed any details. I was satisfied I had read it properly the first time. I went to get Bridget and tell her the news. She was over the moon. 'We had a fantastic day when Daniel and Deirdre got married,' she said. 'Let's hope this one is as good!

I said, 'It will be brilliant, especially if at least some of my siblings could come. We'll just have to wait and see.'

The girls went back to work, and the doorbell rang, so I opened the door. It was Caroline. She gave me a hug and said, 'You are looking great! How are you feeling?' I told her I was feeling good and that I was having X-rays done the following week to see how the jaw was progressing. If all was well, I could have the wiring removed, which would be great. The time had really gone by quickly; it was hard to believe it was coming up on six weeks. I thanked God I had it behind me now. We chatted for a little while over a coffee, and then she looked at the samples and the finished product the girls had just finished. They were doing a fabulous job; they worked well together. Caroline was very pleased with the end result. I explained to her that the orders would be complete before we went to Ireland. She said, 'You are very professional to have everything finished before you go.'

I explained that we could stay for three weeks if we had nothing to worry about. 'Also,' I said, 'I have a few personal details to sort out, so I feel I need the time.'

She said, 'I understand. Take as long as you want. There is no panic. The next season is covered. Why don't ye have six weeks and have a good break?'

'Yes, Caroline, you're right,' I said. 'I think we will. We can well afford it thanks to you.' Before she left she said, 'I have access to some lovely material. If you need anything for personal use just let me know.'

'I might just take you up on that!'

'No problem, just say what you need.' We hugged, and she said she would call before we left. Perhaps we could have dinner.

'Sure,' I said. 'I should be able to actually eat by then!'

I called into the girls next door and explained to Bridget that, if she fancied any particular material for a dress for the wedding, Caroline would oblige. We both decided we would give it some thought. I went back into the living room and let the girls get on with their work. I turned on the telly just to pass the time until it was dinner time. I picked up my jotter and started drawing, trying to come up with something different for the wedding. I had lost a bit of weight, and all my clothes looked a bit on the big side. It was coming into summer so I thought I would design a mini summer dress and a wrap of the same material. I had not decided on the colour yet . . . maybe lilac with cream accessories and cream lining on the shawl. I would have to check to see what Bridget was planning on wearing.

I soon got the invitation for Timmy's wedding and found that they wanted me to be one of the bridesmaids. I got a letter the following day from Daniel saying he had made contact with Angela and Emily, and they were trying to persuade Ann Marie and our aunts, so at least there was something to look forward to. I knew then that I would make an extra special effort with my dress. I wasn't sure I wanted to be bridesmaid. I told Bridget about the latest developments, and she was overjoyed. She reckoned we would have a fantastic time. I wasn't sure how I felt. Sometimes I was over the moon about it all, and other times I wished I hadn't started any of it. It might not turn out the way I wanted it to.

Dave rang and asked me to the cinema. I found myself looking forward to it. I started getting ready after dinner so I would be ready when he picked me up at seven. I just dressed casually and wore a little make-up. He was on time. We caught a bus to the cinema. The film was good; I enjoyed it. He held my hand during the film. I got goose pimples and a tingling feeling. He put one arm around me. I felt safe. I didn't object; in fact, I liked being close to him. I like his masculine scent. I could feel his heart beating. We went for a coffee after and had a chat. I told him that we had made all the arrangements for our holiday. He said, 'I hope it will be a good holiday. Are you looking forward to it?'

'At times I am scared.'

'That make sense,' he said. 'You'll experience all types of emotions until you've got over that dreadful night. It's natural to feel apprehensive.'

I felt relieved when he said that. I felt he understood me. I said, 'David, are you just feeling sorry for me?'

'No, not at all. I really like you as a person, and I would love to get to know you better, if you would allow me to.'

'I have feelings for you, too, but I'm afraid to trust my judgment right now. I'll know by the time I get back from holiday.'

'I'm disappointed, but I fully understand. And I appreciated your honesty.' He kissed me and gave me a cuddle. I wanted to respond, but I thought it better to take a step back. This seemed to be forming a pattern. I hadn't been able to go all the way with John, now it was the same with Dave. *Why don't I know who I want?* I thought. *What is wrong with me? Does everyone have the same problem?* We got the bus home. I told him I'd had a very enjoyable night. He said he had too. I didn't invite him in; I thought it better not to until I was sure of my feelings. He walked me to the house, gave me a hug and a kiss—a long lingering one . . . the sort that asks for more . . . you know what I mean. Deep down I didn't want him to go, but I knew it was for the best. He said he would like to meet me at the hospital the following week to be there for me. I thought that was real sweet of him, so I said yes. We arranged a time, and he left.

When I got inside, I felt happy to be there. I had a nightcap with Bridget, and we went to bed later after a chat. I got up early the following day and went for a jog, came back, and had breakfast. I had received lovely material from Caroline, so I was going to cut out my dress and make it up and see how it looked. I started on it after breakfast. I was very satisfied with the end result. Bridget pressed it for me while I ran up the wrap. The dress was lilac in colour, as I had planned, and the lining of the wrap was cream. I had got lovely cream platform shoes, which gave the illusion that I was taller than I actually was. And I had a clutch bag of the same colour, and also cream feathers for my hair, which I intended to wear pinned up except for wispy bits around my face.

Bridget opted to wear a dress that she already had in her wardrobe and had worn only once. It was red in colour and had a lovely neckline that showed off her assets. She was planning to wear white accessories with it. She always looked elegant in whatever she wore. I suddenly remembered that my twenty-first birthday was in two weeks' time, and I would be in Ireland. I hoped I would have a good one.

The days seemed to be rushing by. Suddenly it was the day of my hospital appointment. I couldn't wait to get the all-clear. I went for a jog as usual and had breakfast when I get home. Bridget wanted to accompany me to the hospital. I told her I was fine, and that I was meeting Dave there. She wished me good luck, and I left and got the bus. Dave was waiting outside for me. As he walked me in, he asked me how I was feeling. I said I was a bit nervous.

I did not have long to wait before my name was called to go for an X-ray. Dave came with me. I had to wait there some time, as it was very busy. We got back eventually and had to wait again. When my name was called I had to go in to see the surgeon. He greeted me with a smile. He studied the X-ray and told me it all looked well. He would remove the clips. He went ahead and did that. It didn't hurt, but my jaw was very stiff. He said I would need physiotherapy. They would show me what exercises I needed to do. He asked, 'How are you feeling?'

'I'm getting on well.'

'You need to be careful at the beginning. Start eating light food until you get used to eating again.'

Dave had waited outside for me. He knew by the expression on my face that all had gone well. He hugged me and said, 'This is great. Now you are really on the mend.' He asked if I fancied lunch.

'I am hungry, but I'm not sure I can manage lunch. Maybe soup and a roll, or perhaps a sandwich.' He said I could choose when we got to the canteen. We walked hand in hand to the canteen. He had lunch, I had soup and a sandwich and a yogurt, and we both had coffee. 'If you have time,' I said, 'I'd like to visit Shakera.' I told him her story.

'That is very sad. I'm not on duty till evening, so I can stay.' I was glad, because I was not sure how she might be.

I went in alone to see her. As I approached her bed, it was evident she'd had the operation. I thought to myself, *Oh my god*. She was pleased to see me, and surprisingly, she was in good spirits. I was amazed. She said, 'I took your advice. I'm going to make the best of my life and enjoy each day. I'm done trying to end it.'

I hugged her and told her how proud I was of her. I hoped everything would work out for her. 'You have my address,' I told her, 'so keep in touch. I want an invite to your wedding!'

She laughed and said, 'You bet! Will you be my bridesmaid?'

'Of course!' We chatted for some time. I told her Dave was outside. She laughed and told me she would be my bridesmaid. I said, 'Why not? Of course, I'm not sure who the groom will be just yet . . .'

'You will soon know.'

'I hope so.' We hugged and said goodbye.

Dave was falling asleep when I came out. I apologized. He said it was okay and asked how my friend was. 'She's good despite having to have her leg amputated below the knee. She was in good form.'

'Amazing,' he said. We got the bus home. I was feeling happy that all was well. All I needed to do was to try to eat a little more gradually. My biggest problem was deciding whom I wanted to spend the rest of my life with. We walked home from the bus. He said he was going home to get some sleep before his shift that night. He gave me a peck on the cheek and left.

Bridget and I were going home in a week's time, so I had a few things I needed to do before then. Bridget said she and Tricia had the order finished, and she had rung Caroline to have it all collected. She was pleased we would have a little time to ourselves before we went home. I agreed with her. It gave us time to discuss things and maybe see what the future might hold for us. I said, 'I'll be celebrating my twenty-first birthday at home!'

'And so you will. Won't that be nice?' We were just taking life easy until the following week when we would fly home. My God, hadn't we come up in the world? This would be our first time flying, and we were really looking forward to it. Caroline had given us a nice bonus. She was very impressed with our work, and she rewarded us well. That's why we had decided to be extravagant and book flights instead of enduring once again the hassle of going by boat.

The post arrived on departure day, just as we were getting ready to leave our flat. I noticed a decorative envelope among the post and knew instantly it was a wedding invitation. I could not wait to open it. I disregarded the rest and proceeded to open the pretty envelope. It was a wedding invitation from Shakera. I read through it quickly. They were getting married the following month. She asked if we could attend, and if I would be a bridesmaid. I sat down directly and sent her a reply, saying of course we would be delighted to attend, and that I would be honoured to be her bridesmaid. I explained we were going on holiday to Ireland and I would be in touch when I got back. It was going to be a small register wedding with only a few friends.

Chapter 9

WE WERE AT the airport over two hours ahead of schedule. We were so excited. We were amazed at the bargains that were to be had in the duty-free shops. There were over a hundred gates in Heathrow, so I can imagine how many shops there were. Some just specialized in perfume. The scent in those shops was absolute heaven. We could have spent the whole day just spraying scent on ourselves; it was as if we were controlled by our noses. We eventually got around to some other shops. We got a lovely smell of food so we decided to have lunch. At least I was able to manage to eat a little better than I had been able to after my surgery. I was a little scared to chew too hard in case my jaw snapped. The counsellor told me that was physiological and that I would soon forget and eat properly.

We checked the monitors and realized we would be boarding in half an hour, so we made our way to the gate indicated on the monitor. It was simple, really. All we had to do was just follow the signs and keep an eye on the monitors for instructions. We couldn't go wrong. We boarded and settled into our seats. I preferred to have a window seat so I could admire the clouds and the countryside on take-off and landing. We were flying into Knock Airport, which was very handy. Bridget's parents could pick us up from there. They lived in Roscommon, which was not too far away. We were flying with Ryan Air. They were the people's aircraft—the one the ordinary people could afford. It was a very pleasant flight. In fact, for our first flight it was ace! We both said we would fly again with that airline. We left a lovely sunny day behind us in London and flew into a dull, dreary-looking day. 'What's the harm?' I said. 'We didn't come for the weather, that's for sure.' We both laughed.

We reached Knock Airport in less than an hour, which was great. Kate was delighted to see us. She almost knocked us over with hugging. It was great to be back again, although deep down I was dreading telling the folks what had happened to me. We went to Kate's house. As usual she had dinner ready for us—a meal fit for a king. We chatted and told Kate and Mike how well we were doing with our work and how lucky we were to be working for Caroline. 'She is a dream boss,' Bridget told them. 'She gave us a great bonus for having all our work done on time.'

After dinner, I said to Kate, 'I need to tell you something. It's about something that happened to me some six weeks ago.'

When I was finished, she was shocked. She said, 'I am so sorry for you, Rose.' She hugged me and held me close. We both cried. She could not believe it. 'And on top of all that, to have your jaw broken in the process!' she said. 'How awful.'

I felt safe in the comfort of her embrace. I said, 'I am fine now . . . on the mend. All I want now is to put it all behind me and get on with my life.' I explained to her, 'I don't actually remember the rape, which is a good thing. I might not be as good right now if I did.'

She said, 'I am amazed at the amount of weight you lost.'

I told her it was only because I couldn't eat properly. 'But now there's no stopping me! I'm really trying to put on some weight.' I told her I had started jogging again and that I felt better for it. And my appetite seemed to have improved.

After a cup of coffee, I decided to pay Timmy a visit, if he was at home. If he wasn't, I would catch up with him later. It felt odd knocking on the door of my old home and waiting for an answer. At first I turned away thinking there was no one home. I started to cry. I hadn't realized how much I missed Dad. I slowly slipped to the ground outside the door and sobbed my heart out—for me, for Dad, for all the sadness, for the mess I was in. I didn't know which man I loved, if any. I got more and more upset as I went back over what had happened to me. It had been so difficult not being able to talk to anyone about how I really felt. I was sobbing so loud I never heard the door open. Timmy couldn't see me where I was sitting by the door. He looked around. He could hear the sobbing, but could see no one. Just as he turned to go back inside, he spotted me. He was taken aback. 'Rose,' he called out, 'whatever is the matter?' I just cried more. I was so upset I couldn't speak. He helped me to my feet and helped me inside. Dad's chair was still by the fire. He motioned for me to sit in it, which I did.

He looked at me. 'What has happened to you? You look terrible. You are like a skeleton! Rose, are you not eating?'

'Timmy, will you please sit down and let me speak? I need to tell you something.' He sat next to me, and I told him what had happened to me. He jumped up from his seat. 'Rose, you should have told me! I would have gone over to you and taken care of you. Why didn't you?'

'I was very upset,' I told him. 'I wasn't thinking straight. I had a head injury, a broken jaw, fractured ribs, and I ached all over, so I just wanted to be on my own, trying to remember what had happened.' I explained to him that I hadn't really known who to turn to. If Dad had been alive, he would have been my first choice, but since he was gone, I had felt so alone. I felt I didn't belong anyplace.

'You shouldn't feel like that. You have me and Daniel, and Deirdre and Clare. She is a lovely girl. See?' he said. 'You are not alone. We all love you. Don't forget that.'

We had a cup of coffee together. He said Clare would be back soon. We chatted for a while. I told him about our work. He couldn't believe we were doing so well. I told him Caroline was brilliant to work for and very generous. I told him about the good bonus she'd given us for finishing her orders in record time. I explained that I did all the designing and Bridget did most of the sewing. We worked so well together. It was amazing we never had an argument. Suddenly I said, 'Timmy, I'm sorry! I never asked about anyone else. I've just been talking about myself.'

He told me not to worry. Those things needed to be said. He said, 'Deirdre and Daniel are good, and Clare and I are good. We're looking forward to our wedding. We're just hoping some of our siblings will show up. I told him we had another celebration too. 'It's my twenty-first.'

'Great! We'll make it special.'

'Thank you,' I said. He asked how long we were staying, and I said a month. He was pleased. I said, 'Timmy, will you tell Daniel what happened to me? It's very upsetting going over it, so I would rather you told him.' He said it was no problem; he understood.

Just as I was leaving, Deirdre came in. She gave me a big hug and said she was glad to see me. She had just popped in to leave something for Clare. I stood back from her. 'When are you due?' I asked.

'Two months,' she said.

I hugged her again and congratulated her. 'How have you found your pregnancy?'

'I feel great, but now I get very tired. I haven't put on much weight so far I go walking every day, and I feel good.' She said they didn't know yet if it was a boy or girl, but they really didn't care. I said goodbye to both of them. I looked around the farmyard before I left. Everything looked great. They had a lovely kitchen garden, full of every type of vegetable. And there was a very pretty flower garden at the front of the house. It was very picturesque. I was sure that it all was down to Clare.

When I got back to Kate's house I had a coffee with Bridget and Kate. She could see that I was upset, so she gave me a cuddle. We sat and had a chat. Kate asked me, 'Have you been in contact with John?' I explained that we used to ring each other every week, but the week after my attack I had asked Bridget to speak to him saying I had a sore throat, which I did not have. I just couldn't speak to him after the attack. Since then I had not spoken to him. 'It must have been my turn to telephone, and I didn't, so obviously he is not bothered.'

She asked, 'How do you feel about that?'

'I am not cut up about it.' That statement amazed even myself! 'I somehow seem to have put him on the back burner,' I admitted.

She laughed. 'You were madly in love the last time you were here.

'Things change. People change . . .'

She said, 'They sure do!'

'I am excited about Dave,' I said. 'I want to tell you all about him. He seems to understand me better than anyone, and I like being in his company. He genuinely seems to care about me. I told him about John, and he hasn't put any pressure on me. Somehow I couldn't tell John what happened to me. Maybe I'm wrong about him and maybe not. I'll meet him and see how things go. I don't hold out much hope. I think it's Dave I fancy the most.'

Kate didn't interrupt me. When I had finished she said, 'You seem so mature. You are a very brave girl.'

There was a knock at the door. Kate answered it, and who should it be but Daniel. He rushed past Kate, hugged me, and smothered me with kisses. 'I am pleased to see you,' he said. When he let me go he said, 'I'm so sorry for what happened to you. How are you doing?'

'I'm getting through it.'

He hugged me again. 'I love you,' he said. I told him I loved him too. As usual, I started crying, but I was crying because I was happy. He said come the weekend we would all go out for a meal and a few drinks. I said that would be good. He bid us farewell and left.

Bridget asked if I fancied a walk. I said, 'Where are we going?'

'To the hotel we used to work in. We can see how everyone is.'

'Great idea,' I said.

As we were strolling along she asked, 'When are you planning on speaking to John to find out how things are?'

'We're only just home. I need a few days to settle in.'

'Rose, it might be better to get it over with, one way or the other.'

'I hate the thought of meeting him. Doesn't that sound daft? A year ago I was mad about him!'

We chatted all the way to the hotel. When we walked in, Liam, the owner, was at the desk. He didn't raise his head, so he was unaware it was us. We said we needed a room for the night. When he said, 'Name please,' and looked up, we burst out laughing. He came round the counter and hugged us, saying it was good to see us. He asked, 'Will ye have a drink?'

I said, 'We would love two cappuccinos.' He told us to take a seat and he would get them personally for us. When he went inside, he told his wife, Nuala, that we were there, and she came round and greeted us. She said, 'We lost two good workers when ye left.' She asked us if we were happy, and we said very happy. We explained what type of work we did, and how we'd come to be doing it, and they were surprised. We told them we were very happy working for Caroline. In the process of our conversation we drank a pot of coffee and two cappuccinos. They invited us to dinner any night of our choice. Bridget let it slip that it was my twenty-first birthday the following week. Liam said, 'No arguments—we will throw a party for you!' I was so excited, I could not believe it.

We were so happy talking and chatting on our way home. We told Kate when we got back, and she thought that was really good of our former employers and friends. We were only just in the door when Daniel arrived. He was out of breath. He had just received a phone call from our sister Angela. She would be delighted to meet up with us. She and our other sisters, Emily and Anne Marie, would be flying into Shannon the following Sunday. They were not so sure if any of our aunts would come; she felt at the time that it would be just the sisters. Daniel was so excited he danced around the kitchen with me. I did not remember Angela; she had left when I was a baby. I felt it would be a very emotional reunion. Daniel stayed and had a coffee with Kate. Bridget and I could not drink any more coffee; we'd had more than our fair share at the hotel. Kate had dinner ready, so we sat down and ate. Daniel chatted for a little while. We told him about the birthday party at the hotel. He said we would have a good night there. Tuesday was actually my birthday, and I was looking forward to it.

After dinner I told Bridget I was going to visit Mam and Dad in the graveyard. I asked her if she'd like to come and she said, 'Yah, of course.' We put on out jackets as it was getting a little cooler now that evening was approaching. It was only early May yet. We set off together and were there in no time at all. The grave looked lovely. Dad had erected a very nice headstone for Mam. It had been cleaned recently, and it looked as good as new. Dad's name had been added. It looked real good. There were lovely flowers in pots. Someone had gone to a lot of trouble to keep it nice. It was one of the nicer graves in the graveyard. We decided to go home. I was feeling tired; it had been a long day, and I just felt I need a good night's sleep. We had a hot drink and we went to bed.

I had a great sleep. I got up bright and early and went for a jog. I loved the peace of the countryside when I went for a jog. In England I listened to my music. I loved American country—Johnnie Cash, Willie Nelson, Don Williams, to name but a few. I liked some Irish artists as well, but my great love were the American artists. I used to sing along with the songs. I could run for miles and not realize I had gone so far. When I was sad, music was the one thing that kept me going and made me happy again.

When I got back, Kate, bless her, had a huge breakfast ready for all of us. She was determined to put on weight on me. It wouldn't be for the want of trying. We decided, Bridget and I, that we would go to Sligo for some shopping. Clare had just popped in. She said she was going shopping, and we were welcome to go with her. We agreed, and she said she would pick us up in twenty minutes if that was okay.

We were ready when she called back for us. We set off on our journey chatting and laughing as if we didn't have a care in the world. Deep down, though, my mind was in turmoil. I felt cheated because I had been raped. I had tried to put it to the back of my mind, but it kept coming to the surface. For everyone's sake, I kept telling them I was okay, and most of time I was. It would just hit me all of a sudden, and I would struggle not to cry. We were in town before we realized. Bridget and I didn't want anything in particular, but Clare had a certain errand in mind. I discovered later she was looking for something for my birthday. I was giving her hints. I liked jewellery boxes—glass ones, ceramic ones, or antique ones. I had all sorts. Dad had bought me my first one when I was about six. I just loved it. After that, if I ever saw an usual one in an antique shop, I always treated myself. I hoped that was what she was going to get for me. Plus it would be easy to talk home, instead of something bulky. We all went in opposite directions and said we would meet up for lunch at an arranged time. The hour and a half seemed to fly, and we met at the restaurant.

Just as were about to leave, I got a phone call from Dave checking all was well, and asking me to give him a ring later on that night. After lunch Clare asked me to come to the dressmaker's with her for a fitting. They had asked me to be bridesmaid, but I hadn't given my answer. Clare tried on her dress. It was beautiful. She had picked lilac for the bridesmaids. The dresses were plain, with a large contrasting bow at the back. I told her I could have made the dresses for her. She said she hadn't wanted to bother me. I said I would be honoured to be her bridesmaid. I tried on the dress. With a padded bra it would be fine. I thought cream accessories would look nice, and she agreed. Her cousin was to be the other bridesmaid. We got shoes to match, and Clare got a lovely going-away outfit. Bridget got new shoes to match her outfit. We met up again for coffee before we headed off home.

We were in good form laughing and chatting all the way home. When we got home, Kate said dinner was ready whenever we needed it. We told her we'd had lunch in town and we wouldn't be hungry until later. Kate told me, 'John rang. He wants to meet you. He'll ring back later.' I had put him to the back of my mind; now I was beginning to panic. I was just making a coffee when the phone rang. I knew somehow that it was him, so I answered it. He seemed distant . . . very casual. It was difficult to put my finger on it exactly. He was surprised I hadn't rung when I got home. I didn't give him any explanation. I really didn't know what to say. We decided to meet for dinner the following night. He would pick me up. I was not looking forward to seeing him.

I sat in the kitchen after the call, just looking into space and thinking about him. I was not sure if I trusted my instincts. Not that long ago I had been sure I was madly in love with him. As time went by, and as we spent time apart, I slowly had come to think that perhaps it had only been an infatuation. Maybe I just needed someone to love me. I had felt lost and unloved since Dad died. I desperately needed affection . . . someone to be there for me . . . someone to hold me and reassure me. Maybe I was doing the same with Dave. Sometimes I found it difficult to understand my feelings. Kate told me to listen to my heart. If only it was that simple. Then again, it might be. She could be right.

Chapter 10

I WAS WONDERING what should I wear for my dinner with John. Something sexy? Something casual? Just over fifteen months ago, I would have been so excited to be going out to dinner with him, but right now I was just dreading it. I knew deep down I didn't feel the same way about him as I had before. I didn't really know what actually had happened. I just knew I was not in love with him anymore. I decided on a pretty flowery print mini dress with a bolero cardigan to cover my shoulders in the cool of the evening. I carried a white clutch bag and wore matching sandals. I just brushed my hair and left it loose. I was just ready when I heard the car outside. I said good night to Kate and Bridget. 'Wish me luck!' I said. And off I went.

He was the perfect gentleman; he held the door open for me as I got into the car. He kissed me on the cheek and said, 'You look fantastic. I think you have lost weight. Not a lot. Just enough to notice. Personally, I thought you looked just right.' He chatted away telling me how he was getting on with his studies and how he was enjoying it so much. He had only another eighteen months left until he graduated. He asked me why I hadn't gone back to college.

I said, 'I'm working designing clothes for a lady who buys all my designs. Bridget and I are doing really well. I may go back to college later and get a degree in fashion and design.'

'You should really do that. When you are qualified you can demand wages that reflect your worth. You should really consider it.' He asked if I was staying long, and then he asked why I hadn't let him know I was coming to visit. Then he barraged me with more questions: 'Why did you stop ringing? Have you met someone else? You did not seem interested. How come you did not ring?'

I finally said, 'I was unwell for some time. If you cared, you would have kept in touch.'

He just said, 'I hope it was nothing serious.' He didn't even ask about the nature of my problem.

'No, not at all. Just the flu.' I also told him I had private things to sort out, and that some of my older sisters were coming home. They would be here for my twenty-first birthday.

We both seemed to relax a little as we chatted on our way to the restaurant. When we got there, he parked the car, and we went inside. He had booked a corner booth. *Very discreet*, I thought. I felt a bit apprehensive being there alone with him. It's funny how circumstances change. When I first met him I just wanted some time alone with him. Now I wasn't so sure. We looked at the menu. He asked, 'Shall we order a bottle of wine?'

I said, 'Why not?' We talked some more about his studies, and about how brilliant the college was, and the campus. I just thought to myself, *Does he ever stops talking about himself?* I could tell he wasn't that interested in me.

I asked him straight out, 'Why have you asked me out to dinner, John?'

He hesitated. Then he said, 'I have met someone else. She is going to college. She's in the same year as I.'

Funny, I was not upset. Deep down, I was relieved. I just said, 'It sounds serious.'

'It is.'

'All the best to you both.'

'Why did you really stop ringing me?'

'I detected something in your voice—as if you were going to tell me something and then decided against it.'

'I'm sorry. I didn't mean to hurt you. I was a bit immature. I felt I would probably meet someone when I was a bit older.'

I did not reply. I thought, *Bloody cheek!*

Our dinner arrived, and suddenly I didn't feel like eating it. He said, 'I detect an air of maturity about you . . . something different about you. I can't put my finger on it.'

I hadn't intended to tell him what had happened to me, but somehow I blurted out that I had been attacked—mugged. I told him about my broken jaw and my fractured ribs. I did not want to tell him of my rape.

'I am so sorry. Are you going to stay at home now?'

'Why should I?' I responded. 'I am happy in my work. I am not going to let a thug determine what I do with my life!'

'I don't regret knowing you. I wish things could have been different.'

I told him I felt the same. I told him that he had been the first guy I fancied, and that I had been crazy about him at the time, but that, as time went on, I realized that he would always put himself first. He was surprised at my frankness, but said, 'You are probably right.' I told him I would like him to be a bit more spontaneous and not so cautious. He laughed and said, 'You haven't known me for long, but you have summed me up correctly!' We both laughed. We felt more relaxed once we had put our cards on the table. He said, 'I have also seen through you. You weren't upset when I told you I had met someone. Have you someone new in your life?'

I wanted to be honest. I said, 'I am not sure. I have met someone. It's early days. I'll have to see how things work out. I thought you were the one, and see how that worked out!'

He started laughing. 'Do you still go dancing? How about going dancing for old time's sake after we have finished our meal?'

'Why not?' I said.

We went upstairs to the ballroom. It was fairly packed. It brought back so many memories. The band started playing a very lively number. He just gestured to me with outstretched hands. I started laughing. We clasped hands, and off we went. We twirled around the floor as if we were the only ones there. Then the tempo changed to an old-time waltz. I thought to myself, *Do I really want to do this now? I wish I were having this dance with Dave.* But, true to form, John was the perfect gentleman. We just glided around the floor. He was a very attractive man. As the Don Williams song goes, 'another time another place.'

We had a fantastic time. We complemented each other on our dancing. I absolutely adored dancing. We sat down for a drink, and we chatted for a while. 'Does your girlfriend like dancing?' I asked.

'No,' he said. 'That's the sad thing. That's one of the thing that attracted me to you—your moves on the dance floor. Talk about dirty dancing! You could leave them all behind. You are a brilliant dancer.' Then he said, 'I just like dancing. I'm not brilliant at it. I just love music, and the dancing comes easy.'

We had one more dance, and the band started playing the national anthem. The night was over. I had really enjoyed myself. We didn't speak a lot on the way home. When he stopped the car outside Kate's house he asked, 'Did you enjoy yourself?'

'Of course I did. The company was agreeable!'

He laughed. I asked him the same question. His reply was, 'Excellent company and witty conversation. We should do this again sometime.'

'This is probably the last time we will meet.'

'Sadly, I know.' He kissed me on the cheek, gave me a hug, and drove off.

I stood outside for a few minutes, thinking to myself, *What a very pleasant evening*. I didn't feel sad or upset. I realized that I had just been infatuated with him. He had been the first guy to make a pass at me. We had nearly got caught up in something that we may have regretted later.

Kate was still up when I went inside. She said, 'Would you like a drink?'

'Sure,' I replied. 'I would love a coffee.'

'How was it?'

'Good.'

'I thought you'd be in bits.'

'We had a great time together. We had a lovely meal, and we went dancing in the dance hall upstairs. We had a fantastic time.'

'Did you tell him what had happened to you?'

'Not quite. I told him I'd been mugged. I didn't want to go into too much detail. I think I was right.' She said I was very mature, and I had handled everything with dignity. I explained, 'Sometimes I get really scared when I think about what happened, but I can't let it rule my life. I have to put it to the back of my mind and get on with things.' I told her about Shakera and what had happened to her. She was amazed at what I had told her. I said, 'I got off lightly in comparison to her. I am not badly off. I have family that love me and the best mam in the world.' I put my arms around her and gave her a big hug.

She said, 'I will always love you, Rose. I look on you as my daughter.

'I am going to ring Dave tomorrow,' I said. 'If it is agreeable with you, I am going to ask him to come and spend some time here with me.

'That's a brilliant idea!' We finished our coffees and went to bed.

I had a wonderful dream; I woke up feeling on top of the world. We were all going to the hotel that night for dinner and to celebrate my birthday. I was really looking forward to it. Bridget had washed her hair and put it in large rollers so that it would cascade down her back. She would look amazing. I decided to do the same later. When I got a quiet moment, I rang Dave. He was delighted to hear from me. I said, 'I have met up with John, and I now know it's you I have feelings for.' He was very happy. I asked him, 'Would it be possible for you to come and join me for a week?'

Without hesitation he said, 'No problem. I will be there as soon as I can.' I was over the moon.

Bridget and I spent the whole day planning what we were going to wear for the party. I was so excited—like a little kid. I'd never had a birthday party before. I thought it was a pity my sisters could not be here for the party; still, they would be there in a couple of days, and Kate said we would have another party when they arrived. It all sounded so exciting. It was like old times as Bridget and I messed about with make-up and tried on different outfits until we decided on what to wear. It was fun. I heard the phone ringing in the distance. Kate came up stairs. She seemed really excited. 'Dave is at the airport and will be here in an hour! He needed directions to get here.'

'Oh my God,' I squealed. 'I am so excited! I'd best get ready quickly.' We would be ready to go to the hotel in an hour, and Kate had arranged for Dave to meet us there. I decided on a pretty red mini dress I had made some time before that. I wore my red-and-white strappy platforms and carried a matching clutch bag. I was glad I'd done my hair earlier. I only had to brush it out, and it would fall into place.

I was so delighted Dave could come. It's nice to have someone special in your life. Even though I was surrounded by friends and family, I still often felt alone. It is difficult to explain how I felt. So, yes, it is nice to have that someone special by your side. We were all finally ready to leave. We were to meet everyone at the hotel. When we got there almost everyone was there. Daniel and Debbie greeted us at the door and gave me a big hug and my present. Timmy and Clare were also there, and there were three other ladies as well. I did not recognize them straight away. On reflection, I thought to myself, *They do look familiar even though I have no recollection of them.* I outstretched my hand to the one nearest me. 'Would you be my sister?' She said, 'I am indeed. I'm Angela. This is Emily, and this is Anne Marie.' We all hugged in turn. It was so emotional. I could not believe they were there. They told me they had come the previous night, but they had been instructed to stay out of the way until the party.

True to form, I was crying. Angela said, 'You are the image of mam.'

I said, 'Dad always said that.' We hugged and kissed each other over and over. It was so good to finally put faces to names. A couple of girls from the hotel whom Bridget and I had worked with were also there. They all gave me a little present, and there was more hugging and kissing. I was looking out for Dave. I was really looking forward to seeing him. I needed a hug from him.

Liam and Nuala had supplied lovely finger food. You would have thought we had worked for them for years instead of eighteen months. They had been lovely people to work for. The band were playing lovely music, but no one was dancing. I went in search of Bridget. 'Come, on let's dance!' We started jiving to a catchy number. We were having the time of our lives. Then the band started playing an old-time waltz. 'Let's sit this one out,' I said to Bridget. But suddenly there was a guy in front of. 'May I have this dance?' It was Dave. He gave me a big hug and a long lingering kiss. I thought to myself, *This is the guy for me.* We waltzed around the floor. I only had eyes for him. I loved having his arms around me, I loved his touch, and I loved his odour. I just loved *him.*

I had a dance with nearly everyone at the party. I really enjoyed myself. It was brilliant. I had a chat with my sisters in between dancing and having a drink. They wanted me to visit them in America, and I said that I would sometime soon. Kate had a beautiful cake made especially for me, which I thought was really sweet of her. I knew she loved me like a daughter, and I loved her dearly. The band played the national anthem, and that was the end of the dancing. Liam came over to our table and said, 'You know, Rosie, the party is only beginning.'

Is it?' I said, laughing.

'It's a private party,' he said. 'Ye can all stay as long as ye wish. There are plenty of beds upstairs when ye get tired.' That was greeted with a loud cheer. Liam went around to everyone and asked them to put money in the kitty. 'When it runs out,' he said, 'the party will be over.' So we all contributed. We thought it was a good idea. He supplied us all with sausage and chips, which went down well.

It was the most amazing night. I will always remember it. There was a touch of sadness with Dad not been there. He would have loved meeting everyone, and he would have been singing with me and saying to everyone that I was special, when he was really the special one. We sat around talking and chatting and catching up on lost time. Life had not been a bed of roses for my sisters. They had worked hard. Luckily they seemed to have married well and were happy.

The chatting and drinking went on well into the early hours of the morning. We hadn't realized that Liam actually did have all the rooms ready for us. Some had not taken him seriously earlier. We could stay the night, which was even better.

Dave loved meeting my family. He was having a ball, really enjoying himself. He was delighted I had asked him to come and visit. He said, 'Does this mean you have given John the chop?'

'It wasn't like that,' I said. 'I met him and I realized I didn't love him. I have feelings for you.'

He said he was glad, because he had very strong feelings for me also. 'I fell in love with you the minute I saw you,' he said. We had a fantastic time. He had booked into the hotel, and he asked me to stay in his room that night.

I said, 'Why not?' We were exhausted by the time we got to bed. The sun was shining, and the birds were singing, and my heart was beating like a drum. We were a bit worse for the wear, so we just kissed and cuddled and went to sleep.

It was way past midday when we woke up. It was lovely to wake up in his arms. We chatted for a little while, then kissed and cuddled. We thought it best to take things slowly, so we got up and showered and went downstairs to meet the gang for brunch. We were starving. Most of the gang were up and eating when we got downstairs. We ordered a full Irish. I was dying with thirst; a cup of tea was the order of the day. We finished our breakfast and chatted. I needed to chat more to my sisters, so I arranged to meet up with them later. Right now I was going to go for a walk with Dave. We went off for a stroll in the woods chatting away. It was if we had known each other all our lives. We found a bench and sat down for a kiss and a cuddle. He asked if we could meet up for dinner, and I said sure thing.

When we got back to the hotel, Kate and Bridget had collected up all my presents and my beautiful bouquets of flowers. I couldn't believe I had received so much stuff! I was going to stay with Dave; the rest were going home. I told them I would meet up with them later. Dave and I had lunch with my sisters; we had a good laugh. We decided to go to the graveyard after lunch and lay fresh flowers for my parents. We took some of the bouquets I received as presents. I gave the rest to Kate; she deserved them.

Chapter 11

I HAD A fantastic weekend—an absolutely unforgettable one! My sisters and brothers celebrated my twenty-first birthday with me. That in itself was a dream. I never thought we could all be together again. My Dad used to say, 'Everything happens for a reason.' If it hadn't been for my misfortune, I would probably never have met my sisters when I did and get to know them. I might not have met Dave either. One never knows.

Dave and I spent our days together and our evenings with the family. One evening we had dinner with Daniel and Deirdre and Timmy and Clare. We met up with Bridget's family another night, and the sisters another night. They showed me photographs of their families. I was surprised to learn I had so many nieces and nephews. I think it was fifteen in total. They chatted to me about Mam, saying that I looked so much like her . . . that I was petite like her and I had long, blonde hair also like her. She had been brilliant at sewing, they told me. She could make anything out of a piece of material. I seemed to have taken that from her—also the love of music and dancing, which I loved. I still wished I had met her, but at least I felt now that I had got to know her a little through my sisters' stories. It sounded as if she had been a very happy person . . . always singing. Dad had adored her.

I would like a relationship like that. It must be a special feeling to know you are loved and cherished. That's what I wanted from my relationship. Dave spent the week with me, which made it even more special. I knew he cared about me, and the feeling was mutual. It was too soon to say yet if it would develop into something more serious. We decided not to have sex until our feelings grew and we knew where we were in the relationship. We had a brilliant time together. We went walking, to the cinema, and dancing and sightseeing. We enjoyed each other's company. We kissed and cuddled. He was worried I would get flashbacks and that I would freak out, so he was very considerate. He wanted to take things real slow, so I went along with that and just enjoyed being together without any complications.

On his last night we decided to go out to dinner, and dancing afterwards. I was really looking forward to that— just the two of us. On all the other nights we had been in a gang, as we tried to fit everyone in before we went back. But I hoped this night would be special, just the two of us. I had a long soak in the bath. I put my hair in large rollers. I liked the effect when I removed the rollers and let my hair just cascade down my back. It looked very nice. I decided to wear a mini dress and platform shoes. That would give the allusion that I was taller. I was just over five foot, so any help was welcome in that department. The weather had been gorgeous during the day, and a little cool in the evenings, but it was still early May, so we could not complain. I got dropped off at the hotel, and we met up there. We went into town on the bus and had our meal. It was delicious. Afterwards, we went off to a nightclub to dance the night away. I met some old school friends, and we had an absolute ball. They all liked Dave and told me he was a cool guy. We met Bridget there also. She was with some mates. So much for spending the night alone together! Still I didn't complain.

We got a taxi home, only I did not go home. I decided to stay with Dave in the hotel. We were all loved up. The idea we had about waiting to have sex went out the window. When we got to the room we could not wait to get our clothes off. We were just mad for each other; we were so excited. He kissed me all over. Boy, did I like that feeling. I had reached new heights. It was total euphoria. I just knew I wanted him, and he felt the same about me. He was really gentle with me. It was absolute heaven. The passion was amazing. We were both saturated in sweat and completely spent, but I did not want him to stop. We fell asleep in each other's arms; it was heaven to wake up to his wonderful sexy body lying next to me. It was then my turn to kiss and caress him. We kissed and cuddled. We wanted each other so much. My body was aching for him. Soon we were having sex again. We were in rhythm together . . . so in tune with one another. We just could not get enough of each other. We went on until we were completely exhausted and deeply satisfied. We fell asleep again and woke up again sometime later. It was sheer bliss. I decided I could live like that for the rest of my life.

We got up and showered and went down for breakfast, only it was way too late for breakfast. We were, however, in plenty of time for lunch, and we were absolutely ravenous. Daniel was going to pick us up later to take Dave to the airport, and I was going with him to see him off. I would see him again in a week's time. Bridget was in the car when Daniel came to pick us up. Joking, he said to Dave, 'We'll be expecting a wedding soon.'

Dave said, 'One never knows. Ask your sister.' We had time for a coffee, then we said our goodbyes and left. Bridget was chatting on the way back home. To be honest, I didn't hear half of what she said. I was so excited. I was thinking to myself, *I think I made the right choice, I'm sure Dave is the one, I'm totally besotted with him.*

Timmy and Clare's wedding was on the Saturday—another big day. It was a pity Dave could not have been there for that. I was delighted to be a bridesmaid. The dress fit me like a glove. I did get a padded bra, and sure enough it did make a huge difference. All the women from the village got together and did the cooking. The party was to be at the house; I thought that was a nice idea. The day of the wedding came all too soon, but all the preparations were made so there was no panic. It was a beautiful day. The service was absolutely lovely, and Clare looked like a princess. We had a fantastic day; it could not have been better. A group played the music, and they were outstanding. They could play almost anything we requested. Timmy and Clare looked divine taking their first waltz together as man and wife. We all applauded and then we took to the floor and had a ball. The Irish sure know how to party. All the neighbours were at the reception. It was great to see all of them. Some I hadn't seen for some time. They were all such lovely people, always willing to help whenever there was a problem. They were all friends with the family. I think I must have danced with nearly all people in the village; we had such crack. The party went on well into the early morning. It was fitting that the reception was held at the house. That's what Dad and Mam had done when they got married. We all went to bed exhausted. The sisters enjoyed themselves immensely; we were all so happy to be together.

The next day was the big clean-up. We all mucked in, and the place was spotless in no time at all. Then we all sat around chatting. Timmy and Clare had left early for the airport. They were off on their honeymoon. Timmy had asked me to put the wedding flowers on Dad's and Mam's graves, so Bridget and I set off and did exactly that. We said a prayer for both of them. I knew it might be some time before we visited again. We were leaving the next day, so we decided to call at the hotel to thank them for the wonderful party and have lunch. We had plans to have dinner with the sisters that night. They were staying for a couple more days. Daniel and Deirdre would be joining us at Bridget's. We didn't intend it to be a late night; we had already had quite a few of those! Dave rang that evening to check what time to collect us from the airport. He said he missed me and couldn't wait for me to get back. We had a lovely meal and, as planned, we went home early. We all had coffee at Kate's. Daniel and Deirdre went home soon after, so we went to bed. I was tired; we had a very busy time since we arrived.

We were up bright and early. I decided to go for a jog. I felt good. I'd had a wonderful sleep, and I was going back to Dave, which was wonderful. I quickly packed my bag after I got up; we had each brought only one bag with us, so we could check it in and pick it up when we got there. I got some lovely delicate cut glass ornaments, which I wrapped up in my towels so that they would not get damaged. I had taken a lot of photographs, and would have them developed when I got back. I took my camera with me everyplace. I photographed flowers and places I visited. When I had time I planned to take art classes just to learn the technique of colouring and shading and anything else that I needed to learn. I could draw anything, but I knew I would feel more confident if I took some classes. A few of the neighbours dropped in to say farewell before we set off. This I always find very touching; it also makes me sad.

We were ready to be off in no time at all. Kate came with us for the spin. We all chatted and remarked on how quickly the time had passed. We said our goodbyes outside the airport. We thought that would be better than hanging about inside. I prefer to go through customs and then relax and perhaps have a coffee. There were not a lot of passengers on the plane. There were plenty of empty seats. Dave was going to pick us up at Heathrow. I was excited about going back, and so was Bridget. We were both feeling the effects of the late nights. We were longing to get back and have a good rest.

Dave was waiting for us when we got in. He kissed and hugged me and told me how much he had missed me. It was lunchtime when we landed, and he wanted to buy us lunch. I didn't feel hungry, so I just had soup and a roll. Bridget and Dave had lunch. We didn't hang about when we had eaten. We just left; we were longing to get home.

When we reached home, I told Dave I was shattered. I wanted to have a snooze for a couple of hours. He said he would call back later in the evening. We kissed and said goodbye. I woke up around eight o'clock absolutely starving after a wonderful sleep. Bridget woke up some time later. She had slept well also. I showered and got ready, as I was expecting Dave to call. Bridget said she was going to make an omelette, as she was not feeling that hungry; she just fancied something.

Dave arrived and announced he was taking me out to dinner. I told him that was good as I was starving. I was dressed casually in jeans and T-shirt. He had made a reservation for dinner. We could walk to the restaurant it; was not too far. It was nice just to stroll holding hands.

There was a bench near the entrance to the park we passed on our way. Dave said, 'Rose, will you sit for a moment?'

'I'm okay. I don't feel tired.'

'I know. Please sit with me.' I did just that. We sat quietly for a few minutes, but then he got down on one knee and said, 'Rose, will you marry me?' I was shocked. I had not expected him to do this! He said, 'Sorry, am I jumping the gun? I just know how I feel.'

'No!' I replied. 'I love you! I would love to marry you!'

He kissed me passionately and said, 'I am mad about you. I love you dearly.'

I laughed and said, 'What about taking things easy?'

'I want to spend the rest of my life with you. The first time I kissed you I knew you were the one.'

'I feel the same way too.' He slipped a beautiful sapphire ring on my finger and kissed me again, telling me again how much he needed me and loved me. Deep down I was thinking, *Please love me forever as I will love you.* He kissed me again—a long, wanting kiss. Then he said, 'Shall we go and have dinner?'

'Yes please!' I said. 'I am starving!' We got settled at our table in the restaurant. He had arranged for a bottle of champagne to be brought to the table. The waiter filled our glasses, and we toasted each other as if we were the only ones in the room. It was so romantic. I felt so happy. We had a lovely meal. I was ravenous. I thought I was too excited to eat, but as the saying goes, I ate a hearty meal.

We walked back to the flat chatting all the way. I was so excited. He asked me when I wanted to get married. I said I was in no rush. Maybe it would be nice to live together for a while to get to know each other. He said that was a good idea. We would have to discuss it. We had a lot to talk about, but there was no rush. We got home and had a coffee. Dave said, 'If you wish, you could move into my house with me. I bought a house a couple of years ago. It needs to be decorated, but we can do that together.'

'That is a wonderful idea! It will be fun to decorate.' I told him I would probably move in the following week after I had sorted out things with Bridget.

We kissed goodbye. Dave left, and I retired to bed. Bridget had gone to bed, and I did not like to wake her, so I decided to wait until morning to tell her my news. I could hardly sleep. I had so many things going around in my head. Eventually, though, I did fall asleep. I got up fairly early. Bridget was still asleep, so I went for a jog, She was having breakfast when I got back. She let out a scream when she saw my ring. She said, 'Why did you not wake me up?' She hugged me. 'Good luck,' she said. 'I hope ye will be very happy.' I was crying I was so happy. It was all finally beginning to sink in.

I joined Bridget for breakfast. I told her that Dave wanted me to move in with him. I asked her if she would be interested in keeping the flat. She said that was brilliant, because James would love to move in with her. 'That's settled then,' I said.

'Where is the house?' she asked.

'It's not that far away. It's only a couple of roads away, near Greenwich Park. You can walk from here.'

'Brilliant!' she said. 'We can still be neighbours. We will still continue working for Caroline, for the moment anyway. We may want to change things down the road, but for now things will remain the same. Speaking of Caroline, we need to meet up with her soon to discuss next season's designs.'

I said, 'I will ring her, and we can meet up for dinner.' Bridget said that would be fine.

We agreed that I would move in with Dave the following Friday. I did not have a lot to move. It was mostly clothes. I was so excited about moving in with him. This is all so new to me. Having the place to myself when he was at work would give me time to sort it out and have it the way we would like it to be.

He took me to see the house during the week. It was a lovely house, screaming out for loving care. I was the one to do just that. I loved having a project to sort out. We decided to paint it all, starting with the bedroom. We were getting a new double bed before the weekend, and Dave painted the bedroom walls a cream colour. The neutral colours are nice, because you can introduce other colours to brighten up the room—bed linen and curtains.

I took on that job. I measured the window in the bedroom and made curtains accordingly. The duvet cover matched the curtains, and I got a rug to complement those colours. The bedroom looked ace even if I say so myself. Dave was really impressed with it. I got the bed delivered on Thursday, and everything was ready for my move on Friday. I moved according to plan, and Dave had a beautiful dinner ready for me—our very first dinner in our own house. Words cannot describe how I felt.

The next room on the agenda was the dining room. The best room in the house was the kitchen. Dave had had a new one put in when he bought the house. It was perfect—all done in pine. I really liked it. We had to decide on a colour for the dining room. I got coffee colour for the chimney breast and a lighter shade for the walls. The effect was stunning. I made cream curtains for the bay window and placed a cream rug in front of the fire. The chimney was open so we could have a fire for a romantic evening.

It was just perfect. We got a new dining room table and chairs. It all looked lovely in the room.

The bathroom was fine for the moment. We decided we could change it later if we wanted to. We were settling in well and were very happy. When Dave worked nights, Bridget came over to stay the odd night, and we still had our long chats. Dave's birthday was coming up so we decided to have a party and invite his parents and his sister and also celebrate getting engaged. I was really looking forward to my new life. I couldn't have been happier.

The party was a success. We just invited close friends and family. His parents were lovely. They could not have been nicer. They gave us money to buy something for the house. His sister was a lovely girl too. Bridget and James were there too. We all had a lovely time. Dave and I were so in love and so happy.

Shakera's wedding was the following weekend. How time was flying. It seemed like ages since we'd got the invitation, and now it was suddenly about to happen. It was to be a registry wedding; only close friends were invited. Dave and I got a taxi to the registry office. We got there with plenty of time to spare, only there was none of the wedding party there. We were a little surprised. We were waiting around thinking it must have been cancelled, when at last we saw the bride and groom walk towards us. She looked lovely in the dress I had made for her. I had not actually seen it on, but she had told me it fitted well, which it surely did. It was full length and ivory in colour, with a short headdress, just as she had requested. They seemed very bubbly. They thanked us both for coming and told us that only his parents were going to be here for the service. We were to meet up with the rest of the party at the restaurant. The service was over in a matter of minutes. We went to the restaurant and met the rest of their friends. We had a pleasant meal, and the company was good. Everyone seemed to enjoy themselves. There were only a handful of people there, but the happy couple did not seem to care. They seemed happy. We all left shortly after the meal. An Irish wedding it was not. I took a few photographs of the couple and asked the waiter to take a group shot before we left. I did manage to chat with Shakera for a moment. She'd had no contact whatsoever with her parents or her siblings. She said it was very sad, but it was the way things were. She was learning to live with it. She managed to walk quite well with her prosthesis. One would never know she was wearing one. Dave and I got a cab home. We felt sad for the bride and groom. They really were on their own. That was one time I hoped love would conquer all.

Chapter 12

LIFE WAS GREAT. Every chance I got I was doing something with our house—painting or making curtains. On Dave's days off we usually went shopping for bargains for the house. It was my project for the moment. I was really into the decorating. I'm sure I must have been boring to all my friends; all I talked about was how wonderful Dave was and how he loved helping me with the decorating. Work was brilliant also. Caroline was so impressed with me she gave me a rise. I didn't even ask for it. Bridget settled into the flat with James, and as they say, things could not have been better. We were all happy with our lives. We were moving in different directions, but still making time for friendship, which was very important.

When Dave was on nights, I often had 'girly nights' in. We'd all cook something and bring a bottle and have a laugh. He worked a week of nights every four weeks, then he had a week off. That week was like a holiday.

I usually worked round his schedule, which worked for us. When I had to come up with new designs, I could be a bit agitated until I had come up with some workable plans, then I was okay. Caroline was brilliant. She would give me a few ideas and leave the whole collection in my hands; she never interfered. I usually created a rough draft of what I was about to work on. I'd take it to her. She never condemned anything; we seemed to totally understand each other.

One day I had lunch with Caroline. She told me she was planning on opening her own clothing factory. She wanted to expand, and she asked for my input and thoughts. The flat had become too small for all the production, and it would be easier on Bridget if she did not have to worry about getting orders out on time. So I thought it would be an excellent idea.

Caroline had been a buyer for a well-known store, and she had finally decided it was time to part company and set up on her own. She wanted to produce her own label and sell them on to whoever would pay her the most. She asked me to go in with her as a partner and still work as her designer. This was a big undertaking. I knew I had to give it careful consideration. I felt excited about the whole idea, but I needed to discuss it with Dave. I had quite a lot of money saved; I could easily go into partnership with her, but I had other things to consider. How much of my time would this take up? Dave had a good job, which he was very happy with, and I was happy just being a designer. I was not sure if I wanted the hassle. I needed to sit down and throw a few ideas into the ring and see what we come up with.

We all met up for dinner: Bridget, James, David and I, and Caroline. We intended to discuss this new project and how it would affect the lot of us. We had a good dinner, then we took our coffee out to the garden to get stuck in with the discussion. Dave had told me to go ahead with whatever I wanted to do. He would back me up in whatever I decided. That was very reassuring. Caroline went over some figures and said we could have a nice little earner if we were to go ahead. We looked over the figures and discussed various things. She said Bridget could stay on as a seamstress, or even better as a supervisor. That would mean more money for her, which was a sweetener. We went over everything until we were fed up with it all. In the end I decided I would go into partnership with her. I would continue to design. Maybe later down the road we could get a student to help out and perhaps bring fresh ideas to the table. We would wait and see how things took off before we made any major changes. We planned to meet up with the solicitor the next day. He would put everything in order and make it legal.

It was exciting—another new adventure. Everything was going well in my life. I was happy. I had put my attack to the back of my mind and did not dwell on it. My life was good. Dave loved me, and he could not have been more attentive if he'd tried. I loved everything about him. We had the house finished for the moment. We had sanded the floorboards in the hallway and varnished them, and they looked fantastic. We had got new wall lights fitted to finish off the effect. Once we got the business up and running, we planned to get married, so Dave said. My life seemed to be filled with good things. I just hoped it would stay that way.

Caroline and I looked at quite a few buildings for our factory. After we narrowed it down to three, we went back again for a more thorough look before we made our final decision. There was an industrial estate at the back of New Cross train station, and it seemed ideal. It was easy to get to by train or bus or car, so that was not a problem. Easy access was very important. We could move into the building as it was; it was in very good condition. All we needed to do was put loads of power points all over the place and install a new transformer. There was a nice set of offices there also. We were lucky. We got all the stock from an auction. We would start off with fifty sewing machines and see how we got on. We interviewed prospective employees together to move things along quickly. It was not as daunting as I'd thought it would be, and in no time we got our quota of workforce. Bridget was to be one of our supervisors, and we employed another girl also. We had all the material delivered. We had employed two cutters and two pressers. We didn't know in the beginning if that would be enough, but we felt comfortable that we had a good start.

We opened on a Monday. We were both so excited. We had managed to get loads of orders. Caroline certainly knew a lot of people in the business, and that helped a lot. Everything went through Caroline and me, so it was all daunting until everything was sorted. I knew we would succeed.

On that first day, everything just seemed to go according to plan. We had asked the cutters to come in early, so that the machinists—the seamstresses—would not be sitting idle. Everything went as planned. By eleven o'clock we were both sitting in the office toasting each other with a coffee, saying business was child's play. Still, we were keeping our fingers crossed. The day went off without a hitch, which was unbelievable. We had been apprehensive about our first day, so we were delighted when it was over.

We decided we would meet up later with our other halves and have a dinner celebration. We were so happy about our first day that Caroline and I both hit the wine when we go to the restaurant. The fellas were laughing at us. Then Dave disappeared for a few minutes. When he returned, the waiter came to our table with a bottle of champagne. We had a toast to our future as entrepreneurs. We all laughed and raised our glasses. It felt so good to be running our own business, and we were only in our early twenties. I was only twenty-two, Bridget was twenty-one, and Caroline was twenty-five. She tried to boss me sometimes, but I didn't let her get away with it. We were friends really; since the day we met we had been friends. I believed we had the potential to make this adventure a success.

At the time I was travelling to work by bus, as Bridget had bought out my half of the minivan. I decided I needed to get a small car for myself. Dave was on the lookout for one for me. Work was going like clockwork; everything was ticking over nicely. The staff clocked in and out, and we employed an accountant and an assistant for all the office work, so we did not have to worry. I had my own office, and I could also work from home if I wished. After all, I was the boss—or at least one of them—so I could decide to go in or stay at home, which is everyone's dream.

Dave and I had breakfast together most mornings. And I usually went for a jog before work. One morning I did not feel too well. I felt a bit faint. I made tea and waited for Dave to come downstairs. I had already decided to cancel my jog. I began to get a bit worried. I had a sharp pain in my abdomen, and it was getting worse by the minute. I took a sip of tea and stood up to call Dave from the kitchen door. That's the last thing I remember. When he came downstairs, I had collapsed on the floor. He called for an ambulance without hesitation. The ambulance arrived within three minutes. That's the beauty of living in the city; one is never too far from services. I woke up on the way to the hospital, wondering where I was. I saw Dave, so I knew I was safe. He explained I had fainted and that I had been unresponsive. 'How are you now?' he asked. I told him I had an excruciating pain in my abdomen. The paramedic examined me and said it was very tender; it could be an ectopic pregnancy. I just thought to myself, *Oh no, not history repeating itself!* I thought of Mam, and I started crying.

Dave was very concerned about me. He said 'Rose, I don't understand why you are so upset.' Between the sobs and the pain, I told him about my mother. He hugged me and told me not to worry . . . that things would work out. He said we had plenty of time to have children—as many as I wanted. I laughed through the pain, which had eased off a little. When the pain became unbearable again, I was given an injection.

When I got to the hospital, I was rushed to X-ray so the doctors could see what was going on. Dave called into work to let them know he would be late because of a family crisis. He did the same for me; he rang Caroline. When I came back from X-ray, I was very drowsy. I struggled to stay awake. The doctor examined me after checking out the X-rays films. He said that, indeed, I had an ectopic pregnancy; I would need to go to theatre. In addition, as I had lost a considerable amount of blood, I might need a blood transfusion. Poor Dave was there taking it all in, and I was just struggling to stay awake.

I must have fallen fast asleep. When I woke again I had been to theatre. I felt very thirsty. Dave was sitting in the chair by my bed. He looked so worried. I stretched out my hand and said, 'I will be okay.' He smiled and asked me how I was feeling. 'All I know at the moment,' I said, 'is that I am very thirsty.' He went to get the nurse to see if I could have a drink. He came back with half a glass of water and told me I could have only sips, as I might be sick after the anaesthetic. I had a few sips and felt sleepy again. Dave said he would see me later. He kissed me goodbye and left.

When I woke up, I was very disorientated. It took me a while to realize where I was and what had happened to me. When I looked around trying to comprehend the situation, I realized poor Bridget was sitting in the chair by the bed. When she saw that I was awake, she hugged me and told me not to worry. She said, 'Sure you don't want a baby just yet.'

I thought about it and, to be honest, I wouldn't have minded. 'I just feel sad that I have lost this one.'

She said, 'Dave was concerned about you. He asked me to come and sit with you.'

I explained, 'I am worried about having a baby—or should I say miscarrying babies. My mam suffered a lot of miscarriages. My menstrual cycle is very erratic. Sometimes it's regular, and then I can go months . . . and nothing.'

'You never said anything.'

'It's something one doesn't discuss. I just thought it would settle down.' I told her they had taken bloods and they would have results by the afternoon. I felt very tired; I just wanted to sleep. The doctor had told me that there was no reason I could not have a baby, and not to worry about it. He told me I was very underweight. He advised me to slow down, rest, and try to put on weight—at least a stone weight.

Bridget said, 'You should take a few weeks off and relax.'

I said, 'The timing is all off.' I felt guilty about leaving Caroline to cope on her own. I was up to date with the designs, but it was the day-to-day running of things that she might need help with. I knew she was more than capable; it was just nice to have back up if a problem should arise. Bridget stayed for quite a while trying to cheer me up. After a while she could see I was struggling to stay awake, so she said she would come back later. I must have drifted off to sleep. When I woke up Dave was sitting in the chair;

he had brought me a beautiful bouquet of flowers. He kissed me and asked, 'How are you doing? I didn't want to wake you.'

I said, 'I feel good now. I'm waiting for the doctor to come back to see me and tell me if I needed a blood transfusion.'

He said the doctor had spoken to him when he came in. I did need a unit of blood; after that they would need to check to see if I needed a second one. He said to me, 'Rosie, you need to take life easy for a while and stop skipping meals. You need to sit down and relax and enjoy your food and stop rushing about the place. Caroline can cope for a while on her own. You'll be in hospital for a couple of days. They want to do more tests on you just to see if everything is okay.'

'Now you are scaring me. Should I be worried?'

'Not at all,' he said. 'I have to get back to work. It may be late when I pop back, but I will see you then, my love.' I dropped off to sleep again. I couldn't understand why I was so tired; all I wanted to do was sleep. I woke up around ten o'clock, and the doctor asked me when Dave was coming back. I told him he was going to pop in later, when he got a chance. He asked me to tell the nurse in charge when he did come back, as he needed to speak to both of us.' That caused me to be really worried. I asked him what was the matter, but he said he needed to speak to both of us. I knew something was not right. I was really worried. *Maybe I cannot have any more children,* I thought. *Dave will surely leave me if that is the case.*

Caroline came by to see me. I told her something was not right, as the doctor wanted to speak to both of us. She tried to reassure me and told me not to worry, but I was worried. I was dead scared. She stayed and tried to take my mind off things. She told me about the business, but I was not interested. All I wanted was Dave to come by so we could get the bad news over with. She left. She knew I was not in form for chat. I felt so upset. All I wanted to do was cry, yet I did not know why.

Caroline must have rung Dave, because he came in shortly after she had left me. He asked me, 'How are you feeling?'

'Very tired,' I said. 'I cannot keep my eyes open.' I told him what the doctor had said.

'Don't jump to conclusions,' he said. 'Let's hear what he had to say first.' He asked the nurse in charge to beep the doctor and let him know we were waiting for him. We were both nervous; we were making small talk just trying to keep each other from screaming. We seemed to wait for ages before the doctor appeared.

He came in and brought a chair with him so he could sit with us. He drew the curtains around the bed. I thought, *Oh my God what is he going to tell us?* He started to explain. 'I was worried when I examined you in theatre,' he began, 'so I had bloods taken for a number of tests, and one showed up positive.' He paused for a minute. 'Don't be too alarmed,' he continued, 'you have leukaemia. It is chronic, but I feel sure I have got it in time. But we must start treatment immediately. There is no time to waste. I will leave you for a few minutes, but I will be back directly.'

I was shocked. I just started to cry. Why was life so unfair? We both sobbed. Dave said, 'I will be there every step of the way.'

The doctor came back directly with some literature that would answer some questions we might have. He said the ectopic pregnancy had triggered the illness; it had been a blessing in disguise. Otherwise, the leukaemia may not have been detected until later. He explained, 'You need to go into isolation. Your immune system is very low. This is just a precaution. We have a bed ready for you.'

I was completely shattered. I had not expected this news. I knew I would just have to put my trust in the doctor and hope for the best. Dave said he would wait until I got settled into the new room before he left. I thought, *This must be dreadful for him. He did not sign up for this.*

I had a lovely room to myself. I just wished this was not happening. I had been thinking that things had been going so well for me . . . it was all too good to be true. I had kind of been waiting for the knock back. Boy did it hit me with both barrels! I just wondered, *Will I get through this, or is it just a matter of time?* We never know what life will throw at us. It would have been so unfair to have only just met the nicest man in the whole world and then die before I really got to know him. How cruel would that be? As I waited for the doctor to return, everything was running through my mind. *I love Dave so much. Why couldn't we get old together? Why did I have to be the one who has to sacrifice everything? I have never misbehaved. I have always worked hard. I had to grow up without my mam. I lost my dad when I was fifteen. How much more do I have to endure? What have I done to deserve all this? Why can't I just be allowed to get on with my life and love my darling and he love me?*

Just then Dave walked into the room wearing a gown and mask. I tried to be offbeat. I said, 'Hi, doctor.'

He laughed, but the tears welled up in his eyes. He cuddled me and said, 'If anything happens to you, I do not know what I will do.'

I said, 'We will beat this together.' The doctor had explained that I would have blood transfusions throughout the night. They would check my blood again the next day and see what my cell count was. I would have to have chemotherapy. If that strategy failed, the next step would be a bone marrow transplant. As I was talking to Dave trying to piece it all together, I realized all had not been well with my health after the rape. I had never fully recovered. I had never put on any weight. I often felt very tired, but when I had been for a jog I would feel just fine. The weight problem used to worry me, even though I had never told anyone. Another symptom was the night sweats. Sometimes I had to get up and change the bed linen and my pyjamas. I didn't think they had been so bad after I moved in with Dave, but maybe I was just masking it.

At the time, all of this was irrelevant. I had to concentrate on fighting this battle. I had to find the strength from somewhere. Dave said, 'I'm going out to get a coffee. Would you like one?'

'I would love one,' I said. 'Please kiss me. I love you, and one day I will give you a baby.'

He gave me the longest kiss, and hug. 'I love you too,' he said. When he left the ward I started crying. I loved him so much. I need him. *Please, God, help me get better. He is the most important person in my life, and I want to grow old with him.* I was asleep again when he returned with the coffee. He laughed and said, 'You are like sleeping beauty!' He stayed with me, and we drink our coffee together.

I said, 'We will have to discuss freezing my eggs so that I can have them implanted again when I am better. The chemotherapy will ravage my body. We will have a better chance of having a family if my eggs are frozen. He agreed with me. I asked him how work was going. Were they busy? He said his partner was going to call around later. I told him I was feeling tired. If he wanted to go back to work, I would be fine. He said he would stay a while. The nurse was coming in every half hour to check my vital signs. I did fall asleep. When I woke up in the morning, Dave was fast asleep in the chair. The nurse said he had come back early in the morning, and she had given him a blanket.

I was to have my first chemotherapy that day, so I expected to be feeling ill. I was not looking forward to it. I decided to keep a journal of my stay in hospital and my treatment and how I felt. It might keep me motivated. I drifted in and out of sleep throughout the day. *Maybe all the days will be like this*, I thought, *and I will wake up feeling better. As if.* Poor Dave was shattered. I said, 'You need to go home and go to bed properly and have a good rest.' When I woke up again I was feeling very ill. I just wanted to be sick, and I felt so week. It was a struggle to get to the toilet, but I did get there eventually.

It was weird being in a room on my own. It would have been nice to speak to someone. There was a large window in the room. I could watch the world go by. I had never been one for watching television, but I began watching breakfast television and various programmes. I just needed to get interested in something. I wanted to wake up and find the whole thing over. It was very frustrating. *Still*, I thought, *maybe it's best that I rest.* The nurse came in to give me an injection of Stemetil to stop me from being sick. I dropped off to sleep again.

Chapter 13

THE DAYS SEEMED to go by in a blur. When I was awake, I was being sick, getting injections, having drips changed, and feeling so weak I was unable to get to the toilet at times. It seemed that every time I opened my eyes, Dave was sitting at the end of the bed. Sometimes I spoke to him, but more often than not I didn't. I just felt as if I was lying there and floating above my body—such a weird feeling. I didn't have the strength to do anything without help. I had never slept so much. I slept for hours on end. When I woke up I felt thirsty. Sometimes I fancied something to eat, and at other times even the smell of food made me ill. When I was alert, Dave was brilliant. He brought me whatever food I fancied. It might be a burger or chicken nuggets and chips, or maybe just sausage and mash. I sometimes woke in the middle of the night having dreadful nightmares. Dave stayed by my bed most nights. If he was there when I woke up, I could go straight to sleep after a dream, but if he wasn't, I found it difficult to get back to sleep again.

The tests showed that the medication was working. It would be a long haul, but at least the treatments had stopped the leukaemia from getting any worse, which was a relief. I felt a bit of hope. I just had to have faith. That's what nurses kept telling me. Some days I felt so awful. I lost a lot of weight, which I could not afford to lose. My hair fell out also. I had got Bridget to cut it short before I started the treatments so that I would not have to watch it all fall away and make me feel even worse.

I had six rounds of chemotherapy, and then I had a break. I had to concentrate on eating. I had to have high-energy drinks. My mouth was very sore, as mouth ulcers were a side effect of my treatment. I needed to keep rinsing my mouth to help it get better. I seemed to be getting my strength back. I could get in and out of bed better. It was not such an effort, and best of all I could do it without help. I did feel a little better. One afternoon, I was in the mood to chat to Dave. Poor Dave. He came in that day with a big smile on his face. When he saw me sitting in the chair, he gave me a big hug. 'You look great!' he said. 'I think you have turned the corner.' He stayed for quite a while until I got tired. He helped me to bed. It was the first day I had stayed up for a couple of hours. He said he would call back later.

I had a wonderful sleep and woke up feeling hungry for the first time in months. I thought to myself, *I must be getting better.* Bridget rang me saying she was on her way in. She asked if I fancied anything. I said, 'I would love sausage and chips, coffee and an éclair.'

She said, 'Brilliant. See you soon.' I had a shower on my own while I was waiting for Bridget to come in. My hair had started to grow, and it didn't look half bad. Better still, I felt good in myself, which was great. Bridget arrived laden down with food, God love her. We hugged and had a laugh. She started crying. 'Rosie, you have come back. You are on the mend.'

'I hope so. I do not want to go through all that again.' I managed to eat all my food, which was a first. I had become used to just nibbling, but finally I felt like eating. I actually enjoyed the food. I no longer had the vile, awful taste in my mouth from the chemotherapy. We had a good old laugh, just like old times. I told her I had heard from Daniel. He'd had the test done for compatibility for the bone marrow transplant. I said, 'Let's hope I don't have to go down that road.'

Bridget said, 'Mam and dad are praying for you, and all our neighbours rooting for you.' She left the best news till last. 'Deirdre and Daniel have a baby boy. They've named him John after your dad.'

'Oh, that is wonderful news!' I said. 'Now I have to get better so I can go home to see my new nephew.'

While we visited the laboratory technician came round to take blood for testing. If everything was okay, I would be cleared to go home for the weekend, which would be brilliant. But I would have to come back Sunday evening. It would be lovely just to go home for a couple of hours. I had been in hospital for six weeks. But the time had gone quickly. I couldn't remember the half of it. Bridget said, 'I'll get two coffees while you are having your blood taken.'

I said, 'Great. I would love a coffee.' My arms were all bruised from all the blood draws, blood transfusions, and injections. I looked like a junkie. Bridget came back with the coffee. She said, 'It will be brilliant if you can go home for the weekend.'

'Yes it will,' I said. 'I am not out of the woods yet. I still have to be very careful. I can't be in crowds in case of infection. I'm not taking any chances. I can't afford too.'

She said, 'I understand.' We had our coffees. I savoured every drop. It was so good to eat and drink without feeling ill, but I was beginning to get sleepy. I said to Bridget, 'I am going to have a nap for a little while.'

'Sure.' She hugged me and said, 'See you tomorrow. Dave will be in later.'

I must have dropped off to sleep. When I woke up, it was getting dark, and the lights were on. I had slept for hours. I was amazed, as I had not felt that tired. Dave came in with sausages and mash. 'Brilliant!' I said. 'You must have read my mind.' He brought me some magazines to read. He asked me how I was feeling. 'Good,' I answered. 'I have great news for you! If my bloods are okay I can go home for the weekend.'

He hugged me and said, 'That's brilliant!'

'That's not all. Deirdre had her baby—a little boy!'

'Brilliant again!' he said. 'Now you are an auntie.'

'Yes I am. And it's wonderful news that I might be able to go home for a couple of hours.' Then I said, 'Dave, I don't want to see people yet. I don't feel up to it. I need to be careful not to pick up any infection; it could set me back.'

He said, 'Don't worry. I know what you've been through. It will be just the two of us for the weekend.'

'That's great,' I said. 'I'm looking forward to it. Will you put a duvet on top of the mattress? I'm afraid the bed will hurt my bones. I have a special bed here. I think the duvet on top of the mattress will be very comfortable. I feel the cold a lot more too, as I have lost so much weight, but hopefully I will start putting it back on again.' He went to the canteen to get chicken broth. I still felt peckish. I had a milk shake as well. We watched television for a while together. I said, 'Dave, as I am feeling better, why don't you go home and rest?'

He said, 'Actually, I feel exhausted.' The next day was uneventful. I had a good rest. The test results came back clear, so I could plan on going home. I was delighted. I rang Dave and told him I couldn't wait until he came in later.

He was also absolutely delighted. I asked him to bring in a warm tracksuit for me to wear on the journey home. It seemed weird saying those words, because at times I had thought I would not make it.

Caroline came in to visit. I told her my news, and she was delighted. She told me not to worry about the business. Everything was going well. Our first orders had gone out that week without a hitch. 'Great,' I said. Then I jokingly said, 'You don't need me at all!'

'Not really,' she said, also joking. Then she got serious. 'I want you back as soon as you are fit. Take it easy and see how things turn out.'

I said, 'Will do. One scare is enough.' Caroline left saying she would be in touch. Only one more day and I would be going home. Time seemed to be dragging. I was to go home on Friday afternoon. My room would be kept for me in case of an emergency. Dave, my darling, would pick me up. I was so excited. It was like I had been given a new lease on life.

At the appointed time he picked me up as arranged, and we went straight home. He had placed scented candles all over the place. The house looked inviting and homely. I knew I would appreciate it more when I felt better. I had a lovely cup of tea. Nothing can compare to a lovely cup of tea. Dave had a log fire in the living room; it looked divine. I found everything overwhelming. I started to cry. I said, 'Dave, will I live to enjoy all this?'

'Of course you will,' he said.

'I hope I do,' I said. We had a kiss and a cuddle. *It's good to be home*, I thought. Dave had rented a video of a film I wanted to watch. We had a light dinner as well—sausages and mash and onions. It was my favourite at the time. We watched the film. I started getting sleepy towards the end, so Dave carried me to bed. The electric blanket was on, and everything was perfect. I think I fell asleep as soon as I lay down. I felt so happy and contented, and with Dave beside me, life could not be better.

I woke in the morning in Dave's arms, where I wanted to stay for the rest of my life. He got up and made breakfast. I just wanted porridge and a cup of tea. He came back to bed for a little while. We chatted, and I fell asleep for a couple of hours. When I woke up again, I watched television for a while. I did not feel like getting up. I was cosy and happy. Dave made soup for lunch, and I ate a chicken sandwich with it. I stayed in bed until afternoon, and I felt all the better for it. It was just nice to be together and talk, listen to music, and enjoy each other's company. We had a fantastic weekend together. I really enjoyed it, and so did Dave. Sunday evening was not long coming around. 'We can do the same again next week, all being well,' he said.

The nurse on my ward was waiting for us. She wanted to know if everything had gone well, and I said, 'Yes . . . perfect.' She checked my vital signs after I got into bed and said everything seemed to be okay. Dave said goodbye and left. I fell asleep directly after going to bed. I had a wonderful night's sleep. After breakfast they checked my blood again. I would have the results in the afternoon. I had breakfast and watched television for a while. Dave rang me to see if I was okay and to say, 'I love you.'

I said, 'I love you too.' Very soon I received a delivery of a beautiful bouquet of red roses from him with a note that said how much he loved me. I got very tearful. *What if I don't beat this? I have to be positive,* I said to myself.

The doctor came to visit me. He told me things were going as planned, so I could go home the next day. Dave was over the moon with this news. He took a few days off to take care of me. I seemed to be doing well and gradually putting on weight, which was a good thing. I had to attend the hospital every week for a check-up, but at the moment, everything seemed fine.

I was feeling better in myself. I took an interest in work again, and I started designing again. Gradually things were improving—my state of mind as well as my body. Dave was an absolute saint. He cooked dinner every evening and brought me tea and toast or porridge or whatever I fancied every morning. Some days I fancied only a cup of tea. I went to the hospital every week for blood tests, and for weeks everything seemed okay.

I started going for short walks in the park, just to get out in the open air and feel alive again. Dave went with me sometimes if he was at home. One morning after having a shower, I got a really bad nosebleed. Thank God Dave had not left for work. It would not stop. He rang the hospital, and they told him to take me in straight away. I had been at home now for three months, so I thought all was okay, but it seemed I had hit a setback. I was given a bed straight away, and the specialist came right in to see me.

They had a chat with Dave and told him the only way now was a bone marrow transplant; he did not know how he was going to tell me. He came into the room. I knew it was bad news. I said, 'Dave, tell me straight.' He explained what he had been told. I was very calm about it. He said, 'I have to contact Daniel straight away and get him to the hospital.' I was feeling tired and despondent and a bit disappointed. I had a blood transfusion later that afternoon. Daniel arrived by evening. I did not see him. Everything was arranged very quickly; they did not want me to get too ill. The surgery was scheduled for the next morning.

The transplant was done, and the doctors were optimistic about the outcome. I was in bed for a couple of days, not feeling my best. Then I began to feel less tired and weak. From that time, I seemed to be getting stronger day by day. After the third day, Daniel was able to visit me. I said, 'Thanks for saving my life.'

He said, 'Wait until you are up and about; then you can thank me.'

Dave was there by my side every time I opened my eyes, willing me to get better. After a couple of weeks, I was feeling much better. After more tests, the doctors were confident I would be fine. I got the all clear, and I was able to go home. I took life easy—very slowly this time. I did not rush things. I was eating okay and drinking those energy drinks. Thankfully, my weight seemed to be creeping up. I was almost afraid to say it, but I was feeling better by the day.

Dave was an absolute rock. He was there day and night for me. He just could not do enough for me. I went for additional tests, and everything was going along grand. My bloods were okay, and I felt good. I just had to hope for the best. I put on a couple of pounds, which pleased the doctors and me. I just had to keep eating and getting better. Hopefully this time I would be fine, and I would get better.

Chapter 14

I MANAGED TO get on fine after my bone marrow transplant. Everything was just wonderful. I managed to put on weight—not a lot, about half a stone, but it was a start. I could tolerate all types of food, and I was enjoying eating my food, which was brilliant. I went walking every day. I hadn't tried jogging yet; I was not sure if I was strong enough yet to start jogging. Dave went walking with me whenever he could. He was so glad to have me back, almost as good as new. My hair had grown back also. I decided to keep it short for the moment. I thought it suited me. It was also a lot handier to manage. I just towel dried it after a shower. I used to spend hours with my hair, thinking it was my crowning glory. Dave has seen me without hair. If he hadn't run a mile then, he would hardly do so now. We were happy and contented with one another, and that was all that mattered. If all went well, we were planning to get married the following year.

When I was convalescing, I had time on my hands—lots of time. I started painting in oils. I found it relaxed me, and I enjoyed it. I was surprised how good I was at it, so I began the process of having an exhibition and selling the lot for cancer research. It gave me a sense of pride that I might be able to help someone with cancer. I was so grateful for the care I had received myself. Everyone at the hospital had been brilliant; they hadn't been able to do enough for me. Dave and his family had been great also. His mum and dad visited often, and they took me under their wing. I loved them to bits.

A year after my battle with leukaemia I felt wonderful. I had my check-up, and the doctors were very satisfied with my progress, so I didn't need to go back again for six months, which was brilliant. I was up to date with my work. I was planning to maybe start going back to work again for a couple of hours a day, just to see how I would cope.

Dave and I were planning to go to the Lake District for the weekend just for a break and a change of air. We were going to leave on Friday afternoon and come back on Sunday. Dave rented a cottage there. We could go for walks and generally relax and just be together. I was really lucky to have someone like him. He was so kind and considerate, thoughtful and loving. I didn't think I could live without him. We had a lovely time at the cottage. The weather was lovely. I did feel tired when we came back—just general tired though, not flat-out tired.

Dave had still been doing most of the cooking. Now that I was feeling better, I needed to start doing things around the house again. I went in to work on a Monday to a round of applause. Everyone was delighted to see me. I had not realized I missed it so much; it was great to be back. I planned on taking it slowly—a couple of hours a day until gradually I felt I could do a full day. On my way home I went to the supermarket and picked up some food for dinner and a bottle of wine. I thought I would surprise Dave. I did grilled steaks, onions, mushrooms, and mashed potato. I set the table in the dining room and lit two candles. He was due in any minute. When he got in, he said, 'Something smells great!' He picked me up and kissed me when he saw the table. He said, 'Welcome back! Rose, you look divine. It's great to see you back cooking again, and better still able to eat it!' He opened the wine and poured us each a glass. 'Here's to us, Rosie, and a long life ahead for both of us.'

I raised my glass and said, 'Thanks, Dave, for being there for me. Cheers!' We kissed and cuddled. It felt so good to have each other. We promised to love each other forever. We decided it would be an easy task.

I was busy preparing for my exhibition at the weekend. I was very excited about it. Bridget helped me to name all the pictures and to price them. I knew they were not brilliant. I understood that all our friends would buy them just for the charity. I was okay with that.

I had been going in to work every morning, and Caroline was delighted to have me back. I was surprised to see she had kept on top of things. It was lovely to be involved again, and of course I missed the crack. I had begun working on new designs, and I was really looking forward to seeing the end result. When I designed something new it was nice to see it made up. It was easier for me to then decide whether to change something or leave it as it was. I had just started designing little girls' outfits, and that was a challenge. I decided to do little boys' outfits when I got the girls' outfits sorted. There was a market for them also. The boys' outfits were a little tricky. It was a whole new ballgame for me. I really liked a challenge, and that certainly was challenging. I decided to design for boys and girls up to the age of ten. After that they are very fussy, and I felt I might not be up to meeting their standards.

Finally I was all ready for my art exhibition. I was proud, and really looking forward to it. All the firms we did business with had been incredibly generous. They had given us fantastic items to raffle so we could make extra money. We got wine and nibbles from friends and neighbours. The police officers at the station where Dave worked made a collection among themselves, and they also held a pub quiz and handed over a cheque to Dave for two thousand pounds, which was brilliant. We were holding the exhibition in the foyer of the council offices. Dave had sorted that for me. It was in a prime location on the high street, so we hoped all the shoppers out at the weekend would pay us a visit.

Bridget and I set off early to open up and sort out some bits and pieces and put out tables for the wine and nibbles. We also had to sort out the pictures. We could only put the paintings on stands, as they would not allow us to deface the walls by hanging them. That was okay really, as we could arrange them accordingly. We were not long opened up when we had a few early birds showing an interest, which was encouraging. Dave said he would call at midday to take me to lunch. He still worried that I might skip a meal. Caroline was also giving us a hand. We decided we would all just mingle with the crowd and try to make a sale if someone showed an interest.

We had a steady flow of customers throughout the morning. We gave out tea and coffee in the morning and planned on giving out wine in the afternoon. I left for lunch as planned. Dave and I went to a nearby restaurant. I was anxious to get back, so we did not delay. When we got back we were amazed. The place was alive with the hustle and bustle of people chatting and generally enjoying the exhibition. The atmosphere was amazing. I found Bridget, and she informed me she had made a few sales. She said some people wanted to meet the artist. I said, laughing, 'I am here now!' Dave was going to stay with me so Bridget could go to lunch.

Everything went well . . . more than well. It was amazing! We had sold all my paintings by five o'clock. We had sold raffle tickets for the other items and had done very well with that too. Caroline had kept a rough tally on what we had made on the sale of the paintings, and we were all surprised. Some of Dave's mates came to help us clean up. We were ready to go at approximately seven o'clock, which was very good. We did a quick check before we left to see how we had done, and believe it not, we actually made ten thousand pounds, which astonished us all.

We all decided to go to dinner together—Caroline and Bridget and James and, of course, Dave and I. We had a wonderful dinner. I was so happy at the amount we had made for charity; it was unbelievable. We sat around for a little while after dinner just chatting. I was feeling tired, so we decided to get a cab and go home. We had a hot drink when we got home, and then we went to bed.

I had a wonderful sleep, and I woke up full of beans. I decided to go for a jog. Dave was not working that day, so he said he would come with me, which I thought was sweet of him. We set off on our jog around the park. Surprisingly, I was not tired. I felt like a new woman. We took it easy on the way back. I enjoyed my jog. When we got back we had a full Irish breakfast, and it went down a treat. While we were eating our breakfast, I came up with the idea of having a fashion show to promote our designs. Dave thought it was a brilliant idea. He said, 'Why not ring Caroline later and run it by her?'

I said, 'I sure will.'

When I rang Caroline, she was so excited, she said, 'Are you sure you are up to it?'

I said, jokingly, 'I have all the work done. Now it's your turn.' She started laughing. We had a lot of planning and organizing to do, but nothing we couldn't handle. We chose a local hotel in Greenwich for the venue. It was ideal. Their fantastic ballroom would be perfect for our show. We decided on our summer collection, so we had exactly a month to get everything sorted. We decided to expand our quota of stock with additional various colours. That would be especially appropriate for a summer collection. We got extra machinists to cover the heavy workload. We were all excited. Everyone was involved. All the shop floor staff were great. Anything we asked of them they delivered. We worked like beavers for the last week, getting everything done.

The night dawned on us like a shadow, but not to worry—we had everything sorted. We hired models from a nearby agency. We really wanted this to be a professional production. We got excellent support. The hall was filled to capacity. We had a few seamstresses on standby in case of accidents. Caroline introduced each model and described what she was wearing. We had a lot of buyers in the front rows, and they were indeed impressed with the collection. We did all the daywear and had a break and then went on to the evening wear and had another break.

I mingled with the crowd. A lot of people knew I had just battled cancer and come out the other side. Most people also knew about the art exhibition I had done, and they were congratulating me for my hard work. There had been an article in the local paper about me and the money I had made for cancer with my efforts. I did not want any praise; I was just glad to be well enough to do that.

We finished off with the children's collection, which all the buyers were crazy about. It was a real hit. We did very well with sales and orders—much better than we'd expected. It was a total success. Caroline and I went around chatting to prospective buyers and thanking our existing clients for their continued support. We had arranged with the hotel to serve finger food when the show finished. We were hungry by this time, but we thought we should wait until it was all over before we had something to eat. It was a fantastic night. We could not have imagined in our wildest dreams that the show would be such a success.

Before the end of the show, Caroline publically complimented me on my work, and the way I had coped throughout my illness. She said I had never let her down . . . that I had always delivered. I had no idea she was going to do that, and I was embarrassed to say the least. She presented me with a beautiful bouquet of roses. I thanked everyone who had helped to make our night a success, and I also thanked Dave for looking after me when I was ill.

When everything was over and people were making their way to the bar or heading home, we went into the restaurant for dinner. We had a great time. All our close friend and colleagues were there. We went out to the ballroom to dance some time later; there was some group playing. I had a wonderful time. Dave and I had not been dancing since my illness. We certainly made up for it! We danced the night away. We had a few lovely old-time waltzes and real smooches. All I wanted in life was for Dave to hold me tight and never let me go. It was very late when we finished up.

Dave, bless him, had booked us into a room for the night, for which I was ever so grateful. We just had to get the lift and go to bed when we got upstairs. Dave kissed me all over and undressed me just inside the room door. We were very passionate. It felt like the first time. We may have been tired, but it didn't matter. We had a very passionate night. He made me come alive. I just loved his hands caressing my body. He just drove me wild, and of course he had a lovely sexy body . . . enough to drive any woman wild. I felt so good . . . so happy. It was as if all the bad times were behind us, and we were going to enjoy life to the fullest. We stayed in bed late and made love again before we got up. I felt so happy and fulfilled.

The next task on the agenda was to set a date for our wedding, which I was really looking forward to.

Chapter 15

I HAD BEEN looking forward to my wedding day for a long time. At one stage, I had thought I would never make that journey, but now it was before me, and I was planning to enjoy every minute of it.

We had decided to get married in Ireland in my home town, which was an added bonus. I was not really that fussed about it, but Dave, God love him, wanted us to get married in Ireland, so that's how we decided on an Irish wedding. It would take place in June. The weather should be good; I should have no worries on that score.

Of course, I decided to design and make my own dress, but I didn't tell anyone but Bridget about it. Bridget was going to be my bridesmaid; I could not get married without her. We booked the hotel where we had celebrated my twenty-first. The service was great there, and I knew all the staff. We decided on Irish beef or salmon for the main course. One cannot go wrong with beef; it's everyone's favourite. Salmon is an excellent choice also. I ate an awful lot of fish. I did like it—especially salmon or brown trout.

Bridget and I went shopping for material for my dress. It had to be something special. I had designed a brocade bodice with a detachable long satin skirt. There would also be a detachable train. I could change the long skirt for a short one for dancing, which would be more appropriate. The ensemble was ivory in colour. When Caroline saw the design on paper she said, 'Is this your latest design? It is fantastic!'

'I'm designing my wedding dress.'

'Oh my God! It is superb. Why are you keeping it secret?'

'Caroline,' I said 'I am scared to make plans . . . really scared something will go wrong.'

'Rose,' she said, 'the bad times are behind you. You have to embrace life and live it to the fullest. Look to the future.'

'I know you're right,' I said. 'I'm been silly and stupid.'

'When the wedding is over,' she suggested, 'you might consider designing a line of bridal wear . . . maybe for the spring?'

'Okay,' I said. 'I have enough on my plate now at the moment. I have to design a special dress for Bridget too. It's going to be lilac, perhaps on the same lines as my dress with a detachable skirt. Maybe with a full skirt and white accessories. I'm going to make a special outfit for Kate also. She was delighted when I rang her and told her we had set the date. None of my sisters can come. They have other commitments, but my brothers and their wives will be there. That's all I need. All our neighbours will be there for the reception. I have made a trouser suit, which has a skirt also, for my going away outfit. So I won't need to bring too much clothing. I don't know where we're going for our honeymoon. It's a surprise, Dave says.'

I was really looking forward to our special day. We planned to go to Ireland a week ahead of the wedding so that any last-minute problems that might arise could be sorted straight away. I was just hoping we had covered everything.

The day arrived at last. It was a beautiful sunny day—the twenty-third of June to be precise, and our very special day. It was especially poignant as we had gone through so much to get there. It was a day I had once sadly thought would never happen. No one could have imagined how I felt on that beautiful sunny June morning.

I got up and had a cup of tea in Kate's cosy kitchen. It was only just gone six, so I decided to go for a jog as I always did. It was a lovely jog—on my own. I loved listening to the birds singing and being in tune with nature. I spotted a fox cub in the field. He stopped and looked at me as if to say to himself, *She is no threat.* They are beautiful animals. When I got back, I showered and came back down to Kate's kitchen. As usual she had a fab full Irish breakfast for us all. Bridget was just after getting up. We all tucked in and enjoyed the crack and the food.

The local hairdresser was coming to the house at nine, so all the women who were having their hair done were getting ready. The activity at Kate's was something else. The comings and the goings was amazing. Suddenly, there was a knock at the door. It was special delivery. Dave had bribed the postman to deliver a single red rose to me. I thought it was very thoughtful of him; it was a lovely gesture. As it is traditionally unlucky for the bride to see the groom before the ceremony, he had opted to stay at Daniel and Deirdre's house the night before the wedding. They would get him to the church before I even left Kate and Mike's. That way, we could avoid seeing each other.

My hair had grown back stronger than it ever was. It was just shoulder length at the time, so I had a half fringe, and I just wanted the ends flicked in—nothing fancy. I was going to wear a little hat with feathers at an angle to suit my small face. I had tried all types of veils, and they had not looked right on me. The little hat had a small veil that could be raised in the traditional way when I reached the altar.

Bridget was all dressed and ready. She looked divine in her lilac dress. When she had helped me into my dress, she said, 'Rose, you look amazing!'

'Thanks,' I said. 'Are you sure?'

She said, 'You look divine.' I weighed eight stone on my wedding day. I looked better in my clothes, and I was even beginning to get some curves at last—something I had longed for all my life.

Daniel gave me away. As I walked down the aisle, all my friends were there, all looking their best. I smiled as I slowly walked toward my darling Dave. *Thank you, God, for this lovely man*, I said to myself, *and for giving me back my life*. I struggled to keep the tears at bay. We stopped, and Dave squeezed my hand as he had done so many times in the past. I smiled at him and he gave me that fabulous wink. I knew my life was only beginning with this wonderful man.

The choir were brilliant. I had gone to school with most of the girls, so they sang their hearts out for us. It was a lovely ceremony. Kate was the first to congratulate us and call me Mrs O'Malley. I just laughed and hugged her. 'Thank you for loving me,' I said to her. 'You don't need to worry about me anymore. I've got Dave to do that now.'

The neighbours had lit bonfires along the route to the hotel. It is a tradition to wish luck to the happy couple. I thought it was very nice of them; it made me very emotional. The hotel had laid on the cars for us, so that was one other thing we did not have to worry about. We were served champagne upon arrival, and we toasted each other and had one long, lingering kiss. Everyone cheered us.

The meal was fabulous—plenty of food, all served hot and delicious. Dave's mate Alex was his best man; they had been mates all their lives. They'd gone to secondary school together and had remained friends since. That's a real measure of friendship. He was a bit of a comedian, was Alex. He had us all in stitches with all the jokes he was telling us—all related to Dave.

I considered myself a modern woman, so I said a few words also. I thanked everyone for coming. Everyone who knew me knew what we had been through, so it was an opportunity for both of us to thank everyone who had helped us along the way. We both toasted all our very dear friends and those who had travelled from England to share in our happiness and celebrate our marriage. Cheers to all of them.

The band were getting ready to play. I couldn't wait to start dancing and work off the big dinner I had just eaten. The staff moved the tables to the side of the room. They were like beavers; they had it all sorted in the blink of an eye. The band played Hello DarlinThat was our queue to take to the floor. We were always messing about, so Dave got up and kissed my hand and asked me for the dance. We took to the floor as if we were the only ones on the planet. We twirled round and round and bowed to each other when we finished. Then we kissed each other in the middle of the floor to a round of applause. When the band started playing again everyone joined in, and we all had a fantastic time. When the band took a break, some of our neighbours sang songs, and others told jokes. I even sang a song myself. I had always loved singing and music.

The day was the best day of my life. I did change my skirt and put on the short one, so I could have freedom of movement in my dancing. We had an absolute ball. I don't think I had ever felt so happy. As the evening approached Dave said to me, 'We should cut the cake.' So we did. After taking some photographs, we slipped away to our room to get changed and 'go away' as they say.

Dave informed me we were not staying at the hotel. He had made other arrangements. It was a surprise. We came downstairs, and I tossed my bouquet into the crowd. Who do you think caught it but Bridget! We all laughed, saying she was next. We said our goodbyes and left. I was so excited; I had no idea where we were going.

We drove for some time. I recognized the road signs. We were heading for Mayo, and I was trying to guess our final destination. Dave had booked us into Ashford Castle for the weekend. I was speechless. I said, 'Dave, can you afford this place?'

He said, 'For you, princess, I can afford anything.' I had only ever seen pictures of the castle, and they did not do it justice. It was a fantastic place. We parked outside, and I said, 'Let's just go for a little stroll. The gardens are beautiful. We shall have to explore and see more of them tomorrow.'

We had a lovely dinner, and the staff were superb. They had a bottle of champagne sent up to our room. The room was lovely. We could not wait to get to bed and make love. It was a huge four-poster. To say it was comfortable would be an understatement; it was fantastic. We had our champagne, and in between glasses we made love . . . beautiful, sensual sex . . . passionate and erotic. We satisfied each other in every way possible. We eventually fell asleep.

We woke up during the night and continued where we had left off. We were still spent from earlier, so it was less urgent . . . more caring and thoughtful, yet passionate. I was just so happy and contented to be with the man I loved and adored.

We got up late, not surprisingly. We were rather tired, so we decided to have a lazy day. We had breakfast in our room and we made love again. This time we were not tired; we were wide awake, and we could not get enough of each other. It's true that the best things in life are free, and that's for sure. I had never felt so loved and cherished in my life. I had no complaints. I loved every minute of it, and hoped it would last for the rest of our lives.

We got up and showered and went for a walk through the wonderful woods. We made love in a secluded spot, and that was wonderful—and daring. (I had always dreamed of making love out of doors!)

We had a wonderful time. We even went out on the lake. It was absolute heaven. When we came back we decided to walk down to the village and have lunch there. There were lots of little bistros and restaurants there in the lovely village of Cong. We went back to our room to rest after walking back to the castle. We had a nap and made love again before we got up for dinner. We decided to stay in the castle for dinner, and it was superb—fit for royalty. There was a harpist playing as we sat in the lounge having a drink. It was simply lovely; she made us feel she was playing for us alone.

We had one more day there at the castle, and we decided to drive out around the countryside. Dave was amazed at the scenery. We drove on through the village towards a little place called Clonbur, a nice, pleasant village. We stopped at the hotel and had a coffee and then continued on our way admiring the scenery as we went through a place called Cornamona. We continued on to Maam, another delightful place, though a bit on the rugged side. We stopped and had lunch. This was also a nice place; the food was excellent—real cuisine.

We had a wonderful time; we continued on till we arrived in Galway city, another lovely place. After a coffee in a lovely coffee shop, we decided to make our way back to the castle for our last night. We had a very pleasant journey back. We stopped in Cong village for a drink before we returned to the castle. There were two guys playing and singing in the bar, and they were very entertaining, so we stayed a little while and listened to them. We went back to the castle for dinner. We had brown trout that had been fished locally. It was very tasty. We had a bottle of champagne, which Dave ordered. We laughed and chatted and enjoyed just being together.

Before we retired to bed, we went for a walk around the castle. It was a beautiful night. We just drank in every aspect of this very special time of our lives. We knew we would look back on it and say, 'Wasn't it so special?' We had a nightcap before we went to bed.

We woke up in the morning fully refreshed and looking forward to our lives together—a journey we both could not wait to embark on, come what may.

We went back to see Bridget's parents before we left for London. We planned to stay one night with them and fly out the next day. They were delighted and surprised to see us. As usual they hugged and kissed us and brought us in for a cuppa. We told them all about the castle, and I showed them photos I had taken. There was no need for words; they knew we'd had a wonderful time.

We met up with the rest of the family at the hotel for dinner. It had been our plan to try to have an early night, if that is possible in Ireland when friends get together. We had another fantastic night, and it was not too late when we said our goodnights. We were up early next morning to say goodbye to all before we left for the airport.

We had a fantastic time. I was so delighted that Dave suggested we get married in Ireland. It could not have been better. It was the best day of my life so far, and hopefully the beginning of a long and happy life together.

Chapter 16

MARRIED LIFE WAS absolutely wonderful. People say that marriage is just having a piece of paper that makes the union legal, but it's much more—a whole lot more. I found that Dave was much more thoughtful in every way. When we made love, he made sure I was satisfied and that I always climaxed. We had a fantastic love life. I could not have wished for a better partner.

Work was also going well. We had loads of orders, and we seemed to be getting them out on time, which was good. I started designing kiddies' clothes and was quite excited about it. Caroline was impressed so far with what I had done. We decided to have some of the designs made up to see how they looked.

Bridget announced one day that she and James had just got engaged. I was so delighted for her. She seemed to be in my shadow and doing her own thing quietly. I congratulated her and said we would have to go to dinner that night to celebrate if she had nothing else planned. She said she needed to check with James and that she would let me know later.

Caroline and I arranged to have a bouquet of flowers delivered to her. All the girls who worked with her wanted to get her something. They took up a collection among themselves and got her a bottle of champagne. We opened a bottle of wine in the office and toasted their health. We had a laugh and a giggle. Bridget told us they planned to get married the following year. She said to me, 'You have plenty of time to design me a fabulous dress!'

I said, 'Sure! No worries.'

It was Friday, so we didn't need to worry about staying out late. We arranged to meet up at our house and have a drink before we headed out on the town. We got a taxi into town. Dave had booked a restaurant down by the river. We had eaten there before, and the food was superb. We had a fabulous meal. Everyone was so happy. We had quite a lot of champagne—not just one bottle. Dave is fond of his champagne. We were all feeling merry. It was too early to go home, and we were not ready to go home just yet, so we decided to go to a wine bar. We met up with some of the gang who worked for us, and we all decided to go to a club. We had a whale of a time. We danced all night and had the best of fun. We were all a bit worse for wear by the time the club closed, and we had to scramble to get taxis home, but we eventually managed. We stopped at the chippy on the way home for the usual orders— sausage and chips or burgers and chips. We were all in the best of spirits. Despite the witching hour, we were in no mood for going home. We decided to go back to our house and have a few more drinks. It was one of those nights when everyone was on a high and in the mood for a good booze up.

It was early morning before we called it a night. Bridget and James stayed in our spare room, and we went to bed exhausted. As one can imagine we were not in a hurry to get up the next day. We did eventually surface, and Dave, bless him, took over the kitchen and did us all a fry up. We began to come alive after we had eaten, so we decided to go for a walk and blow the cobwebs away. Bridget and James had a coffee, and then they decided to go home.

They had decided not to have a big wedding; just a few friends and family . . . nothing elaborate . . . just a quiet day with the people that meant the most to them. Everyone has his or her own ideas of a perfect day. Not everyone likes a big wedding. I loved our wedding, and the photo album was lovely . . . well done. A local guy did it for us. He also did a video of the ceremony and the guests, which was really nice.

Bridget explained the type of dress she desired—again, nothing fancy. I was thinking a plain line, with emphasis on the neckline, with, perhaps beading. Maybe empire line with a bow at the back. Long sleeves in leg-of-mutton style with beading along the cuff to match the neckline. She was tall and elegant, so straight lines in her dress would show off her lovely figure.

She wanted me as matron of honour. She chose fuchsia as my colour, which was good with my colouring. She wanted a veil and a train; they just appealed to her. I knew she would look lovely whatever she wore.

I had been going for my check-up every six months. After this next one it would be every year. So far everything had been good. During my visit, we had a chat with the consultant about getting pregnant. It had been two years since my treatment. At the back of my mind I was scared of a relapse. It was difficult to forget about what I had gone through, even though the surgeon had been reassuring me. I would need to have in vitro fertilization (IVF) treatment to get pregnant. I'd had my eggs frozen, as I was hoping to become a mum in the future. I felt that the right time had come to get pregnant.

The doctors advised me to take another year out before I got pregnant to give my body time to get back to normal. I thought about it. *So, what's another year?*

We had our fashion show for the children's designs, and that was a runaway success. We sold practically our entire stock in one night. This show was very similar to the other fashions shows we had put on. Caroline and I wore our own designs for the show, which was a clever idea, because we got loads of orders for them also. We had a very successful night. We partied well into the night with all the clients and staff.

I decided to design maternity wear. I figured it might come in handy if I managed to get pregnant. Caroline laughed when I told her. She was planning to get married soon. She also wanted a small family affair in a register office. She said, 'Wouldn't it be really funny if we were all pregnant together?'

I said, 'Yah . . . hilarious.' We both laughed. She had always said she did not want children, but she seemed to have changed her mind. She even often said she would like two. If I could manage one, I would be more than pleased. Caroline never planned anything. She would just make decisions out of the blue. I was sure she would do the same thing with regard to her wedding.

I was feeling well, and I had maintained the weight I had put on. I seemed to be stagnant at eight stone. I suppose that is not a bad weight. I just bordered on five foot, so if I were any heavier I would probably fall over. On the other hand, Caroline and Bridget were both around six feet with figures to die for.

I finished designing Bridget's wedding dress, and I had it made up, unknown to her. It was to be a surprise. I asked her to come into the office one evening before she went home. I said that Caroline and I both need to speak to her. When she came in, we were both having a coffee, and the gown was hanging on a rack at the back of the office. We asked her to help herself to a coffee, but first would she try on the gown, as we'd had it made up for a client. We put paper on the floor to keep it clean. She obliged and tried it on. It fitted her like a glove. She absolutely loved it. It was ivory, and it looked superb on her. We had shoes for her to slip on just to complete the outfit. The full-length mirror we kept in the office was invaluable at times. She stood in front of the mirror totally mesmerized. She said, 'I love it! Who is it for? Who is the lucky lady?' I told her she knew the bride well. She said, 'No, I don't.' I put her out of her misery and said it was hers—from Caroline and me. She screamed with delight. The dress had a detachable train that fastened at the waist. When it was removed, the dress became an evening gown. I never believed in having a gown for one day and never wearing it again. This way, she would be able to get some wear out of it. She could also wear a different colour sash around her waist, and she would have a completely different gown.

Bridget was so excited she could not wait to tell James. Caroline rescued a bottle of wine from the office filing cabinet while Bridget took off the gown. We both toasted her and James. We told her now all she had to do was name the day. We told her to get to it that night and set a date. She said she would. We carefully put the dress away for the moment, and we decided it was time to go home.

Nothing exciting happened in the forthcoming weeks. We were turning out the orders, and everything was pretty normal. Bridget did get back to us with a date. Her wedding was to be on May Day. We had exactly two months. She decided she did not want to wait any longer. I knew the feeling. We were all going to chip in and help her organize it. They had decided on the Bromley Court Hotel in Bromley. It was a very nice venue, and there were beautiful gardens for photographs. The register office was just round the corner.

Kate was delighted with the news, but a little disappointed the big day was not being celebrated in Ireland. But that's what Bridget wanted, so they respected her wishes. James was a banker, and they had put a deposit on a new house. They were planning to move in the week before the wedding, so they had a lot happening all at the same time.

Bridget came to the house one night when Dave was working, and she looked very upset. I took her into the living room. I could clearly see she was agitated, and I could not understand what could be the matter, unless they had broken up. I kept thinking, *Please let it not be that.* She sat down and I asked her if she wanted a drink—tea or coffee. She said no. I sat down next to her. 'Is everything okay? Is there a problem?'

She started to cry and blurted out, 'Rose, I'm pregnant!'

I didn't know what was the best thing to say. 'Have you told James?' I asked.

'No, not yet. What will his parents think?'

'Well, they know you didn't do it all on your own!'

'My mum and dad will be very disappointed with me.'

'First you have to tell James. I'm sure he will be delighted, and so will his parents You get on well with them, so there shouldn't be any problem.' I hugged her and continued, 'Your parents love you, and they will still love you—and your baby.' Then I said, 'How do *you* feel about the baby? You are the most important one in all this.'

'I would love to have a baby. It's going to be a little sooner than we had planned, but I will embrace motherhood.'

'That is the most important thing,' I said, 'and I feel sure James will welcome the baby also.' She seemed to settle down a bit. She said she would love a cup of tea, so I went off to the kitchen. We sat and chatted about the baby. I told her, 'You are so lucky. I may not be so lucky, because of my treatment.'

'I am so sorry, Rose, and insensitive.'

'Not at all,' I said. 'Let's hope all will work out well. Maybe we'll be pregnant together!'

'That would be lovely—a new experience for us,' she said. 'We grew up together, and now our lives are changing.'

The day of the wedding came round very quickly. James had been delighted with the news that Bridget was pregnant. Yes, it was a bit sooner than they had planned, but no worries. They loved each other, and they would cope. He told her that, since his mother lived not too far away, she would be only too willing to help. That helped put Bridget's mind at rest. Her parents were not too upset either. They knew the couple loved each other, so they were delighted for them.

The wedding was lovely. Small weddings are nice, because you soon get to know everyone. Afterwards at the hotel, the meal was great and the music was great. A good time was had by all. Bridget was a beautiful bride, and the dress looked great on her (it needed to be altered only a little to accommodate junior). The only problem was that she had been sick in the morning and had not been in the mood for having her hair done or even getting dressed. But in the end everything worked out well. They went to Paris for a couple of days, and they both enjoyed it.

Caroline decided to train up another supervisor to take the pressure off Bridget. We told Bridget, if she was not feeling well in the mornings, she should come in later when she felt better. That seemed to please her. She did not want to be letting anyone down. We told her not to worry.

I went to see the specialist to find out about having the IVF treatment. He agreed that, if I was happy about going ahead with it, he could do it the following week, but he warned me it might not work. We would have to wait and see. Dave was with me. We said we understood. He said it could be done in A&E (accident and emergency), but that I would need to rest for a couple of hours and take things easy.

We went to the hospital the following week and had the procedure done. We did not tell anyone about it. We were hoping we would have to do it only the once. The gynaecologist explained they had to use more than one egg, and we could end up with multiple births or none at all. It was a very tense time. We just had to put it at the back of our minds and get on with life and hope for the best.

Time seemed to crawl by. One month went by and another and another. It wasn't so bad after all. We went back to the hospital and had some tests done, and would you believe? I was pregnant. I could not believe it. Dave was over the moon. He nearly smothered me in kisses. We were so excited, we wanted to shout it from the rooftops. 'It's the best news we could ever get,' he said.

The doctor was not sure, but he thought there could be more than one heartbeat. It was possible that I was having twins! That was the icing on the cake. I said to Dave, 'How will we cope?'

'Don't worry,' he said, 'we will cope.'

I rang Bridget and told her she was not alone . . . that I was also pregnant. She let out a scream. 'Brilliant!' she said. Everything was happening together. We were both pregnant.

Then Caroline decided to get married. As she had mentioned before, it was going to be low key. That was just as well as Bridget and I were both huge Bridget was about two months ahead of me, but if I were going to have twins I would naturally be the bigger one.

Twins were confirmed on our next visit. I was told I needed to take things easy and rest as much as possible. If I was worried about anything, I was not to hesitate to call the hospital. We went away feeling a little apprehensive. We had a coffee on the way home. Dave said he could not describe how much he loved me. He loved the idea of becoming a father. He could hardly wait. Having a baby together was an added bonus to our relationship. 'But if it doesn't work out, I will still love you, no matter what,' he said. I told him I wanted to give him our baby. Just to have it to hold would be great. I just hoped it would work out. He kissed me and said he loved me more than ever. I told him I felt the same . . . that I could not put into words how much I loved him. We kissed one long, lingering kiss.

It was a great pregnancy, I felt good . . . a little tired sometimes, but I never felt ill. I could eat anything. My hair looked great, and I was just glowing. Bridget, on the other hand, had a horrible time. She was ill most of the time. She could hardly keep anything down. She was slow to put on any weight. I was putting weight on gradually. My bump was out in front. Bridget put on weight around her hips towards the end. We used to laugh about our cravings. I fancied tomatoes and ice cream, and Bridget fancied gherkins and cheese. We both had a fancy for various flavours of ice cream. Our partners, God love them, were always rushing to the late-night mini mart for some type of food for our cravings, which often were hilarious.

So, Bridget was ahead of me, and then Caroline fell pregnant three months behind me, so we all did end up being pregnant together. Bridget went a couple of days over her due date. We all went to the hospital excited about the event. She was not unduly long in labour. She delivered a beautiful, healthy baby girl, whom they called Rosemarie. She had dark hair like her mother.

I was beginning to feel awkward around that time. My tummy seemed to be getting very big. The doctors had decided to do a section instead of a natural birth. Because of my past history, they felt it would be safer to do it that way. They didn't want me to be stressed in any way, so we went along with their advice. I went for a walk most days. Not a long walk, just gentle exercise. And I went swimming throughout my pregnancy. I had to go to the hospital every week during the last month; they were monitoring me very closely.

During one of my visits they decided they would take me in the following week an section me. The doctor felt the babies were a good weight and it would be the best option, considering my past medical history along with my mothers. At the time, I was very uncomfortable. I couldn't get to sleep or sit in a comfortable position. so this was a very welcome decision as I was both physically and mentally stressed. It would not be long now before I met my two babies.

We went in early in the morning on the appointed day. My blood pressure and other vital signs were good; there was no cause for concern. Only my past medical history was a source of worry. They performed the section and delivered two beautiful boys, each weighing over six pounds, which was very good for twins. We named them Jonathan and Gareth

Dave was very proud of them—and me. We were very happy to finally have them in our arms, safe and sound. I felt good. I was a little sore where I had the clips, and a little tired. I felt I could sleep for a couple of hours. The nurses took care of the babies the first night and let me get some rest, which I didn't say no to.

Caroline had about three months to go before her baby was due. She had put on quite a lot of weight and looked like she was carrying a boy, as she had a big bump in front.

Dave's mam had offered to help when I came home from hospital. Dave had also got time off work for six weeks to take care of us. Between the three of us, we figured we would manage well enough.

We planned on baptizing the boys shortly after we came home. We left the hospital together after a week. My stitches had healed very well, and I didn't feel uncomfortable except when I was nursing the babies. They were very quiet and were feeding well. Dave and I both got up at night together to see to them. Dave's mam was great during the day with them. She even took them out in the fresh air, which helped them to sleep. They boys were lovely. We both could not stop admiring them.

Bridget was a good mother. Kate came to visit and stayed for a couple of weeks to help her out. Her little girl is beautiful. It was rather odd to have little babies to take care of now, instead of all the wining and dining we had been doing for work purposes. Life had certainly changed for all of us, but it was an experience we would not have swapped for the world.

Poor Caroline was still waiting; she still had about eight weeks left before she would have her baby in her arms. Still, time would pass, and she would have her baby. She did go into labour just a couple of days after her due date. She delivered a little baby boy who weighed almost eight pounds. She called him Daniel, and she was over the moon with him. So now we all had what we wanted most in lives—our very own little babies . . . safe and healthy. In our case, we had two little babies!

We hired a manager to run the business while we were on maternity leave. We had not decided what we were going to do long term yet. I was sure we would make some changes. For the moment, we were going to enjoy our bundles of joy and see what the next chapter in our lives would bring us.

I had a letter from Shakera one day. She had kept in touch occasionally. They had a little baby girl, and Shakera was over the moon. She sent me some photographs. The baby was indeed an angel. She had her mother's dark features. Shakera said all was well, and that they were very happy. I sat down directly and answered her letter, brimming with excitement about our own good news. I also enclosed a few photographs of our delightful little boys. I asked her to come and visit when the babies were a little older and more settled. We could catch up on some gossip. I posted my letter to her later that afternoon when I went for a walk. I would anxiously await her reply. They lived across London. They seemed to have moved around a lot; maybe they might come and stay for a weekend. *Who knows?* I thought.

Chapter 17

WE WERE ALL helping each other out with the babies and having good laughs at our mistakes. We tried our best to keep each other sane and keep our stress levels down. Caroline and I decided we would establish a crèche in the factory and employ two children's nurses to take care of our babies. That would leave us stress free to continue our work. Also, the babies would be close by so we could pop in on our breaks. I thought it was an excellent idea.

Dave and I had always said that two would complete our family. I felt good in myself. I had maintained my weight at around eight stone, which was good. The boys were healthy proper mischief makers. We would not have wanted it any other way. We were blessed to have them.

Bridget and Caroline were planning their second pregnancies. Even though Caroline was a brilliant businesswoman, she wasn't half bad as a mother either, and Bridget was devoted to her little angel. It was fun to see the little ones playing together. Little Rosemary was stuck in there with the boys, but she was a mucky kid. We didn't care. Who needs a perfect child? There were other young mothers who worked with us who welcomed the childcare addition to the workplace. Everybody thought it was a brilliant idea.

I tried to be independent and wanted to do everything myself. Bridget explained to me that it just was not possible. I should learn to delegate. It would make life easier. So I tried to put that into practice, and it actually worked. It was often a little difficult when both of the boys started crying together when they both needed feeding. They simply wouldn't take no for an answer. Jonathan would listen to music while I tended to Gareth, who could be very impatient and demand my attention. If Dave was around, he would sit down with one on each knee and keep them occupied until I sorted out their feeds. I breastfed both of them for two weeks, just to give them a good start. I was advised by the medical staff not to do it any longer. I thought I would be pulling out my hair when Dave went back to work, but quite the opposite. I enjoyed the experience. The boys were an absolute delight to have and to cherish.

Bridget was a natural with her little angel, but then again she had only one. I remind Caroline of that too, if she started moaning about something. We finally got the crèche up and running. It was an absolute gift. We had two nannies as well as two part-time nurses. The front of the nursery was done in glass, so we could actually see the babies without having to go right in. There was no need to fret about them. If I may say so myself, I think it was one of my better ideas.

The business was doing well. Because of the crèche, we never had to advertise for staff. The child-friendly facility was like a magnet to prospective staff members.

The twins were finally on solids and doing well. I didn't need to go for a check-up for three years, which was wonderful. After that it would be five years.

I often thought of my friend Shakera and wondered how she and her family were getting on with life. I had lost contact with her when I was going through my illness. I had been unable to communicate with lots of my friends. I had to be so careful of infection; therefore, I had to sacrifice my friendships or risk infection. It was not easy to get back on track. Commitments seemed to get in the way of friendships.

Shakera had never answered my letter in which I had told her about our sons. I had awaited a reply, but it never came. As is so often said, 'life goes on', and it sure does, and sometime a lot quicker than we like it to. But sadly we have no control over time.

The babies were teething and were often frazzled, but we would get over that. It was only a blip. We were enjoying married life to the fullest and the many blessings that life brings. Dave's parents were brilliant. They often took over the care of the twins completely for a weekend and let us go away and enjoy our own company without babies. It was good to spend quality time together. We really appreciated it. The twins loved their grandparents, so we didn't have any worries.

We went to Paris for our anniversary. It was so hard to believe that we had been married for four years. We took care of Bridget's little girl to allow them to have a well-earned break. It was great to be able to go away for a weekend and recharge the batteries. We did not send the children to nursery; we had all the facilities in the crèche. We also added a room on next door for toddlers, so that they could interact with other children their own age, which was vitally important for their development.

I stayed at home for the first year. I needed to cherish every moment. We felt so blessed having our children under the circumstances. I couldn't believe the years were going by so quickly. We got into a routine, and it was pretty easy with the two of us working together, much easier than I thought possible.

Soon our little boys will be five and need to go to primary school. Caroline and Bridget were both pregnant and expecting their babies within a month of each other.

I loved David with all my heart. It was different to the love I felt for our children. It's really difficult to explain. Love and motherhood just change you completely, making you whole and a better loving person. It was amazing to gaze at our children while they were sleeping and realize they had been born out of love. That really is something special. I knew from my past medical history that I would not tempt fate and have any more children.

Bridget gave birth to a little girl. She was very disappointed it was not a boy. I was annoyed with her. I said, 'She is healthy and beautiful. What more do you want?'

She said, 'Yes, you are right.' They named her Kate after Bridget's mother, and of course her parents came over to take care of Rosemarie while she was in hospital and to help her out generally when she got home. They stayed for some time to help out; they were absolutely brilliant.

Caroline was huge the second time around. We were all thinking she would have a little girl. She was fed up. She just wanted the baby in her arms. Well, she would have to wait until the baby was ready.

Dave, bless him, had been fretting about me thinking that I was broody and not saying, because my best friends were having babies. But, no. It didn't bother me. As far as I was concerned, my family was complete. I did not need any more. My babies were darlings. They were finally at school, and they loved it. I dropped them off every morning on my way to work, and I picked them up at three. They were always happy and contented and in the best of form. They were proper little boys, always mucking about and getting dirty. They were in their element playing in mud and water and generally getting filthy. We had a fine big garden. They played there all the time. They seemed to have great imaginations. They could be on the moon, or in the jungle. They could be super heroes. Watching them took me back to my own childhood when my imagination used to work overtime. We used to have the time of our lives, Bridget and I.

I sometimes looked back and thought of all that had gone on in my life, and I thanked God for giving me a wonderful husband and two wonderful children.

Bridget and I still had a great relationship. It was amazing that we had never fallen out. We always respected each other and never took each other for granted. Maybe that was our secret. I would be lost without her friendship.

Caroline was a wonderful partner in business and a good friend also. We helped each other out, which means a lot in life. She gave birth to a boy, and she was over the moon. He was a bit unwell and was kept in hospital while she went home, which did not go down well with her. She was convinced there was something seriously wrong. He was not feeding well and was generally a very unhappy baby. I was beginning to think that Caroline may be right. She did eventually get the paediatrician to do more tests, and he discovered the baby had a hole in his heart and may need surgery at a later date. He would have to be monitored closely. She was more at ease after she was aware of his problem. He had to remain in hospital for a little longer. He was intolerant to any milk except his mother's, so naturally she spent a lot of time there with him. She expressed milk for him for the night feeds, and she would go back early in the morning to attend to him. They baptized him and called him Jack. He did not seem to be thriving at all. To me he seemed a very ill baby.

Caroline and her husband Kevin got a phone call late one evening just as they were going to bed. Little Jack had pneumonia. He was gravely ill. Could they come immediately? They had been there for only a short time when he passed away. I had gone over to her house to stay with Daniel. When they came home, Caroline was beside herself with grief; they both were. She blamed herself, saying she should have taken things easy and looked after herself better. I knew only too well where she was coming from. I had been down that road; it can be a lonely one.

My heart went out to her. All I could do was be there for her. She had to work it out for herself. Time is indeed a great healer, but we do not usually realize it during times of stress and sadness. They had a lovely service for him. We all took care of Caroline and helped her out as much as we could. Little Daniel had lost a brother, which he did not fully understand. Still, he was only six, so it was difficult for him to understand. It was difficult even for us adults.

Poor Caroline was in such a bad place. She would get through it, but at the time she was hurting, and hurting real bad. She did not even get dressed some days. We all rallied around her and tried to get her to snap out of it, but our efforts did not make much difference.

We were pretty busy at work. Orders were coming in nonstop. There was lots to be done. We could really have benefitted from Caroline's help. I hinted to her that we needed her at work, but she didn't take the bait.

Dave was great—always there to lend a hand. He would juggle his shifts to suit me and take the pressure off me. He was so very good to me. He took the boys swimming on Saturday mornings and to soccer school in the afternoons He loved quality time with them. I often met them in MacDonald's for lunch, and we would all walk home together, playing I spy and having a laugh.

At the age of seven, Jonathan was excellent at soccer; he absolutely adored it. He could happily play ball all day, nonstop. Gareth was good at swimming; he loved it and was a real water baby. Both of them were good scholars; they loved their studies. Jonathan was good at maths, and Gareth was good at English. He won trophies for debates and essays, and he even had published articles in children's magazines and won prizes for them. They were both very mature for their age. They were very good at amusing themselves. Sometimes if I was busy at work, I would pick them up from school and take them to work with me. They were never a problem.

Caroline finally came to terms with her loss and came back to work with us again. Fingers crossed, she told us she thought she might be pregnant again. I did hope she was. She needed a baby so much.

I was feeling well in myself. I had my check-up, and the doctors were really pleased with me. I had never put on much weight even though I had a good appetite. I could eat practically anything, but gaining weight seemed to allude me. I felt healthy, and that was all that mattered. Some people seem to think that, if you are not carrying weight, you are unhealthy, which in fact is opposite to fact. I still found time for early-morning jogs. I had always loved the outdoors and had always been fond of walking or jogging.

A group of ladies from work formed a group of ramblers, and we all walked or jogged for cancer. We usually managed to raise five thousand annually, which was wonderful, as everyone had been touched in some way or other by cancer. We get a lot of pleasure out of fundraising. We all had a good time, and we all helped each other out.

Bridget was seriously thinking of relocating to Ireland. It was ironic; she got word one morning that her dad had passed away in his sleep. We were all going for the funeral. Poor Bridget was devastated, especially as she had planned to return. Life can be so cruel. Poor Kate was very upset; she could not believe her dear Mike was dead. Bridget told us she and her family would come back after the funeral, put the house on the market, and return home. She asked me, 'Will you do the same?'

I told her, 'No way. I am happy. I have no wish to leave and go back. Back to what? All my friends and family are here. I love living in London. I like going to Ireland for a holiday, but I always like to get home, and home to me is in London. That's the way I feel, and I am not going to apologize for it.' I couldn't imagine life without Bridget, but we were no longer children, and we could always find each other at the end of the telephone.

It took the best part of a year for Bridget and James to sell their house. In the meantime, Kate lived with them. She loved living in London. She knew it was only temporary; they would all be off to Ireland when they had sorted out everything. We would have one hell of a party when they left. It would be one of the last things we would do together. We had all been so close throughout our lives. Separating would be a wrench.

We did, indeed, have a wonderful party. We invited all our friends and the entire workforce that had worked for us down through the years. We laughed and cried and reminisced about our lives. If we were honest, Bridget and

I had had a great life in England. We had never been out of work, and we had made a pretty good living for ourselves. We had been able to send our children to private schools, and that in itself was some achievement. It was not a bad time for Bridget to go back. Her kids had just started secondary school, so it wouldn't be that disruptive for them. Most kids find it easy to adapt to situations; they are better at it than we adults.

We all wished them luck in the new phase of their lives, and we promised to visit as soon as they had settled in. The huge furniture van arrived very early the next morning. We had helped them over a couple of days with the packing and marking of all the boxes. It had been exciting, but also sad. The lorry was packed by lunchtime and set off. We took the family to our house for lunch. We said our goodbyes, and suddenly my lifelong friend was gone, and life would never be the same without her. I just sat down and opened the floodgates. I just cried and cried

Caroline soon fell pregnant again, and she was delighted. She decided to take a backseat and take life easy this time round. She felt good, and she was relaxed, although she suffered with morning sickness at the beginning. But soon she was over that stage, and it was easy sailing, hopefully. She was expecting her baby on Christmas day or thereabout, depending on when the baby wanted to make an appearance. Dave and myself were hoping that this pregnancy would be okay. We thought of Caroline as family and families always looked out for each other. We decided that, because Caroline was expecting her baby so close to Christmas, I would cook for all of us. If Caroline went into labour during the dinner, they could slip away quietly., All going well when the baby was bore we could bring Daniel to the hospital. That was the plan anyway. We had a wonderful dinner, and nothing happened. We all had a few drinks, except the expectant parents. We played games with the children, and Dave and I took a quiet moment to tell each other how much we loved each other. And, of course, Caroline finally went into labour.

We sorted the children out, and Caroline went to the hospital. Things quietened down a little. We had our tea and started sorting out the sleeping arrangements for the children. When that was done, Dave poured us a glass of wine. We all relaxed in front of the telly and waited for the phone call. No one was really saying very much; we were not even interested in the television programme. We were all just secretly hoping all would go well for Caroline. Kevin rang after a couple of hours to say they had a little girl. Mum and baby were doing well. Dave took the call. We had all been scared to get the news, but thank God it was good news. He opened a bottle of champagne, and we toasted the new arrival, and of course the mam. We waited for Kevin to come back before we decided to go to bed. Everyone stayed at our house that night. I think the kids were too excited to sleep; it was late when we all got to sleep.

It was late when everyone got up the next morning. Kevin did not tell Daniel about the baby till after breakfast. He was really excited; he wanted to go right away to visit. We persuaded him to wait till after lunch. Kevin did visit. We all planned to go in the afternoon. Dave went to the shops to get some presents for the children to give the baby, and also something from us. We had a light lunch, and off we went.

Caroline was in good form, and the little girl looked beautiful. They named her Louise. At the moment, she looked just like her mam. Caroline would be going home the following day, and she couldn't wait. 'Now,' she said, 'my family is complete.' They christened little Louise the following week. It was a low-key affair with just family and close friends.

Dave asked me if now I felt broody. Did I want another baby? I think deep down he did himself. 'No,' I told him. 'I do not. My family is complete.'

We all just got on with our lives. Nothing eventful happened . . . just the everyday stuff that adds up to family life. We had a few holidays in Ireland as the boys were growing up. They loved visiting and playing with their cousins. They considered it an adventure. They used to help rounding up the sheep and lambs and rolling up the wool at shearing time. Life was moving on, and we were getting older without realizing it. The boys who are now twelve spent their first summer holiday in Ireland without us parents. They did enjoy themselves. They told us it was the best holiday ever! They even met their first loves. They came back different people, more grown up . . . happy and contented. They were to start secondary school at the beginning of term. They were looking forward to a new chapter in their lives, and so were we. They were both still good at athletics and sports. Jonathan said he would like to be an accountant or work in a bank when he left school. Gareth had stuck with his first love, English. He read no end of books. He aspired to be a journalist. Both boys studied hard at school. We were blessed; we never had to ask them to do their homework. It was always done when I got home from work.

Caroline and I had a long discussion. We decided to sell the business and take life easy. As it was, we had been taking life reasonably easily. We had staff now to do all the work, but we thought it was time to take the money and run. Maybe we would buy homes in the sun. Who could know? We had various meetings with our accountants and agreed on a price. Then we put the whole thing on the market. Within a couple of days a big firm snapped it up, along with the entire workforce. We made a hefty profit . . . more than we could ever have imagined. We were now millionaires. Didn't that have a lovely ring to it? It was amazing how life changed. I had never realized for one minute how successful our business would become. It had provided us with a fantastic lifetime. We could retire now and send our children to university and provide accommodation for them. There was no need for them to live in hell holes. We could afford to buy them whatever they wished. That was a choice we'd never had. Somewhere along the line in our lives we had made the right decisions, and as the old saying goes, 'the rest was history'.

It was still a wrench for to get used to Bridget not being there.

Chapter 18

THE FIRST COUPLE of days after Bridget and her family left were awful. I was all the time ringing her for really trivial things. I felt as if I had lost my comfort blanket. She was doing exactly the same. We used to laugh about it at the end of the day. Gradually the phone calls were not as urgent or as frequent. We were like children as we settled into our own routines without each other. We were getting there at last.

The school holidays would upon us in a couple of weeks, so we are all going to Ireland to stay for a little while. The teenagers would have some fun and so would the adults. We stayed for three weeks. Dave had to go back to work after two weeks, and the boys and I stayed on the additional week. We had a fabulous time. We really did unwind. We walked and went mountain climbing, sailing, and swimming—all the things teenagers love to do, but the parents never have the time to do with them. The younger kids went wind surfing and rock climbing. They played football and went swimming. It was all fun. Bridget tried to persuade us to stay permanently, but she didn't succeed.

After spending the time with Bridget and her family, we went home contented and happy. Funny, I no longer needed

Bridget to be there all the time. I knew if I really needed her I could ring. We had succeeded in making the final cut, and our friendship had survived. She was happy with her family in Ireland, and I was happy with mine in London. I did not miss work either. I hadn't done any painting in oils for years, so I took the easel out of mothballs again, and was totally happy. My health was good. I felt good in myself. Dave and I were very happy. He was a wonderful husband and dad.

The boys had almost finished secondary school. Gosh, where had the time gone? Jonathan was going to go to university to get a degree in banking. We knew he would succeed; he seemed very determined. Gareth, on the other hand, was going to continue with journalism. He had secured an apprenticeship with a well-known newspaper. We were very proud of him. They both had jobs in the local supermarket while they were going to secondary school. They worked during their holidays and managed to save money. Now they were quite the young men, very careful about their appearance. We felt we must have done something right. They were both very polite and had impeccable manners. Now, it sounds as if I am boasting; it's only that we were both very proud of our sons.

Gareth was having the time of his life. He was reporting on local events, and he loved it when there was a deadline. He found it exciting having to finish on time. He loved the buzz of rushing to events and reporting on them as they unfolded. He reported on a big fire in a warehouse, and his boss was very impressed with him, telling him he was a natural. He wanted to work in television when he finished his contract with the newspaper. He said that was where the money was, and the real excitement. We have no doubt he will.

Jonathan finished his degree in college. He got a top job in one of the leading banks. He works hard and enjoys the buzz of the banking business. He has moved into the private sector of investments and now has his own clients. He loves visiting his clients especiall in their own environment.

I could not possibly sit at home all day and do nothing, so when I had finished a decent number of paintings, I decided to hold an exhibition and sell them off for cancer as I had in the past. The Macmillan Cancer Support nurses worked tirelessly for the most vulnerable people in our society. They were my chosen charity. I could work at my own pace, and at the end of the day I felt I had achieved something.

I had a friend who worked in an art gallery. I often met her for lunch. She liked my style of painting and often had put one of my painting on display in the window. They always sold within a couple of days. That gave me a great feeling of pride.

Dave talked to me and told me he had decided to take early retirement. I said, 'What will you do to pass the time?'

'I have a wonderful idea,' he said. 'I will take woodwork classes and learn how to make picture frames for your paintings.'

'Brilliant!' I said. 'You can turn the garage into a workshop.'

'No,' he said, 'I will put up a prefab at the end of the garden.'

'Yes, good idea,' I told him. He said he had a few loose ends to tie up first, but he would be officially retired in a months' time. He said, 'I have made plans for us to go on a Caribbean cruise for a whole month. We owe it to ourselves.'

'I totally agree with you,' I said.

He said, 'For once, Rose, you are not going to make any posh frocks for the cruise. We are going to splash out. We'll go uptown, dine out, and shop till we drop.'

'Oh, Dave, I like that idea,' I said. 'We could get used to the high life!'

'Don't we deserve it?' he said, and he planted a kiss on my lips. He opened a bottle of wine, and we had an early night.

We went uptown one day and had lunch in a posh restaurant. It was really nice. We hadn't had lunch together for ages—dinner, yes, but not lunch. I really enjoyed it. Dave said we must spend as much time as possible together and do things together. One never feels the years rolling by.

We would be celebrating our silver wedding anniversary on the cruise, which would be heaven—just the two of us. He was such a romantic. He always planned something special for romantic occasions. He reached across the table, took my hand, and kissed it. He still gave me that tingling feeling with just the touch of his fingers. It was as if the years just evaporated, and we had just met. I loved him to touch me, even if it was only holding hands. I just loved him to bits.

We had a fantastic afternoon shopping. If I tried on a garment and he liked it, we bought it. If he didn't, it stayed on the shop floor. We had such a laugh. Dave bought some nice clothes too. We had a wonderful time. We decided to go to a wine bar for a drink. Of course Dave ordered champagne. I had to laugh because that was just Dave. We toasted each other between kisses and cuddles.

We decided to go for dinner. Again, we went to a nice restaurant. We had lovely steaks washed down with more champagne; we did enjoy each other's company. We had a fantastic day's shopping and a wonderful evening. We got a taxi home as we had quite a lot of shopping. By the time we reached home, I was really giggly and happy; Dave was too. We had a nightcap and then retired to bed.

We had a fantastic night of lovemaking; one would not think we had been married for twenty-five years. It felt as if we had married only yesterday. We were in no hurry getting up the following morning. We made love again before we got up. We just lazed around the house for the day. It was nice to relax in each other's company and not have to rush off someplace. We had both worked hard while the children were growing up, often not seeing each other for a couple of days if Dave was on nights.

I saw Caroline occasionally. We would meet up for lunch and have a laugh and a giggle. Her family was growing up too. She was getting a little bored; she wanted to start another business. I started laughing. 'Count me out!' I said.

She said, 'No, nothing like before. I'm thinking of investing in an art gallery.'

I perked up my ears. 'Oh, I might be interested.'

She laughed. 'I knew you would be . . . anything to do with art.' I told her I had been painting a lot and had been enjoying it. I told her I sold them to raise money for cancer research. She said that was brilliant. Maybe she would do something for cancer also. She would need to think about it. I told her about the cruise we were taking to celebrate our anniversary. She said, 'That is brilliant! Enjoy.' I told her I intended to.

The day wasn't long approaching for our cruise. We flew to Stockport and picked up the cruise ship there. We were both very excited; this was something we had never done before, so we had been looking forward to it. The ship was slowly filling up. We made friends with a couple who were similar in age to us, and we hit it off straight away. We went to our cabin and arranged to meet them later in the bar. The ship was absolutely gorgeous. It was like a floating hotel with all the trimmings, and all the staff were very helpful. We met Peter and Anne at the bar. They were seasoned travellers and had been on numerous cruises. They knew all the pitfalls and all the good bits. We had a drink with them and enjoyed their company. We didn't want to spend too much time with them; we wanted to be on our own and enjoy our own company.

We dressed in evening wear for dinner. Dave wore a dinner jacket, and he looked real dapper in it. We felt very important going down to dinner. We were really enjoying ourselves. We were asked to sit at the captain's table, and that was an honour to us. The conversation was intellectual and engaging, and at times very funny. All in all, we had a good time, and the evening had just begun. There was a brass band playing in the dance hall, and they were fantastic. They were accompanied by a well-known singer. Tom Jones was on for tonight. He was brilliant in concert. He just sang his heart out. We danced the night away. We both enjoyed it immensely; it was just fantastic.

The food was also brilliant. We could choose whatever we wished for breakfast, and there was a set menu for dinner. During the day if we are peckish there was always food in the dining room. We could just help ourselves. We meet up occasionally with Peter and Anne for a drink in the afternoon or evening. We both went swimming in the mornings and then had breakfast. We sometimes played tennis in the afternoon or watched a film and pretended we were teenagers again, sitting in the back row. We could do almost anything on this cruise. We even went dancing in the afternoon, and that was lovely.

We were having an absolute brilliant time doing all the things we always said we would do but never did because life got in the way. It was amazing to wake up in the morning and think, *What can we do today?* It was like a permanent adventure; we were both so excited. We could stop off at various stops along the Caribbean coastline and go sightseeing, or we could stay on board. There was always so much to do; we never got bored.

I didn't know if it was all the activity or whether I was a bit under the weather, but I was beginning to get tired easily after about the first week. I didn't say anything to Dave. I didn't want to spoil things for him or get him worried. I started getting up a little later in the mornings for my jog. Dave often came with me. One morning I felt weak . . . unable to run. I asked Dave to get me a coffee. I said we could run in a little while. He came back with the coffee, and we just rested for a while. I thought I felt okay, so we started off on our jog. We were jogging at our ease when suddenly I collapsed. I don't remember anything except waking up later in our cabin. I was absolutely frozen with the cold, and I was finding it difficult to focus. I could hear voices. I was familiar with one of them. It was Dave. After a little while I could see him. He did seem a little blurred, but I knew it was him. There was a doctor there, but to be honest everything seemed a little confusing to me. I could not figure out what had happened to me. The doctor was speaking to Dave. I just wanted to sleep, which I did apparently for a couple of hours.

When I woke up, I felt fine—hungry, but okay. Dave was there waiting for me to wake up. He said, 'You gave me a scare.'

'Sorry. I didn't mean to do that,' I said. 'Have you eaten?'

He said, 'No way. I was too worried about you. I stayed with you until you woke up.'

I said, 'I feel fine now. Let's go and have some lunch.'

'Good idea,' he said.

I had a shower, and we were ready to go in no time at all. We got to the dining room, and the aroma of food was overwhelming; I could hardly wait for the food. We both had a chicken salad and continental bread. I loved all the different kinds of bread available on foreign holidays. I just had water to drink; I felt very thirsty. Lunch was delicious, and we had a coffee afterwards. We sat for a little while in the sun, and it was just lovely to chill out. Dave was reading the paper, so I dropped off to sleep again.

When I woke up, I could not believe I had been asleep. Dave didn't say anything; he just continued reading. We were having a good old time, and we made loads of friends. We went dancing every night after dinner; we were really enjoying ourselves. I was getting a chance to wear my fancy dresses and show off just a little. All the ladies were dressed in the most elegant styles every night. We were having fun, but for some reason I was feeling a bit under the weather. I was finding it a bit of a struggle to keep going at times. I was beginning to worry because I had not felt like this since I had been ill some years before. We had one week left, and I was just longing to go home. I didn't tell Dave how I felt; he would have been fussing about me, and I could do without that. I never liked anyone making a fuss about me.

I had a feeling I could be getting ill, as I did not feel in good form. I felt tired, and all I wanted to do was sleep. I didn't feel like eating. I knew I would have to pay the doctor a visit and have some tests done when we go home.

We both got a lovely tan from lying out in the sun. Maybe we had over done it the first couple of weeks, trying to fit it all in. I read loads of books, something I never had time to do when I was working. It was a bit weird having time on my hands and not having to rush all the time. I had spent all my life rushing from pillar to post, as the saying goes. I felt the days dragging now that I had no timetable to keep too. I wondered how Dave would adapt to being his own boss. He had spent most of his life, as I had, governed by the clock. That is a habit that is not easy to break.

We had taken the cruise to try to break the routine, I think. Well, for a start, we managed to stay in bed a little later than usual. We had always been creatures of habit. We had always been a very loving couple, so we did not need to get to know each other again like some couples do when they retire. We were always kissing and cuddling.

There was a wonderful banquet on our last night; it was just fantastic. I thought I would never forget that cruise; it was so special. I kept my best frock till the last night. It was black with sequins on the bodice. I was never blessed with natural curves. I had always been on the skinny side, so it was not easy trying to look sexy in a frock, but nowadays there were so many different bras to improve what you have got—or haven't in my case—so the end result can be stunning. Miracles do happen! Dave told me. 'You look amazing, Rose. I could fall in love with you all over again.' I thought that was sweet. He said, 'Nothing is going to get in the way of me making love to you every day for the rest of our lives.'

I said, 'That suits me. I will hold you to that,' and we sealed it with a kiss. We had a wonderful meal and a great night dancing to all the latest numbers. I still loved dancing, even though I could not dance as much because it made me out of breath. We met up with Peter and Anne. We swapped partners throughout the night. We had a fabulous time. It had been a dream of a holiday. Life indeed was great with my darling Dave. I would not change a thing. He had always made me feel special; we had never had an argument. We had nothing to argue about. We loved each other and our children. I was never short of love or money. Isn't it wonderful to be able to say that? I always felt so privileged. But life has a nasty habit of throwing something into the works and upsetting one's plans. That's how it was with my health.

Chapter 19

WHEN WE GOT back home from our cruise, I felt exhausted. It took me some time to come back to normal. One night when we were sitting in front of the fire I said, 'Dave, I'm worried. Something is not right. I feel exhausted I need to see the cancer specialist.'

Dave said, Don't worry Rose 'We will face it together whatever comes.'

We both went to the appointment together. I had bloods taken and various tests done. I was told they would rush the results through as quickly as possible, as I was a former cancer patient. I was feeling very down in myself. I just couldn't believe this was happening once again. I had worked hard and reared my family. Now it was supposed to be my time, and what happens? Just my luck—or my lack of it.

We went to the coffee shop and had a coffee before going home. We sat in the coffee shop wondering what to say to each other. We were probably both thinking the same thing. I was just gazing around when I spotted a guy having coffee at the table next to ours. He was with a young lady; she could be his daughter. I said to Dave, 'That looks like Shakera's husband, Michael, at the next table.'

He looked around. 'Indeed it is.'

'I need to go and speak to him.'

'Go ahead,' he said. 'I'll remain here while you chat with him.'

As I approached his table I said, 'This is not the best place to bump into people.'

He said, 'It sure isn't.' He stood up. 'It's Rose, isn't it?'

'Yes it is,' I said. 'How is Shakera getting on?'

His answer astounded me. 'She is at peace now. She passed away a few minutes ago.'

I sat down at the table. I did not know what to say. I was shocked. 'I'm very sorry,' I said. When I got my composure back, I said, 'I am truly sorry.'

He explained, 'She brought shame on her family by marrying me. They never forgave her. They tracked us down and made our lives hell. For that reason, we spent our lives moving. We have been living on welfare for the past number of years. Our lives were an absolute hell. A few months ago Shakera's stump started paining her. She had to start using a wheelchair to rest it. She was told at the hospital that the bone had become infected and her leg would have to be amputated further up. She was devastated. She said she could not face any more surgery. She asked me to take care of our daughter, Alexia.' He looked lovingly at his daughter. 'She said we would be better off without her. I begged her not to do anything stupid. I could not watch her all the time. One day she was waiting at the pedestrian crossing. As a bus approached she dashed across in front of it. She suffered horrific injuries. That was three days ago. She passed away this morning.'

I was shocked to hear their story. I thought they had been happy. By the looks of things, they had never been allowed to. I told them we had an appointment that we needed to go. I said my goodbyes and joined Dave at our table. I relayed the story I had just been told. He was shocked also. He stretched his hand across the table, took my hand, and kissed it. 'Don't worry, Rose. You beat it once before. You can do it again. I will be with you all the way. We will fight it together.'

We were both completely flat. Nothing could lift our spirits. 'I don't think I have any fight left in me,' I said. 'If only I had been given more time to do all the things we said we would do . . . more time to love you and be with you.' I just stopped for a minute and then continued, 'Dave, listen to me. I sound so selfish! What am I complaining about? I've had a wonderful life. I have the love of a wonderful man. We have two beautiful children who are now responsible young adults, and they love me dearly. So what am I moaning about? It would have been the icing on the cake to see them married and perhaps produce a grandchild, but one does not get to have everything in this life.' I took Dave's hand in mine and kissed it. 'I am not going to feel sorry for myself. We are going to enjoy every day we have together. Shall we walk home and enjoy the lovely afternoon sunshine?'

He smiled at me and said, 'That's the spirit, girl. We are in this for better or worse, so let's make the most of it.

It was coming up to Easter, so the boys would be home for a couple of days. It would be nice to have the whole lot of us together. Jonathan had a girlfriend at the moment. She had been to our house lots of time. She was studying law and was a very delightful person. They both got on well together, but had no future plans, until their studies were out of the way. Gareth was pretty much the same. He had brought lots of girls home, but he never seemed to be serious about any of them. Perhaps he had not met 'the' one yet. Both boys were happy in their careers, and that was very important. I was sure they would meet the right partners and settle down in their own time.

We were waiting for results from the hospital, but we received a message that the results had been inconclusive. They would have to be repeated, just to eliminate any doubt. After the tests were done again, I was told the results would not be available till after the holiday. I did try my best to get some sort of an answer as to what they were querying. The symptoms were not the same as the ones I'd experienced with my leukaemia. I felt tired, and all my bones ached as if someone has been stamping on me. I seemed to hurt all over.

I still rang Bridget every week, and she decided to come and visit for a couple of days at Easter. I was looking forward to it. We still chatted a lot and told each other everything.

Caroline had gone ahead and invested in an art shop. She was doing very well with it. She put my paintings on show, sometimes giving them get pride of place in the window. It was lovely to stop outside the window and admire my own painting. I felt such a sense of pride. I loved painting, especially in oils. When I was going to school I used to always paint in watercolours. After I had the cancer, to pass the time, I did a course in oils, and to my surprise I loved it. And I discovered I was pretty good at it. It was great that I could make money for cancer doing something that I loved. Dave, bless him, as promised, started his classes to learn how to make frames for my paintings. For someone who had never done any woodworking before, he was very good. He even surprised himself. We were able to afford to buy nice fancy wood for the frames, which enhanced the paintings.

Bridget came to visit. I had not told her about the query on my health, as I had not wanted to influence her decision about coming to visit us. We had a lovely weekend. Just before she was due to return home, we told her of my dilemma. She was shocked and very upset. She wanted to stay longer. We told her we would keep her informed as soon as we got the results. She would be the first to know. She was not happy going home at all, and to be honest I was very sad to see her leave.

With the holiday weekend over, it was time to go and get those dreaded results. We stopped off at a coffee shop on the way. We were too early, and we didn't want to be waiting around at the hospital more than we needed to. Each of us was trying to keep the other's mind off the issue at hand, and so we were babbling about unimportant things. While we drank our coffee, we discussed all aspects of the current political agenda, even though neither of us was politically minded. We both laughed about the rubbish we had been debating. We had a cuddle and then left.

We got to the hospital with time to spare and had to wait some time for the specialist. Our names were called, and we were ushered into his office. We could tell by his body language that the news was not good. He continued moving papers around his desk. We both sat down. He started explaining that the first tests had been inconclusive. I said, 'Tell us what you have found, not what you did not find.'

He smiled a nervous smile and said, 'It looks as if you I have bone cancer. It is very aggressive. Treatment does not seem to be the answer as it's in an advanced stage. I can put you on steroids, and perhaps you could have one or two rounds of chemotherapy, which would halt it for a little while. I am very sorry, but there is nothing more I can do.'

Dave was gripping my hands so tight that they were beginning to hurt. I struggled to get them free. Nervously Dave asked, 'How long has she got?'

The specialist hesitated for a few moments, looking at both of us. I spoke next saying, 'We would prefer to know how long.'

He said, 'At most, I would say three months. But I could be entirely wrong, and you could get a year or even longer. I do not like giving a time to people. I am not God.' We understood that entirely, though he may have been the next best thing. We thanked him and left his office.

When we got outside, the triage nurse had a chat with us. She explained that we could do a lot in the way of diet to help my condition. She said I should include a lot of vegetables and fruit in my diet. I should liquidize vegetables and drink the juice frequently during the day. It should be as green as possible. That was very good for the immune system. In addition, I needed to remain healthy and try not to pick up cold or flu germs, as they would zap my energy and make me feel lethargic. The doctor had written me a prescription for steroids. She advised me to take them and to eat plenty of protein. She said not to drink any alcohol, and to take particular care with my oral hygiene. They also advised me to take painkillers if my bones were painful and to relax and not to let any pain get on top of me.

We left for home feeling a little dejected, but also a little optimistic. I said to Dave, 'Let's go to a restaurant for lunch. I am feeling fine right now, and there will be days when I won't feel like going out . . . or won't be able to go out. Let's make the most of the time that I have.'

'Of course,' he said. We had a very pleasant lunch. We did not speak of cancer. We chose healthful food and drank water. We were happy with that. We both had fruit salad for desert and our usual coffee to finish. I decided to cut down on the coffee . . . maybe just one a day. When we got home I was not feeling down in the dumps. Oddly, I felt pretty up beat. I knew my prognosis was not great, but I also knew that feeling sorry for myself would not improve things. I started a new painting, and I did quite a bit before I got tired. Dave made a liquidized fruit and veg drink for me so that I would have a good intake of vitamins. It was an acquired taste. In fact, at first it tasted revolting. But after a few sips it seemed to grow on me. If it would help, I knew I could tolerate it.

I was still able to go for my run in the morning. Sometimes I found I had to go a little easier, but all in all I could still go out and exercise, which was great. I felt fine. I could eat most things, and I was particularly careful with my oral hygiene. Last time round my mouth got very sore and tender, and it was extremely difficult to eat. Even having a drink was sometimes difficult. Hot and cold drinks both would sting. I was trying to prevent that happening on this occasion. The fruit and veg drinks seemed to be helping me, as I felt quite good.

We were both just plodding along. One evening we had an in-depth discussion. Dave did not want to go into any detail about my affairs, but it was something that needed to be sorted. We had a long chat and discussed my affairs and wishes. It is always best to be prepared for the inevitable. No one likes discussing those things, but I wanted to have things in order. It would be less of a hassle for those left behind.

We told the boys also and prepared them for the end. They were both terribly upset. I told them I was privileged to have known and loved them and to receive their love in return. We loved them both dearly and respected them as the fine young men they had become. I also told them not to be afraid to love and be loved, as love was the one thing that I always had in my life. Like a comforting blanket, love is always there when you need it.

I had had a most extraordinary life. I had earned my living doing what I loved most—designing—and I had been well paid for it. I had always been in a position to work. We had never been short of money. We had been able to send our sons to private school, and we had always had the best of holidays. Beyond that, of course, I'd had some wonderful friends. I'd been blessed with a loving husband who loved and cared for me and always treated me like a lady. Yes, life had been good to me.

We shouldn't wallow in self-pity. We should look back on all the wonderful things we did in life, and we should look forward to all that we can still do. I liked to go walking or jogging every day and observe nature. I liked to take the camera with me on nature trips, and perhaps snap a squirrel climbing a tree or maybe some birds building a nest. There were lots of things to see if one really looks. I developed my photographs and painted them in oils. I couldn't wait to paint them and see how they turned out. I liked bold strong colours. When we went to visit Bridget it had been the season for the lambs I used to love watching them playing, running, and jumping. Yes, nature is brilliant; nothing can compare to it.

I painted most afternoons and listened to music, another love of my life. I absolutely loved country music. I listened all the time and sang along at the top of my voice. I knew hundreds of songs. I also loved dancing, but I didn't really have the energy for it now. We had been dancing off and on since my diagnosis. Sometime I had loads of energy, and other times I could only manage an old-time waltz.

But, again, who can ask for anything more than the love of your life waltzing you round the floor, holding you tight and whispering sweet nothings in your ear, or just nibbling your ear as the music wafts towards you from a distance.

It's true the best things in life are free. It's a pity people do not appreciate life more—and each other. We should be content with what we have got. When we find someone to love, we should love that person as if he or she was the only one in the world. We should make him or her feel special. I loved life. I had always loved life. I tried not to take people for granted. If someone did me a good turn, I always returned the favour in some way or other. I was blessed to have a talent to paint. I could raise money for charities, cancer being the one that was nearest to my heart. Everyone knows someone who has had it, or if they are lucky is living with it. Either way, it touches everyone. I was able to raise money without any fuss, which suited me fine.

I went to the hospital every week for tests to see how my situation was. The good news I was that it had not got any worse. It seemed to be stable. I did not feel too tired, and I was not in much pain. I thought I might carry on for a little bit longer. Inside me a little flame of hope is still lightining and secretely I am hoping to prove the doctors wrong and live a little longer than they anticipated. I am in awe at the wonderful life I have lived so far yet at times I feel this illness is casting a shadow on it: but. Who knows? God may be on my side for once.

Chapter 20

Six months after that terrible day I was told I may have only three months to live, thank God I was still alive and kicking, as the saying goes. I felt great. Don't get me wrong. Some days I did not have the energy to get out of bed, but I pushed myself and I did get up. It may have been a little later than usual, but I would make the effort, and I usually felt better for it. My appetite was not so bad. I had lost a little weight, but nothing drastic. My mouth was good also. It was not sore. That was one thing that would get me down—not being able to swallow comfortably. It can be very painful, but so far I was okay.

I managed to do a bit of painting every day. I found it very relaxing, and it gave me a great sense of pride to finish each one. I often thought to myself, *This will probably be the last one*, but somehow I still kept going.

Caroline was brilliant. She visited me most days or evenings, and she often brought me a little something like a cream cake or cheesecake—my passion in deserts. Sometimes I just couldn't eat it; just to look at it was often enough.

Dave, bless him, was an absolute rock. He went with me to the hospital every time I had to go for my treatment. I had a few sessions of chemotherapy. I was violently sick after each one for a couple of days. I could not tolerate it. I refused to have anymore. Dave did most of the cooking for us. Sometimes I could cook, but not very often. Sometimes the smell of cooking made me nauseous.

The boys came and stayed every weekend and brought their girlfriends with them. They were brilliant for cheering me up. Gareth's girlfriend was a lovely girl. She was studying to be a solicitor. She told me she was taking a year out, because she had just discovered she was pregnant. I could not believe what she was telling me. One of my wishes was to see my grandchild before I die. That would have been the icing on the cake, but unfortunately it was not to be. Gareth rang during the week telling us that they had lost the baby. They were very upset, and they would not visit at the weekend. We were also very upset. It just was not to be.

One evening, Dave was preparing dinner while I was reading in the living room. I heard a noise like someone falling over. I called to him but didn't get an answer. I rushed into the kitchen and found him collapsed on the floor. I checked his pulse; it was very faint. I called an ambulance; it arrived in a matter of minutes, but it was too late. He was already dead. I was in total shock. I could not believe it. He had to be taken to the hospital for a post-mortem to see what he had died from.

I called Jonathan and Gareth; they could not believe what had happened. I called Bridget; she said she would come as soon as she got a flight. I couldn't believe my Dave had died. He had never complained, ever. I would have to wait a week for the results of the post-mortem.

Dave and I had all the arrangements made for my own funeral. I even had the hymns sorted. I didn't think I could plan another funeral. I never thought he would be gone before me. However, when you have to do something, you find the strength somehow.

The hospital rang to say they had the results of the post-mortem, would I like to go in and get them? I made an appointment for later that day when the boys would be able to accompany me. We got there at three o'clock and were seem immediately. He had had a massive heart attack and had died instantly. Further tests showed that he had cancer also. There were tumours throughout his body, the primary one in his chest. If he had lived, he would have been in dreadful pain.

I was devastated. I never realized he was ill, and by the looks of things he didn't either. I was glad he hadn't suffered. He had always been very fit. I was surprised about his heart. The doctor explained he must have got twinges, but chose to do nothing about them. Poor Dave, always thinking about others and not himself. He was the most unselfish person I have ever known.

The boys were devastated. They could not believe their father had passed away, and neither could I. It was like a nightmare. I just did not know where to begin. His parents were still alive and in good health; they were also devastated. They had always been very good to me . . . had always been there to lend a hand. I could not have had nicer in-laws if I had tried. God love them, they would miss Dave terribly, as we all would.

We left the hospital in shock. We had a coffee in the foyer and discussed what arrangements we needed to make. The boys were so upset. I had to put aside my own grief and console them. I did not know how we were going to get through this, but I supposed we would have to. The worst thing was that I was on borrowed time myself. I didn't really know how long I had, but I was supposed to be making the best of every day. We never know if it's our last.

I knew I had lost my best friend, but I had fantastic memories. We'd had a wonderful life, full of love. He would have done anything for me. We had started each day with a kiss and ended it the same way. I know I was truly loved, and that in itself is a treasure.

The boys made all the arrangements for the burial. It was a family service with just close friends. Of course, all Dave's colleagues wanted to attend, and they duly did. We invited all our friends back to the house for refreshments after the service. Friends and family had also come from Ireland. Everyone had been shocked at his sudden death.

When everyone had gone and the boys had gone back to their lives, that's when I realized what being alone was all about. It was scary. I had to leave the radio on all the time just to inject sound into my life and break the silence. The boys kept ringing me up to see if I was coping and if I was eating. Of course I wasn't coping. And how could I eat? All I wanted to do was die. I was living in a limbo, just getting up when I felt like it. Nothing seemed to make sense anymore. Why did Dave have to die? And so suddenly? Why does life have to be so cruel?

Bridget wanted to stay on for a little while with me, but I persuaded her to go home and let me sort out things my way in my own time. I was determined to bounce back again, but I was not ready to do so yet. I was still trying to make sense of it all. But there was no point in trying to make sense of life. Things just happen, and we have to accept them.

I started getting up a little earlier and going for a walk in the park. I was just trying to get some order back into my life again. Dave would have said, 'Get up and do something.

It's good to be alive.' How true that is. I missed him terribly. I found myself crying every minute. I didn't know where all the tears were coming from. Was there any chance I might run out of them? No way.

We had got on so well. We were best friends as well as husband and wife. I discussed everything with him, always wanting his approval and usually getting it. Even if he disapproved of something I wished to do, he always came round to my way of thinking. He never denied me anything. He was always generous with his time and money.

I had to start painting again and try to organize an art exhibition in memory of Dave. I wanted to raise some money for heart research. Maybe I could organize some sports event. He used to work with deprived children one day a week and play soccer with them. He had left his mark. He did love being involved with children, so maybe I should get off my bum and do something. I had to put my thinking cap on. I decided to mention it to Caroline. I felt sure she would help.

Caroline called every day to see if I was doing all right; she was indeed a good friend. We decided on a soccer blitz as our fundraiser. We would donate the money to the club Dave had started some years before. We were very lucky. All our friends helped out, and we made a substantial amount, which was brilliant. I made a little speech and thanked everyone for their support. Dave's friends got together and erected a plaque outside the soccer grounds in his memory, which was a lovely gesture.

I was finally beginning to come to terms with Dave's death. I didn't cry as much. I tried to concentrate on the good life we'd had together. Sometimes it was not easy. A song on the radio or something someone might say could make it difficult to hold back the tears.

The boys arranged it so that one of them was with me every weekend. I kept telling them that I was okay, that Dad would not want me to be moping about. I still went jogging every morning, and I felt really good. I didn't feel as if I had a death sentence hanging over me, but I did.

I had lots of good friends, and there was always someone calling. I sometimes went out to dinner with friends, but when I came home I would get a little emotional. I just had to remember he was not coming back. I had to get used to that fact.

A friend and I started visiting patients in hospital on a voluntary basis. We got great satisfaction from it. We would meet up for lunch later and have a chat. I found it took my mind off things.

Soon my bones started to hurt a little, and I noticed a lot of bruising on my limbs. Since Dave died, I had not been having my vitamin drinks as much. He used to blend all the different vegetables and fruits for me, and they used to make me feel good. I knew I should start doing them again. I felt they would do me good.

When I went to the hospital for my scheduled appointment they were surprised at how well I was. They were, in fact, amazed, especially that I was able to eat. They put me back on the steroids again. They told me I needed them. I told them I would not have any more treatments. When my health started to deteriorate, I would not have any more chemotherapy. Certainly without Dave I could not go through with it. I knew myself. I might look good, but I did not feel in good form. I ached all over, and was still bruised. They tried to reassure me at the hospital that I was fine. They told me to return in three months. I had also been getting nosebleeds. I found it difficult to sleep. I started taking painkillers to ease my bones.

Caroline still visited often. She asked me to ring Bridget and ask her to come and stay for a little while. I asked her if she thought I really needed her, and she said she thought I did. She said she did not want to alarm me, but in her opinion I had lost a significant amount of weight. She asked me if I was eating. I said I had not been eating a lot, but I was drinking the drinks I made in the blender. I told her one of the boys always came home for the weekend, and I was managing during the week. She said she would ring Bridget directly. Bridget said she would love to come for a chat.

Jonathan stayed for the weekend, and Bridget arrived early on Monday morning. I had not eaten much over the weekend; I just hadn't fancied anything. I had tried, but all I had managed was soup and a little bread. My mouth had got a little sore, which made it difficult to eat. Bridget had never been one to mince words. She told me I looked dreadful. She felt I should contact the hospital and maybe get them to take me in. I protested immediately. I told her I was not that bad. Maybe I had lost some weight, but all in all I did not feel so bad. As soon as she arrived, she asked if I had eaten. She made porridge for me and insisted I eat it, or at least make an effort. I did just that, and I managed to finish it. I asked her if she would go for a little walk with me, and she said of course. We set off on our walk, slowly at first. But I managed to get strength from someplace, and we did have a nice walk through the park. We sat on a park bench for a little while and resumed our walk home after we had rested. I felt good after we got home. We had a coffee and we watched television. I dropped off sometime later. When I woke up, Bridget had lunch ready. I made a good attempt at eating it. I felt hungry, but soon after eating, I felt bloated and nauseous, and I vomited all I had eaten.

This became a pattern. I was unable to keep food down. Bridget sent for my GP. He was an old family friend. He told me all he could do for me was make me comfortable. 'Are you in pain?' he asked.

'Sometimes,' I said. 'It has not got that bad yet.' He wrote me a prescription for morphine and other pain relief. He told me to take the pain medication and not be a martyr and suffer unnecessarily.

I was able to keep down yogurt and light meals, but not anything with meat or vegetables. I could manage a boiled egg, but no toast, as my mouth was quite sore with mouth ulcers. I kept rinsing my mouth, but it did not seem to be improving. I was sleeping for longer periods also. I felt so tired and exhausted. The two boys took some annual leave so that they could be with me. It was so sad. It seemed like only six months since they had lost their father, but somehow a year had gone by. Now our sons were just waiting for me to join him.

Eventually I was unable to get out of bed; I was just too weak. My sore bones made it difficult for me to get comfortable, but then I got a wonderful inflatable mattress from the hospital, which helped a lot. I lost a lot of weight. I was down to only about five stone now. I was very frail. I could manage to sit up for only a couple of hours on some days. I found myself just drifting in and out of consciousness, especially when the morphine kicked in. The mornings were the only time I was lucid. As the day passed, my pain became more intense. I had my own nurse. I could afford her. She was truly lovely. Bridget could not cope. She went home for some time and came back again to be with me. Daniel and his family came to visit me, but I was not in form for visitors. Timmy and his family came. Kate passed away. Bridget did not tell me till later. I was in no condition to go to her funeral. I was upset about that; I loved her dearly.

I woke up one morning unable to breathe. The nurse sent for the doctor. He came immediately. He said I had pneumonia and that I would most likely die from it. He put me on oxygen and upped my morphine. I said goodbye to my beautiful sons and their girlfriends.

I see Dave sitting in the chair in the corner of our bedroom. He smiles and outstretches his hand to me. I close my eyes and drop off to sleep. I can't complain. I did have a good life with the man of my dreams. I would like to have lived longer. That's human nature—to never be satisfied and always want more.

I see Dave in the distance now. His hand is outstretched, and he is walking towards me, smiling. We hug and kiss. I am happy to leave this life knowing I will be with him again forever. I have no worries about my wonderful sons. They are settled in their chosen careers, and they appear to have chosen loving partners. I know they will miss me, but life goes on. I know they will be okay.

I am happy to see Dave. He is waiting for me with that lovely smile on his face.

Lightning Source UK Ltd.
Milton Keynes UK
UKOW05f0854240614

233951UK00001B/1/P